My Fair
Duchess

Megan
Frampton

AVONBOOKS

An Imprint of HarperCollinsPublishers

This is a work of fiction. Names, characters, places, and incidents are products of the author's imagination or are used fictitiously and are not to be construed as real. Any resemblance to actual events, locales, organizations, or persons, living or dead, is entirely coincidental.

MY FAIR DUCHESS. Copyright © 2017 by Megan Frampton. All rights reserved. Printed in the United States of America. No part of this book may be used or reproduced in any manner whatsoever without written permission except in the case of brief quotations embodied in critical articles and reviews. For information, address HarperCollins Publishers, 195 Broadway, New York, NY 10007.

First Avon Books mass market printing: March 2017

ISBN 978-0-06-241279-9

Avon, Avon & logo, and Avon Books & logo are registered trademarks of HarperCollins Publishers in the United States of America and other countries.

HarperCollins is a registered trademark of HarperCollins Publishers in the United States of America and other countries.

17 18 19 20 21   QGM   10 9 8 7 6 5 4 3 2 1

To Scott and Rhys. I love you.

Acknowledgments

Thanks to my editor, Lucia Macro; my agent, Louise Fury; my critique partner, Myretta Robens; and my first reader, Erin Cox. You guys all make my writing so much better, and I am so grateful.

Author's Note

Yes, it is extremely improbable that a woman would inherit a duchy. But it is not unprecedented! The first Duke of Marlborough had two sons who predeceased him, and four surviving daughters. He was able to get a special act passed through Parliament that would allow his eldest daughter to inherit the title. How cool is that? I started thinking about what it would mean if a woman were to inherit but no one had thought to train her up for it.

Dear Aunt Sophia,

How are you? ~~I am desperate.~~ I am doing well. As you know, I am now the Duchess of Blakesley. Don't ask me to explain how an unmarried woman could inherit such a title. The solicitors explained it four times, and from the little I understand, it seems my ancestors received some special dispensation to allow any direct heir to inherit, regardless of gender. ~~My father, God rest his soul, was too errant to prepare me for that, or any, possibility, and I have no choice but to appeal to you.~~ Since that ridiculous scenario has occurred, I am at the London town house preparing to take on my new position ~~for which I was never prepared.~~ I am writing you to ask if you have any advice for navigating societal waters, I am quite adept at swimming (the second footman taught me when I was twelve), but this is a very different kind of pond. A veritable ocean, one might say. ~~And I am drowning.~~

If you would be so kind, please send along any recommendations for ~~anything~~ hiring staff, assembling a proper wardrobe, ~~how not to annoy the Queen,~~ managing several country estates, and any other thing I might have overlooked ~~in my desperation. Have I mentioned I have no idea what I am doing?~~

Normally I would consult a book if I were at a loss in

any situation, but there don't appear to be any manuals on what to do if you are an unexpected duchess.

Sincerely,
~~Genevieve~~ Duchess

P.S. If there is such a book, please do share the title!

~~P.P.S. Even though I will probably fall asleep, those kinds of books are so dull.~~

Chapter 1

"There's only one solution," Lady Sophia said, passing the letter to Archie as he felt his stomach drop. And his carefully ordered life teeter on the verge of change. "You'll have to go to London to sort my goddaughter out." She embellished her point by squeezing her tiny dog Truffles, who emitted a squeak and glared at Archie. As if it was his fault.

He resisted the urge to crumple the paper in his hand. "But the festival is in a few weeks," Archie said, hearing the desperate tone in his voice. He did not want to ever return to London. That was the purpose of taking a position out here in the country after leaving the Queen's Own Hussars a year prior. His family was there, and his father, at least, had made it clear he never wanted to see him again. What's more, he did not want to assist a helpless aristocrat in some sort of desperate attempt to bring order to their lives. Even though that was what he was doing in Lady Sophia's employ. But working for her had come to have its own kind of satisfactory order, one he did not want to disrupt.

"There is work to be done," Archie continued, hoping to appeal to his employer's sensible side.

Although in the course of working for her he had come to realize his employer didn't really *have* a sensible side, so what was he hoping to accomplish?

"Didn't you tell me Mr. McCready could do everything you could?" Lady Sophia asked. "You pointed out that if you were to get ill, or busy with other matters, your assistant steward could handle things just as well as you."

That was when I was trying to get one of my men work, Archie thought in frustration. *To help him get back on his feet after the rigors of war.* And Bob had proven himself to be a remarkably able assistant, allowing Archie to dive into Lady Sophia's woefully neglected accounts and see into her investments, neither of which she paid any attention to.

Lady Sophia placed Truffles on the rug before lifting her head to look at Archie. Who knew, in that moment, that he was doomed. Doomed to return to London to help out a likely far-too-indulged female in the very difficult position of being a powerful and wealthy aristocrat.

Perhaps it would have been easier to just get shot on the battlefield. It certainly would have been quicker.

"It's settled." She punctuated her words with a nod of her head, sending a few gray curls flying in the air. "You will go see to the new duchess and take care of her as ably as you do me. Mr. McCready will assist me while you are away."

Archie looked at the letter again. "This duchess is your relative?" he asked. That would explain the new duchess's equally silly mode of communication. An "unexpected duchess," indeed. What kind of idiot wouldn't have foreseen this circumstance? And done something to prepare for it?

"She calls me aunt, but she is not my actual niece, you understand," Lady Sophia explained. "She is my goddaughter; her mother married the duke, the duchess's father. It is quite unusual for a woman to inherit the duchy."

"Quite," Archie echoed.

"But it happened, somehow, and since I don't know anything about being a duchess . . ."

Because I do? Archie wondered. But there wasn't anybody else. She wouldn't have asked Lady Sophia, of all people, unless there was nobody else.

Or if she was as flighty and confident as her faux-aunt. A scenario that seemed more and more likely.

"The only thing Mr. McCready can't do is attract as much feminine interest as you do, Mr. Salisbury." She sat back up and regarded him. "Which might make him more productive," she added. She leaned over to offer Truffles the end of her biscuit.

Archie opened his mouth to object, but closed

it when he realized she was right. He wasn't vain, but he did recognize that ladies tended to find his appearance attractive. Lady Sophia received many more visitors, she'd told him in an irritated tone, now that he'd been hired.

Bob, damn his eyes, smirked knowingly every time Archie was summoned to Lady Sophia's drawing room to answer yet another question about estate management posed by a lady who'd likely never had such a question in her life.

Archie responded by making Bob personally in charge of the fertilizer. It didn't stop Bob's smirking, but it did make Archie feel better.

"And you will return in a month's time so you can be here for the festival."

"Sooner if I can, my lady." If this duchess needed more time than a month, there would be no hope for her anyway. Country life suited him; he liked its quiet and regularity. It was a vast change from life in battle, or even being just on duty, but it was far more interesting than being the third son from a viscount's family. A viscount who disowned his third boy when said boy was determined to join the army.

Meanwhile, however, he had to pack to head off to a new kind of battle—that of preparing a completely unprepared woman, likely a woman as flighty and often confused as Lady Sophia, to hold a position that she was entirely unsuited for.

Very much like working with raw recruits, in fact.

* * *

Dear Duchess,

You are probably surprised to receive correspondence from a gentleman you've never met. ~~I assure you, I am not in the habit of addressing strange women, either.~~ Lady Sophia shared your letter with me, and asked that I pen a reply, since your aunt is ~~scattered~~ naturally quite busy. ~~I hope to God you aren't as silly as she, but judging by your letter, that is a forlorn hope.~~

I am your aunt's steward, and my duties include assisting Lady Sophia with any planning and business dealings. I am on my way to London to see how I might be of assistance to you.

You can expect me in three days' time.

Respectfully,
Mr. Archibald Salisbury, Capt. (Ret.)

"Three days' time?" Genevieve heard herself squeak. When did she start *squeaking*? Squeaking was not something she had ever done before.

Then again, she'd never been a duchess before. Maybe it was some understood thing that duchesses squeaked, and now that she was one, she did as well. And if that was the case, then she wouldn't need Mr. Archibald Salisbury, Capt. (Ret.) after all. It would just be intuitive. Rather like when she just knew that choosing to read *The Miser's Daughter* was far preferable to *Threshing and Other Exciting Farm Things* or whatever other boring tomes resided in the library.

"What is happening in three days' time, dear?" Genevieve turned and smiled at her grandmother, who was sitting in what was now referred to as the duchess's sitting room, even though it had been her father's study. Apparently female dukes—also known as duchesses—didn't need to study.

But she would. She did wish there was some sort of book she could just read on the subject, as she'd asked her godmother. *Duchessing and Other Very Specific Occupations*, or perhaps *How to Duchess Without Being a Dullard*.

"A Mr. Archibald Salisbury"—*Captain, Retired*, she added in her head—"is Aunt Sophia's steward. And she is sending him here to answer some questions I have."

"I can answer questions," her grandmother said indignantly. "Why, just this morning Byron asked for breakfast and I gave it to him."

Byron looked up from her grandmother's lap and regarded Genevieve sleepily, one paw stretched out.

"If only it were that simple, Gran," Genevieve replied in a fond tone. She looked back at Mr. Salisbury's letter. "We will have to see if this gentleman can be of assistance." And if he couldn't, she would just have to blunder along as she had been.

Her grandmother lifted her head in Genevieve's general direction. Her grandmother was almost completely blind, which made it difficult to ask her opinion about anything Genevieve might wear. Among other things. "You will know best, I am sure." She accompanied her words with a warm smile and a pet on Byron's head.

It was heartening, if also terrifying, that her grandmother had such confidence in her. That the staff back at home in Traffordshire—where she had spent the first twenty years of her life— were also so confident, even though she had had no training in how to be a duchess beyond having Cook address her as Your Highness during the two weeks Genevieve had insisted she was a prin- cess from the country of Snowland.

She should have spent less time imagining that cold possibility and more time facing the reality that she would be inheriting the duchy.

But it hadn't seemed real. And that was the problem. Nobody had thought it would happen, even though long ago their family had had a bit of royal legerdemain that allowed women to become duchesses in their own right provided there was no direct male heir. Genevieve had male cousins, but she was the heir.

She hadn't even had a proper debut in Society; her father had ignored her letters asking about it, and she had been just as happy to stay in the country. Who would have helped her through such an event, anyway? And if the purpose was to find herself a husband, probably some man who would pay her father for the privilege of marriage to her? No, thank you.

Her father had remarried after Genevieve's mother's death, and it seemed certain that her father would have a son to inherit the title anyway, so nobody had thought Genevieve would be the duchess. If they ever thought of her at all. But he had not had another child, and then his wife had died, and now he was gone, too. The only ones who had paid her any type of attention were the servants in the house she'd grown up in. Who'd loved her, and been kind to her, and who'd brought her books, and biscuits, and smiled as she explained the intricate plot of the novel she'd just read.

But who didn't have any clue of what it would take to be a successful duchess.

Although she should be grateful she hadn't learned how to be any kind of ducal entity from her father, who had apparently been terrible at the whole thing.

He was far more interested in sampling London life to pay attention to pesky things like estate management. Genevieve's strongest memory of her father was of him kissing her cheek and making some sort of inarticulate approving noise at her.

Thankfully the estates were wealthy enough to withstand her father's excesses, but she also guessed that they would need some assistance if they were to thrive. Another job for which she was ill-suited.

Which reminded her that she was about to get some help in the form of the unknown Mr. Salisbury. Help that she sorely needed, even though apparently it also made her squeak.

She rang the bell, making both her grandmother and Byron jump. She heard footsteps, then the door opened to admit her butler.

"Your Grace?"

Thus far, Chandler had treated her with the

utmost external respect, but Genevieve had caught an expression of disbelief on his face at times he'd thought she hadn't been looking at him.

She couldn't fault him for it; it was the same expression that she had when she looked at herself in the mirror.

She pretended she was the princess of Snowland again. It was easier than dealing with the reality of who she was now. "A Mr. Archibald Salisbury is arriving in a few days," she said in what she hoped was a suitably frosty tone. "He is my aunt Sophia's steward, and he will be attending to my affairs until we locate a suitable person for the position." Was she explaining too much to him? Not enough? Why didn't she know? Oh, of course, because she hadn't been raised to become a duchess. It had been thrust onto her, through a variety of mishaps and unfortunate demises.

"Yes, Your Grace. I will place your guest"—and was it Genevieve's imagination, or did the butler seem to sneer the last two words—"in one of the guest rooms on the third floor."

"Excellent. Oh, and," she added, as though it was an afterthought, "Mr. Salisbury is not precisely a guest. But he is to be treated as one for the duration of his stay."

"Yes, Your Grace," he replied, bowing. She thought there was a tinge more of a thaw in his manner—because she was behaving as a duchess ought? And since when did she care so for the opinion of people she'd just met, and who worked for her?

Since now. Since she'd recognized that even the

barest hint of talk would undermine her position and her ability to carry out her duties.

She hoped Mr. Salisbury was as stuffy, appropriate, and efficient, not to mention boring, as his letters implied. The last thing she needed was someone else to upset her peace of mind.

"Your Grace?"

Genevieve paused in the act of dropping a bit of cheese for Byron, whose expression of expectation turned to disgust as Genevieve's hand stilled in mid-air.

"Yes?"

She and her grandmother were in the duchess's sitting room again, since her grandmother was most comfortable navigating her way around the furniture here. Genevieve knew she would have to redecorate eventually—all the furnishings were worn, or old, or both—but she was hoping to be able to keep everything in the same basic location so her grandmother wouldn't fall.

"Your Mr. Salisbury is here." Chandler's sharp eyes focused on Byron, and his gaze narrowed. He had not said so in so many words, but he did not have to—it was clear he did not approve of Byron's being in the household. Of course, he probably didn't approve of Genevieve, either, so she couldn't pay heed to his opinion on either of them.

"Do show him in, Chandler."

She took a deep breath and settled her hands in her lap, her thumb and index finger rolling the crumb of cheese into a ball as Byron continued to glare at her. Drat, and her hair was likely untidy. She'd felt it unwinding when she came to the room, but then her grandmother had needed help with some yarn, and then Byron came begging, and now the likely very proper and properly dull Mr. Salisbury, Capt. (Ret.) was about to come in, and he would be shocked at her impropriety. And her hair.

Although as far as impropriety went, an unmarried duchess living on her own with only her grandmother and a hungry cat as companionship was far worse than untidy hair.

"Mr. Salisbury," Chandler said, then stepped aside to let the gentleman in.

Oh goodness.

The man was so tall it seemed he filled up the entire doorway, blocking out the light that streamed from the large windows in the hall. All she saw was an enormous shape that looked vaguely manlike. And then he came into the room and Genevieve was able to focus, and then it felt as though he'd blocked out all the air from her lungs. Even though he hadn't, he was just standing there holding his hat in his no doubt equally compelling hands.

But the rest of him seemed so improper it really did take her breath away, now that she could see him. Properly. He was so ruggedly good-looking it seemed impossible, and yet here he was—dark hair with just a hint of a curl, a strong blade of a nose over a full mouth, blue eyes that gazed at her unrelentingly. As though he could see inside her soul.

Which Genevieve knew perfectly well could be characterized with the word "confused."

And his build was—well, "impressive" was one word for it. Genevieve imagined there were other words, far less proper words, words that deliberately untidy-haired women would know. He was tall and also broad-shouldered and lean-hipped, and he stood in her sitting room with an easy grace that nonetheless seemed as though he could move at any time. To attack, to defend, to—

Not that. She could not even think that.

"Your Grace?" His eyebrows had drawn together, and he was looking at her as though she were an oddity he had run across, and wasn't certain he liked.

That was the expression she'd seen on most people's faces since inheriting. It shouldn't discomfit her; on a less impressive gentleman it wouldn't. But him, with his height, and his looks, and his general (no, *Captain!* her mind corrected hysterically) air of command—well. Well, it seemed as though she could be discomfited after all.

And here she thought the worst part about being a duchess was the whole inability-to-handle-anything part.

She really was obsessing on her own lack of suitability. She'd have to improve soon or she would mire in self-doubt. *No miring, Genevieve!* she reminded herself.

"Yes, Mr. Salisbury," she said, keeping her voice low so it wouldn't tremble. Or squeak. "Thank you so much for arriving, and so promptly, too."

She glanced toward Chandler and nodded. "That will be all."

Her butler withdrew, closing the door behind him. Leaving her with him and—"Oh goodness, please allow me to introduce my grandmother."

"The dowager duchess?" he said, walking forward to bow in her grandmother's direction.

Gran giggled and held her hand out. "Heavens, no, I am Lady Halbard. My daughter was the duchess's mother."

How, in goodness' name, could Gran tell that he was so good-looking? Because she was preening, at least as much as a sixty-year-old woman could. Which is to say she was wriggling in her seat and smiling in a nearly coquettish way.

The only time Genevieve had seen her grandmother behave that way before was in the presence of the butcher, who had apparently been quite comely in his youth, when Gran had much better eyesight.

"It is a pleasure to meet you."

Gran wriggled some more, and Genevieve found herself almost wishing she were ten years old again, and could roll her eyes with impunity.

"Would you excuse us, Gran? Mr. Salisbury and I have some business to discuss."

Her grandmother began to rise, and Mr. Salisbury reached out to hold her elbow as she stood, a delighted smile on her face. "Byron and I will leave you alone. Byron!" she called, even though the cat had yet to acknowledge he had a name, much less that anyone was in authority over him.

"Byron?" Mr. Salisbury asked, that look of confusion on his face again.

"Byron. Named after the poet. *Childe Harold's Pilgrimage*?" Gran replied.

"Ah. Of course," Mr. Salisbury replied. In a tone that implied it was a ridiculous conversation. Which she couldn't argue with.

"The cat," Genevieve explained.

"Ah!" As though he'd confirmed with himself the conversation was indeed ridiculous.

"I spoke with him once," Gran said dreamily.

"The poet, not the cat," Genevieve said hastily.

"He was the most handsome man," Gran continued. Apparently Gran had long been a connoisseur of masculine beauty.

"Let me help you, Gran," Genevieve said, going to her grandmother's other side. The one not currently occupied by the handsome observant man. Not Byron, but Mr. Salisbury. And now she was doing it. She shook her head at herself as she began to walk.

"Thank you, dear." Gran patted Mr. Salisbury's arm. "It is such a pleasure to meet you, I am hoping you will be able to help my granddaughter with whatever she needs." And then to make matters worse, she punctuated her vague and somewhat leading words with a knowing chuckle.

Genevieve felt her face start to burn in embarrassment. Gran wouldn't see it, of course, but he likely would. The realization of which only made her face burn brighter.

They waited until the door shut behind Gran, as Genevieve tried frantically to get her face to cool.

"Well, Your Grace," Mr. Salisbury said, crossing his arms over his chest. "What do you need help with?"

Oh dear, Genevieve thought. That was certainly an open-ended question. And he looked so forbidding, standing there being all handsome and tall and no doubt keenly aware of how much of a failure she might end up being.

Where should she begin?

Dear Duchess,

~~Your staff is a disgrace.~~ In reviewing your current situation, I would advise you to keep only a few members of your current staff, hiring new staff who are better able to ~~do their jobs~~ maintain the household as it ought to be for someone in your position, ~~unusual though it is~~. I have enclosed a list of the senior staff I believe should be kept on:

The butler, ~~whatever his name is~~.

The rest should be let go immediately. Will you need a list of the necessary positions? ~~Of course you will. Forget I asked. I will write up the list now.~~ The immediate staff needed will be a housekeeper, a cook, a head groom, a coachman, and a steward. They will be able to hire the staff needed to work under their supervision.

Respectfully,
Mr. Archibald Salisbury, Capt. (Ret.)

Dear Mr. Salisbury,

~~Why are you writing me a letter when we are existing in the same household?~~
Thank you for the correspondence ~~although I am still baffled as to why you are writing. Do you loathe my appearance? Think a woman should never be a duchess? Despise cats?~~. I appreciate your advice, and would ask your opinion as to the best way to go about making the changes you suggest. ~~Should I fire them all at one time? Am I even the one who should be firing them?~~ And why is Chandler the only senior staff member who passes your muster?

Yours,
Duchess

Chapter 2

"Because he's the only one who seems to have any idea of how important a duchess's household is," Archie said as he burst into the room where he'd first met her. The duchess. The woman who was inexplicably (even though she had explained, but all that had done was to make him think her ancestors were as muddleheaded as she was, to write such an inheritance requirement) the head of this household, of the lands, of the fortune held by the Blakesley duchy.

And stopped short as he realized he was doing just what he'd accused everyone but the butler—Chandler, he recalled now—of doing. Of treating her not as the most important person in the area, since Queen Victoria was unlikely to pay a visit, but as someone he could command. As though she were serving under him.

But that was the purpose of his being here, wasn't it? For him to treat her as a recruit, even though she was absolutely lacking in any kind of ammunition. In her case her ammunition would include the properly haughty attitude, a suitably efficient staff, and, judging by the gown she'd been wearing when he first met her, an appropriately grandiose wardrobe.

He still wasn't certain why she needed his help, but he had to acknowledge she most definitely did.

She sat on the sofa as she had been that first time, a hoop of some sort of lady's sewing thing in her hand. Except it didn't appear as though she'd been doing the work; she had the hoop on her lap and was looking off in the distance, her eyes snapping to his face as he spoke.

He hadn't expected her to be so . . . young. And attractive. And unmarried. Although he should have guessed all of that (except for the attractive part), thanks to Lady Sophia's explanation.

She wasn't precisely beautiful; Archie had been around plenty of beautiful women, and he'd felt the natural pull of their appearance, but it wasn't the same as this. Instead, it was as though she was magnetic, exuding some sort of element that drew him to her. Did elements attract one another? He had no idea.

And that, he thought sourly, was why he had never done well in his studies. He much preferred dealing in reality: there was a need for a group of armed soldiers to do something, they were assigned to do it, and off they went. No need to worry about what was attracting what.

Except now.

And he would not allow any of that to deter him from his assignment.

"Good morning, Mr. Salisbury." The magnet-in-question was regarding him with a nearly amused curiosity. No doubt because he had—to his own disgust—just spent far more time than he ever had before thinking about how he felt around her. He did not want to feel, he just wanted to *do*.

He knew, from interrogating the staff, that not only did the duchess not have the aforementioned wardrobe, she didn't have her own lady's maid. As though he couldn't tell that from how she was dressed; her clothing was in some sort of disarray, which on a different woman he would have called artless. But in this case, he thought it was just careless. Her gown was crooked on her body, as though someone had just flung it at her and she'd thrust her arms in any which way. His need for order and things in their place meant he wished he could go right her. Which would mean placing his hands on her body and . . . adjusting.

He would not allow himself to adjust.

He cleared his throat and sketched a bow, hoping he could just do the job he had sent himself here for and leave directly after. Perhaps in penance he would assign himself the fertilizer job.

"Good morning, Your Grace." He paused, an odd feeling of—discomfort?—coursing through him. He never experienced discomfort. He knew his place, his position, his duties, and he did them. "Thank you for your reply to my letter."

"Please sit, Mr. Salisbury," she said in a low voice. A gentle wave of her hand accompanied her words. "I will ring for—"

"No," Archie blurted out. "I have no time for tea, nor am I thirsty. Thank you, Your Grace," he added, somewhat belatedly. "If you want some?" he said, making a vague gesture toward the bell.

Her cheeks turned a bright shade of scarlet. Interesting. Perhaps she was just terribly shy, and he was reacting to her discomfort.

That must be it. Not that she was some sort of magnet, and him some sort of attracted-to-a-magnet element. It was that he was being sensitive to another person, something else he didn't think had ever happened. But that possibility was better than the alternative.

"I have no need of tea." She didn't meet his gaze as she spoke, instead staring off into the corner so intently he, too, swiveled his head to look.

Nothing there but some sort of over-ornamented light fixture, the kind Lady Sophia favored.

"Well, then," Archie said, returning his gaze to her. He assessed her, given his marching orders. He would have to mold her into what she was to become; it was important he understand what raw materials he had to work with. She was young, startlingly so, given her position, although likely not more than a few years younger than he. Her greenish-brown eyes were large, and slanted at the sides, giving her an elfish expression. Her hair was dark, a rich mahogany brown like a horse he'd had once. Shadow, he thought its name was. It was dressed very plainly (her hair, not the horse's), not in those fussy curls many women favored that made no sense to him. Why bother obscuring your vision with your hair?

But now he wished she had bothered, since the simplicity of her hairstyle showed off the delicate bone structure of her face as well as her elegant neck. He did not want to be thinking about delicate, elegant anything, unless it was a particularly astute battle maneuver.

That was all this whole thing was, he had to keep in mind—a battle maneuver. A way to maintain his honor and ensure the future of the country through equipping a duchess to handle her responsibilities. A tactic, a strategy. Nothing more.

He took a deep breath and focused on planning, staff, wardrobe, and preparedness. Not on magnetic charm, or delicate simplicity, or anything like that.

Not on that at all.

Mr. Salisbury was, curse him, just as good-looking now as he was the first time she'd seen him. And also apparently averse to sitting.

Genevieve had hoped that her impression had been augmented by her general proximity to a gentleman—she had seldom come in contact with one. An actual gentleman, not gardeners and grooms and such. The ducal estate where Genevieve grew up didn't even have a butler in residence; her father had decreed one unnecessary when it was only "the girl" living there.

And then Mr. Salisbury followed up his impossible good-lookingness by marching in here as though he owned the place, when she barely thought *she* owned the place. And she actually did. It shouldn't annoy her, but it did, that he was so firm in his opinion about her staff after only a few days, far more firm than she was, and she had been here for nearly a month. Albeit a month she'd spent wondering what in God's name she was supposed to do now that she was a duchess.

Apparently she was supposed to decide that some people could keep their positions and others could not.

Of course, he was a Captain (Ret.), so perhaps firmness was a requirement of the military? She presumed so. It would be awkward to be on a battlefield and pause to look at your fellow soldier in arms and ask, "Should we attack? I think we might want to attack, but what do you think?"

And he just as firmly did not want tea, and she found even that annoying. Who didn't want tea? It was a British institution! It was the beverage over which decisions were actually made! She felt the burn of self-righteous anger flow over her, and knew a relief that at least she wasn't still thinking about how attract—

Oh mudpies, she was. In addition to being frustrated that he did not want a hot liquid.

"Would you like something else to drink?" Genevieve found herself asking in a definitely not firm voice. And wished she could take the words back right away. This was not helping her on the path to duchessdom.

He frowned, and she was delighted to see he, too, could be less than firm. As though he were weighing the options in his mind and considering, not just knowing what he wanted straightaway. "No, thank you," he said at last, in a voice that seemed to imply she was an idiot for asking.

So much for being less than firm. That was more than firm. It was firm to the utmost.

Her cheeks began to burn. Again. Was this going to be her permanent state? Blushing every time Mr. Salisbury did or said anything, or anyone (such as her grandmother) did or said anything around him? Was she to be in a constant state of acute Salisburyness?

The sooner she learned how to do what needed to be done, the better. She did not want to Salisbury her way through life. Her cheeks would fall off in a heap of embarrassed flame. And she'd never get tea.

So instead, she asked. They both knew she didn't know what she was doing; it wasn't as though he would be surprised by the question. And asking was one step closer to getting an answer. "What qualities do you believe a duchess's staff should have?"

"Loyalty, efficiency, capability, and a sufficient amount of respect." When he did speak, it was with authority, as though it was painfully obvious. Perhaps it was. Perhaps she had been walking around unaware of knowledge that everyone else had. Or maybe it was just he. And he was an impressively . . . firm sort of man.

Which then just made her cheeks flush again.

But she didn't—she couldn't—think about any

of that. Not when she had to learn how to be a duchess. And not a terrible duchess, as her father had been a terrible duke. She had seen her father's tenants' expression and voices when they'd talked about things that hadn't been done to the lands because of her father's neglect. She'd seen the results of that neglect in the children, who'd given her accusing, and hungry, looks when she and Cook had gone to town to do the shopping. When she'd been old enough to do anything, she had helped where she could, but it wasn't enough.

She hadn't wanted this responsibility, had been nearly horrified when she'd realized she would be the new head of the family, but as soon as the dust—and her nerves—settled, she'd felt an odd yearning to do something right with her power. To make the Blakesley title respected, not derided.

And to do that, she needed the help of Mr. Salisbury, since his opinions seemed sound, even though she felt another odd feeling within her when she saw him.

"Where should we start then?"

He blinked at her, then his face cleared. "Oh, with the hiring." Had she really taken that long to answer him? Probably she had; contemplating his general splendidness could likely take all day. Did other ladies do that, just sit and gaze at him? Was that what her aunt Sophia did?

And if so, why hadn't her aunt Sophia warned her? Although that would be an awkward letter to write:

Dear Genevieve,

> *I am sending my steward to assist you. Do not be alarmed, but he is incredibly good-looking, and it is probable you will find yourself at a loss for words when you look at him. Please try not to stare too much; it does seem to make him uncomfortable.*

She stifled a snort, altering it at the last minute to a clearing of the throat. She hoped. Even if Aunt Sophia had had those thoughts—and Genevieve rather doubted she had; Aunt Sophia's main concern was for Truffles, her dog; she couldn't very well share her thoughts with Genevieve. She probably didn't even share those thoughts with Truffles, who it seemed, from her letters, had her utmost confidence.

"I've drawn up a list," Mr. Salisbury said, dropping a piece of paper on the table beside Genevieve. Then backing away, as though she were going to bite him.

Did ladies often bite him? she wondered. If so, she couldn't blame them. He did look quite delicious.

She picked the paper up and scanned it. It was what he had written to her in the letter, only with a few indications of what the general duties would be—"prepare menus and meals" next to "Cook," "handle all driving duties" beside "Coachman," and so forth.

Genevieve nodded as she read until she realized just what she was reading.

Did Mr. Salisbury think she was stupid as well

as ill-equipped for her new position in life? Judging by what she was reading, he did. Now she was glad she hadn't gotten him tea. He did not deserve a beverage either hot or cold.

It appeared that he had not trusted that she would know what a "Cook" did; he had gone ahead and added "prepare menus and meals" next to the position, as though Genevieve might think a "Cook" did anything else.

And now she felt her face start to burn again, only this time it wasn't because of the good-looking man in the room. That is to say, it was because of him, but not because of his good looks.

"Mr. Salisbury," she began, and she heard how she squeaked, again, and she closed her eyes and took a deep breath, hoping she could settle herself. "Mr. Salisbury." That was better; she sounded not quite so hysterical. "You seem to be under the impression that I have no idea what I am doing."

She kept her gaze locked on him, wishing she could unflush her cheeks, but unwilling to drop her eyes. And it seemed he felt the same way, since they just gazed at each other, neither of them speaking, just . . . looking.

She rather thought she got the better part of the bargain. She got to look at him, while all he had to look at was she. She knew she wasn't hideous, but she was definitely not in the same range of attractiveness as Mr. Salisbury; doubtless there were other people who were every bit as good-looking as he, and she would grow accustomed to such beauty over time. Perhaps if she could inure herself to looking at impossibly good-looking people—such as, for example, Mr. Salisbury here—she would be better equipped to face Society.

And then she giggled at the thought of presenting the idea to him. He seemed to already have a poor opinion of her intelligence. To then ask him to sit while she stared at him for several hours a day would confirm that.

His lips flattened into a thin line at her laughter. Oh, and now she had offended him. This was going splendidly.

"Pardon my bluntness, Your Grace, but it doesn't seem as though you do know what you are doing." He spoke firmly again, damn him, and Genevieve nearly nodded her head in agreement before she realized just what he'd said.

It was true, but it wasn't very polite to say it.

"Then perhaps you should return to Lady Sophia."

"Why?" He looked genuinely puzzled.

Genevieve felt the bubble of anger rising through her whole self, starting somewhere around her shins, so that by the time it exploded out of her mouth it had built and grown. "Because you are doubting my abilities! Because you have done nothing but be dismissive of me since you arrived!"

"I've only arrived three days ago," he said in a clipped tone. "I haven't had much of an opportunity to dismiss you. And you yourself told your aunt in your letter—the letter that prompted her to send me to you—that you were unsure about what to do. What else was I to think?" He crossed his arms over his chest and raised one eyebrow.

She wished she could yank it back down again.

She threw her hands up in exasperation instead. At him. At herself. Because he was right, even though he was incredibly rude about it. "Fine." She did not squeak. She was startled to hear herself sound almost dismissive. She closed her eyes and took a deep breath. *Count to ten, Genevieve, and then—*

"I am sorry, Mr. Salisbury." She spoke in a calmer tone, biting her lip in an effort to keep her voice from rising up into squeaking territory again. "It is just . . . overwhelming. All of this. And I do need help, and I appreciate your coming here"—*even though I did not ask you to*—"and perhaps we can work together and then you can return to Lady Sophia. I am certain she has duties for you that require assistance."

He nodded once. And the eyebrow came down, thank goodness. "That is all I want as well, Your Grace." He gestured to the piece of paper Genevieve still held. "And I likely should apologize to you. I have yet to entirely adjust to civilian life, and sometimes I forget that I am not in charge of a regiment. My suggestions can sound like orders, your aunt has told me. Shall we proceed?" He accompanied his words with a conciliatory smile.

And Genevieve felt her knees buckle, which was remarkable given that she was seated.

He was remarkably handsome when his expression was neutral, but when he smiled? Oh mudpies! He was blindingly handsome, so attractive that she wondered if there was a row of flattened women in his wake, unable to raise themselves from the ground after beholding his splendor.

And yet it wouldn't do to think too much about that, not only because he was a steward, not someone she could possibly have any kind of interest in other than his stewardship. Even if she could throw caution to the winds—or her reputation to Society, which was nearly the same thing—he showed no interest in her at all that way anyway, in fact seeming to think she was slow to comprehend perfectly obvious things.

Things such as a duchess in her own right would never allow herself to marry a gentleman, no matter how handsome or capable he was, if he wasn't an appropriate match.

She heard an odd sound emerging from her mouth, and realized it was a snort. Oh no. Even she knew duchesses did not snort.

"Your Grace?" he said, sounding doubtful.

Of course. He was likely now questioning not only her capability, but also her sanity. Or her lungs.

The sooner they were done with each other, the better.

"Thank you, I accept your apology. Let us begin to discuss what needs to be done, shall we?" she said, her tone as bright as she could make it without sounding, well, *insane.*

"Excellent," he replied, looking skeptical for a moment, then back to that blandly neutral expression.

Dear Duchess,

~~*I am writing to you again. I know we are in the same house. No, I don't know why I keep writing. Perhaps because I do not wish to seem as rude as I know I can be.*~~ *It is understandable that you wish to present yourself to Society in as good a light as possible. I would therefore urge you to* ~~*just be quiet and listen to me*~~ *clear out your schedule so we can work with one another toward that goal.*

Goals, in my experience, are only achieved when one has set them. ~~*Obviously.*~~ *Perhaps we could meet* ~~*anytime but teatime*~~ *at your convenience to establish these goals and lay out a* ~~*battle plan*~~ *strategy to meet them.*

Respectfully,
Mr. Archibald Salisbury, Capt. (Ret.)

Chapter 3

The knock at his door came only thirty minutes after he'd asked one of the soon-to-be-let-go footmen to deliver the letter. Either it was coincidence, or perhaps the footman was actually doing a good job and should be kept on.

"Enter," he called out as he stood from the desk he'd been working at. Lady Sophia had sent her own letter with perhaps seven questions phrased fifty-seven different ways, and he was trying to summarize his answers so he wouldn't have to take the time to answer each and every single one.

He could hear Bob's laughter from here.

"Mr. Salisbury?" Of course it was she, since the only business he had here was with her. Not that he was disappointed; far from it. But that meant he did not want to examine what he felt instead.

He strode over the door and opened it. "Do come in, Your Grace." She entered, and he kept the door ajar, looking around the hallway. He did not want the servants to gossip, even though he was also technically a servant. There was no one in the hallway, however, so if the visit was brief, it would not be remarked upon.

He walked around her to pull the chair of his desk out for her, the only place to sit beside the bed. He would not suggest they sit there.

"Oh no, I don't need to sit, I just came by to ask a question." And even though she'd said she didn't need to sit, she punctuated her words by plopping down in the chair and glancing around her with what appeared to be great interest.

Of course. She had likely never been in a gentleman's bedroom before.

At least, he assumed not. He knew so little about his new recruit.

Archie remained standing, clasping his hands behind his back and staring down at her. He wished he could tell her it was entirely and totally inappropriate for her to burst in here like that, not to mention looking at his shaving kit with such curiosity, but there was something natural in the way she did it. He didn't want to ruin that for her, to make her even more self-conscious about who she was.

Plus he had to admit to enjoying it.

"Sit down, won't you?" she said after a moment, her brow wrinkled. "You look all large and . . ." She fluttered her hands. "Large," she repeated, "looming over me. It's hard enough to do this."

He perched on the edge of the bed. "Do what, Your Grace?"

Instead of replying, she held a piece of paper out to him, her cheeks starting to turn pink. He leaned across the short distance between them to take it, recognizing it as he drew it closer. "This is my letter. To you," he said, in case she didn't understand that part.

She rolled her eyes and crossed her arms over her chest. "I know it is your letter, I brought it to you."

"Yes?" Was there a problem? Also, he should make sure that footman wasn't fired. Because he was remarkably speedy.

"Why are you showing me my letter?" he asked in as mild a voice as he could muster. Which didn't sound very mild to his ears.

She snatched it back from his fingers and tapped her index finger on it. "Because"—*tap*—"you keep writing me when"—*tap*—"we are in the same household. Why is that, Mr. Salisbury?"

Archie opened his mouth—again—to reply, but couldn't. The moment hung there between them, too still and too silent.

He got up from the bed and began to speak. Even before he knew what he was going to say.

"I don't believe you know who I am, Your Grace." She looked puzzled, naturally enough, since he had introduced himself. Even before they'd actually met, in fact. Just as he'd known she had newly acceded to this position for which she had not been prepared. He hadn't known her, though. And she didn't know him.

He started to pace, then realized he shouldn't be so rude as to turn his back on her. So he planted himself right at the end of the carpet, willing himself not to move for fear of being dis-respectful. "My family didn't want me to buy a commission. My uncle understood why I wanted to go, and so he helped me pay for it. But what I wanted, what I really wanted," which he hadn't even known himself until he began speaking, "was there to be order in the world. For things that were right to be right, and for things that were wrong to stop being."

He paused, grateful she didn't interrupt. Instead, she listened, her expression thoughtful, her hands folded in her lap atop his letter.

"And I find it so much clearer when I can write things down, see them as words. I like that I have time to react and prepare—real-life battle is never so expected." He'd grown to hate the chaos. Or maybe he always had hated the chaos, and was doing his best to change that. But this, this organization of sending a letter, then getting a reply—it felt safe. Organized. And correct.

And now he understood why he'd chosen to take a position as a steward, where he could organize things to his heart's content.

"That makes sense to me," she said at last, accompanying her words with a brisk nod. "I should not be so self-absorbed as to think your letter writing had anything to do with me, and that you might possibly dislike me."

"I don't know you well enough to dislike you." That sounded a lot harsher than he meant it. But it was the truth.

She didn't take offense, however; she just chuckled and glanced somewhere past his head to the corner of the room.

He was smarter this time, not turning his head

to see what she was looking it. Did she find him unpleasant to look at? He knew he was regarded as handsome, but could it be that she didn't find him so?

That made him curious to discover just what she thought of him.

Only he shouldn't want that, not when he was just here to do a job. A job that, should he perform his duties correctly, would mean that she would never have cause to speak to anyone of his low stature again, except in a purely professional capacity. Certainly not coming into his room to sit in his only chair with a bed—*his* bed—conspicuously in the room as well.

"Since we are to be working together, we should get to know one another. Shouldn't we?" And she accompanied her question with that direct stare of hers (direct when it wasn't directed toward the corner of the room), and he felt a flare of sexual interest at her words.

Of all the times to be reminded that he was a man with a healthy sexual appetite. It was not appropriate, not at all, but she looked so—courageous, and enthusiastic, and she still looked awry, and he wanted nothing more than to straighten her clothing. Perhaps by removing it entirely and then putting it back on, after a healthy interval of close examination.

Stop that, Salisbury, he warned himself.

It didn't do any good, no matter how accustomed he was to obeying orders.

"And how do you wish to go about getting to know one another, Your Grace?" he asked, taking a cue from her and looking not at her, but at the wall behind her. Unfortunately there was a portrait that appeared to have been done by somebody who thought red was a good color for—well, for everything, so the effect was far more jarring than if he had just looked at her.

Not that she was jarring. Except to his peace of mind. That was very jarred.

He needed to do the job and return to the safety of Lady Sophia, Truffles, and all the admiring ladies.

She smiled at him, nearly flooring him with the brilliance of it. An openmouthed, exuberant smile that hinted—no, that proclaimed—that the woman who wore it was a delightful, intriguing person. That she was, in fact, a magnet disguised as a female.

And he was the element, or whatever it was, that was entirely attracted to her.

"We cannot let anyone go until we have a replacement." Genevieve spoke decisively, not mentioning to Mr. Salisbury that she felt terribly for the current staff—it wasn't their fault they had served under her father, who probably treated his servants as he did his daughter. Either ignoring them or . . . ignoring them.

And she had spent most of her first month hiding out from everybody, which meant that she, too, was ignoring them, but it wasn't because she was more interested in seeing how irresponsible she could be. "In fact," she said, trying to sound as though she'd just thought of it, "I would like to see how they do, now that you are here, and I am preparing to enter Society." Until she said it, she hadn't realized just how much the thought terrified her. Which meant she should probably do it sooner rather than later, so as to get it over with.

That entering Society was like seeing a dentist about a sore tooth nearly made her laugh.

"Should we go down to the sitting room and start making plans and lists and such?" She had no idea what those plans and lists and such would be, but she felt confident that Mr. Salisbury would know.

"And perhaps we can set up some sort of timeline for implementing the changes," she continued as they walked down the hall.

"That is sensib—" he began, sounding surprised. His words were interrupted by a flurry of footsteps on the stairs, with no fewer than three people (two, minus Chandler) scampering up.

"Your Grace, these people would not—" Chandler began, only to be drowned out by the shriek of the female who had reached the landing. She was tall and lean, not as tall as Mr. Salisbury, but definitely taller than Genevieve, and she wore nearly as many ribbons as it seemed she had years.

And she looked to be a healthy age. The result of all that festooning made her look like a Maypole, and Genevieve felt a giggle start within her, but stifled it at Mr. Salisbury's stern look.

Duchesses, apparently, did not giggle. At least not according to her Duchess Expert in Residence.

"And you are?" Mr. Salisbury said, his lip curling. Could pure, arrogant confidence assist in derailing a potentially scandalous situation?

That might explain why he was the Duchess Expert.

The woman's mouth opened, and her eyes widened, and she tilted her head back slowly, as though surveying him inch by handsome inch.

Genevieve wished she could be so bold. She'd like the chance to embark on that kind of appraisal as well.

"I am Lady Houghtsman; I am the duchess's second cousin."

"Once removed," the gentleman added, sounding out of breath. He stood behind and slightly to the side of the lady, and he was just as lean as the woman who was presumably his wife, but nearly as short as Genevieve. He had removed his hat to reveal a few strands of black hair, inexplicably brushed from one side of his head to the other as though his head was imitating a thatched roof. "And I am Lord Houghtsman." He stepped in front of his wife, rotating his hat in his fingers. "We came as soon as we'd heard about your father's untimely death; we are so sorry for your loss." He didn't look sorry, but then again, neither did Genevieve. It was hard to be sorry for losing a person you barely knew.

"It is a pleasure to meet you," Genevieve said, starting to curtsey. Mr. Salisbury's hand shot out and gripped her elbow, stopping her from the movement. She turned to him to protest, only to swallow her words when she saw him shake his head slowly.

Oh. She was not to curtsey too deeply anymore, was she? She was no longer the forgotten relation back in the country. She was now the Duchess of Blakesley, and she needed to command respect.

Although she did not appreciate Mr. Salisbury manhandling her as a reminder of that fact. Something she would tell him later on.

"Would you care for—?" she began, only to feel him grip her elbow even tighter.

What did he have against tea, anyway?

And could he stop treating her like a child?

"The duchess is not currently receiving visitors," he said, his voice even lower than it was usually. It sounded as though it emerged from his knees.

"That is what I informed them, Your Grace," Chandler said in his most supercilious tone, not sounding breathy at all. At least Genevieve hoped it was his most supercilious tone; if it were any more supercilious it might end up being a noise only certain members of the aristocracy could hear. Rather like when her grandmother could tell tea was on its way, even though Genevieve hadn't heard a thing.

Was the duchess squeak part of that as well?

"But the duchess is family," the woman said, striding forward and seizing Genevieve's hands in hers. "And we have come all the way from Thirsk."

The grip on her elbow lessened, and she resisted the urge to rub her arm to increase the blood flow. "If you will allow the duchess a few moments, she will receive you in the second drawing room." He nodded toward Chandler, who seemed to accept the orders, making Genevieve wonder if it was the fact that he was male, that he spoke in utter confidence, or that he looked as if he could thrash anyone who disobeyed him that made Chandler accede so quickly.

Perhaps all three.

It made her feel all peevish.

"That is excellent, thank you, Your Grace," Lord Houghtsman said as his wife's eyes narrowed and her mouth opened. Chandler held his arm out, directing them back down the stairs, leaving Genevieve, her sore elbow, and a profoundly grim Mr. Salisbury alone on the landing.

"It is worse than I thought," he said in a low voice, even before Genevieve could utter a word. He turned and gave her an accusing stare. "Do you have many of these sorts of relatives? The type to just show up and expect things?"

She felt immediately defensive, even though she hadn't done anything wrong. Except to have, indeed, many of these sorts of relatives. "Yes. I do." She nodded vigorously. "From what I have heard and observed myself, all of my relatives are these sorts. The sort that arrives and expects things." Which was why she had been raised by servants.

"This is the sort of thing I wish I had known earlier," he said in a clipped tone.

She cast him a furious look. "When we were exchanging secrets? 'Oh, Mr. Salisbury, I cannot stand the taste of lemon and I have many horrible relatives.'" She planted her fists on her hips and glared at him, her whole self positively trembling with ire. "It is not as though those are the kinds of things one shares with someone one has just met." Except he did share some of himself with her, she had to admit. But she couldn't think about that now, or how his confiding in her had touched her.

To her surprise, he gave her one of those woman-flattening smiles. "Yes! That is how you need to feel to navigate these waters. Just like that."

She raised an eyebrow. "Are you telling me that to be a proper duchess I should be angry?" She let out a rueful sigh. "And here I thought it was just a matter of treating people fairly, being respectful, and having a working knowledge of what I'm dealing with." She paused, considering. "Those qualities are what are required of a good servant, not a good duchess. Isn't that what you said?" she asked. And no wonder she was so bad at the duchess part. The people who'd taught her how to be were kind, usually treated people fairly, and knew what they were doing. And were servants.

Apparently the opposite of what she was supposed to be now.

He hesitated, but eventually nodded in agreement.

"Well," she continued, feeling suddenly weary, "it appears I have some relatives to attend to." She lowered her foot onto the first step down. Only to be stopped again as he spoke.

"Let me help." He sounded earnest. Intense. And not as though he were ordering her, but as though he were asking her.

When she was able to catch her breath and meet his gaze, she didn't feel flattened—she felt the opposite, almost buoyed by the fierce look of concentration he had in his eyes. "Yes. Thank you," she said at last. She didn't know what more help he could give—or exactly what kind of help he was offering—but she knew whatever it was, she wanted it.

Although that did not mean she wanted him. It did *not*.

"Yes. Thank you," she said, and Archie felt something inside him relax, the feeling he had prior to a great battle. Knowing what he had to do, and knowing that he would do it. She was not flighty, as he'd first assumed. He'd unfairly judged her by Lady Sophia and the other ladies he'd met. But she was ignorant of everything she was to be doing and also acutely aware of her ignorance, which made her gaffes even more painful. Everything she'd written and said to him had been an admission of her need for help, and yet it had taken them until this moment to speak the truth to each other:

Let me help.

Yes. Thank you.

Six words in total, but it already felt as if they meant the world to him.

He wanted to see her as the woman she would become. As the woman he would help her become, the confident, assured woman he knew was lurking underneath the hesitancy and the wrinkled gowns. He hoped she wouldn't lose the joy and the good heart she displayed so clearly—her obvious plot to keep her inefficient staff employed for just a bit more time, her kindness in taking in not only her grandmother, but her grandmother's cat, her exuberance when she tracked him down to ask him questions—but he would have to help her hide that heart so people wouldn't take advantage of her.

Which reminded him—Lord and Lady Houghtsman were only the first of what was likely to be a long line of relatives with their hands held out.

They walked down the stairs, pausing in the main hallway.

She wrinkled her nose as she glanced at the door of the second sitting room, which was in need of a fresh coat of paint. Like the rest of the house, it had seen better days. He would have his work cut out for him in order to return to Lady Sophia by May Day.

"I believe we have kept your grasping relatives waiting long enough." He couldn't help himself; he stepped forward and smoothed her sleeve, then gestured to her waist, where the fabric of her gown was bunched up. "You might want to fix that," he said in a rough voice.

"Oh," she said, looking down, her cheeks turning pink. "My lady's maid is—well, she is not a lady's maid." She accompanied her words with a hasty straightening of her gown, which helped a little. Archie doubted the Houghtsmans would even see her gown, so fixed on the sight of the pound signs they had dancing in their head.

It was up to him to keep their daydreams from turning into reality.

"Your Grace," he said, watching as her eyes widened in alertness, "these Houghtsmans, they do not have your best interest in mind."

To his surprise, she uttered something that sounded a lot like a snort. Accompanied with an eye roll. He couldn't help but laugh in response.

"Do you think so, Mr. Salisbury?" She spoke in a mocking tone. "I am certain they are very concerned for the best interest of my wealth, and all the influence a duchess can wrangle. I am certain that, if asked, they would volunteer to shepherd my funds through many different endeavors, only taking a paltry sum for their trouble." She rolled her eyes again. Somehow it made her look even more appealing, even though he normally did not like a whimsical female. Except this one was proving to be the exception to many of his rules. She shook her head. "Honestly, these relatives of mine are the worst. Let us go deal with them, Mr. Salisbury." She took his arm as she spoke, wrapping her fingers around his forearm and nodding decisively. "I might not know how to manage a duchess's household, or dress befitting my rank, or even attend a ball, but I do know how to spot a feckless relative. Lord knows I have enough experience with them," she muttered as they walked out of the room and toward the second sitting room, where Chandler stood, preparing to open the door.

Chandler glanced from her face to his, nodding to both of them. "The Houghtsmans have asked for sherry, but I told them I would wait until you arrived, Your Grace."

Chandler, Salisbury could tell, was as determined as the duchess to maintain the proper dignity.

"That is excellent, Chandler," the duchess replied. "We will not be serving sherry. I hope our guests will not be staying long." She lifted her chin as she spoke, and Salisbury wished it were appropriate to yell "huzzah" or something equally exuberant at her show of spirit.

Instead, he smiled at her as Chandler opened the door. And was startled at his own reaction when she returned the smile.

Almost as though he wanted to claim that show of spirit for himself.

Dear Mr. Salisbury,

~~I have succumbed to your method of communication because goodness knows if I try to say this in person I will likely squeak.~~ Although I realize you had the best intentions, please do not attempt to guide my behavior when we are with other people. I know full well that I can and will make mistakes. I will own those mistakes, and I do not want anyone to be seen to be in command of me ~~even though you are a Captain, Retired~~.

Duchess

Chapter 4

"Your Grace," Lady Houghtsman said as they entered. Both of them rose, and Genevieve noticed that Lord Houghtsman was fondling a porcelain shepherdess that was on the table beside the couch they sat on.

She felt sorry for the shepherdess.

The second sitting room wasn't as shabby as the rest of the house, but it looked as though it had last been decorated about fifty years before—the wallpaper was yellowing, and the furniture appeared to have been made for very small people. She winced as she envisioned Mr. Salisbury, and all his height, sitting down in one of the chairs. But since he seemed to sit down so seldom, that was likely not an issue. "Thank you for waiting." She deliberately did not sit, either. Not just because the chairs looked uncomfortable. "What is the purpose of your visit?"

Lady Houghtsman beamed at her in approval. As though she was a child who'd just successfully calculated a sum, or rolled a hoop for a few minutes without stopping.

Not as though she were a duchess able to wave a hand and make things happen.

She really wanted to be—or at least appear to be—a hand-waver, thing-happening person.

"We came, as we said, since we wanted to offer our assistance during this difficult time. My husband has had some small success consulting on various investment opportunities, and we know that you would benef—"

"No, thank you," Genevieve said before Lady Houghtsman could finish.

The lady blinked at her, a few ribbons fluttering mournfully as her head moved.

"No . . . thank you?" she repeated.

"No. Thank you. I understand you wish the best for me, given my situation, and I will certainly consult you if I have need to." Which will be never, Genevieve promised herself. "I appreciate your coming all this way." She darted a mischievous glance at Mr. Salisbury. "You could have just written a letter."

"Er, well, we were hoping we could stay for a few days."

Lady Houghtsman was definitely not shy, Genevieve had to admit that.

She made herself look regretful. "I am so sorry, my—Mr. Salisbury here has just hired workmen to begin some much-needed repairs. We simply don't have any room," she said, gesturing helplessly.

Even though it was clear that there were no workmen at present. The Houghtsmans, both of them, glared at Mr. Salisbury as though he was the one behind Genevieve's refusal.

Which he was, partially, but she was too well-aware of her family's shenanigans to allow any of them under her roof.

Excellent; it appeared she was finding her duchesslike backbone because of her ne'er-do-well relatives. Maybe she should just hire a few of them to pester her for money in order to keep herself haughty.

"Well, I suppose we will find a room at an inn," Lord Houghtsman said, taking his wife's arm when it seemed she was about to argue the point.

"I think you should." Mr. Salisbury didn't say anything more than that, but he didn't have to—his tone made it clear just what would happen if they didn't leave.

Ribbons flying every which way, Lady Houghtsman left without another word, just eyeing both Genevieve and Mr. Salisbury as though they were up to something.

We are not, Genevieve wanted to shout at her.

Even though she already wished they were.

"Well, that went well," Genevieve said in a wry tone as she picked up the manhandled shepherdess to examine it more closely.

It almost sounded as though Mr. Salisbury was stifling a chuckle. That was a bright spot to the day, wasn't it? Making him laugh?

"I underestimated you, Duchess," he said. His words and the way he said them made her warm all the way down to her toes.

Toes that still had ugly, practical shoes on them, but warm toes nonetheless.

"Underestimated me how? I require specifics." And then she grinned at him, delighting in the moment they seemed to be sharing. A moment caused by the first of what was likely to be an infinite number of horrible relatives, but a moment, at least. There weren't likely to be many moments. And then he would leave, and she would have to share a moment by herself.

Which didn't make any kind of sense.

He smiled back with a lazy twist of his mouth. "Being in command." Which somehow made her shiver, though she didn't know why. "Sticking to what you wanted, which was for them to leave, even though it was uncomfortable."

"Oh, that," she said with a wave of her hand, even though she felt her insides practically light up with the praise. "I have practice with that, at least."

He tilted his head in an unspoken question.

"Well," she began, "I was the only representative of my family, at least the only one in the country, and so when any relatives appeared on the doorstep hoping to find my father in residence, I was the one who had to deal with them." She shrugged, as though it was nothing. Even though it was something. "And I couldn't give them what they wanted, so I insisted that they leave." She met his gaze and smiled. "Until Gran arrived. She didn't want anything, she just wanted"—and she felt her throat get tight at the memory—"me."

None of the other miscreant relatives wanted her. They barely wanted to even look at her. When she was too young to understand she kept hoping one of them would want to take care of her, would want to treat her as someone who was part of a family. Their family. But they never did, and she came to realize that the makeshift family that surrounded her—the small group of servants, eventually her grandmother—were the only ones who truly cared for her.

If they could have given her a come-out, and helped find her a suitable husband, she knew they would have. She'd wished more times than she could remember that they were her real family, and that the distant gentleman who paid no attention to her was no relation at all.

"I am sorry." He sounded sincere. The words felt as though they splintered into her, and she took a quick breath.

"It is fine," she said quickly. Even though it hadn't been fine, not until after she had come to understand that Gran didn't want anything of her, nor of her father, whom she referred to as "that man who married my daughter."

But she had Gran now, and Byron, she supposed, and a motley group of servants back at her old home knowing she could do this. So she would. She couldn't let any of them down, not with so much at stake.

"You know you can depend on me to assist you any way I can." He spoke in a firm tone of voice, not at all intimating anything but what he'd said. And still Genevieve felt herself start to heat up from the inside, and then she felt her face start to turn pink again.

She turned away so he couldn't see her. "Thank you, Mr. Salisbury." She took a deep breath, exhaling through her nose, willing her heart to stop racing and her imagination to stop . . . imaginating. She might sound like a horse that had been galloped too long, but that would be preferable to his noticing how pink she got every time she encountered his Salisburyness. Which was coming to mean a much different thing than she had first envisioned it.

He hadn't expected that show of spirit she'd exhibited with her relatives. It was unnerving, how seeing her like that fired him up, made him want to go to her and—well, he wanted to taste some of that spirit for himself, only that was entirely inappropriate.

And then she'd turned away, and he'd felt colder, as though she had rebuffed him somehow, only there wasn't anything to rebuff.

He had returned to his room to organize his list of what he needed to do, which was ending up being a much larger list than he had originally thought it would be.

And now he had to make a list of who on the staff should be retained, and who should be let go—he was beginning to think that perhaps only a few of them should go, since it was clear they had never had good management. Chandler clearly had done what he could, but there was only so much a butler could do when the owner of the establishment obviously didn't care.

But she cared. And she cared about the welfare of all of the people in this house, even the ones who didn't shovel out the grate properly, or broke glasses, or salted the food excessively.

Although he didn't know if she would retain someone if they allowed her precious tea to get cold.

But he did have immediate vacancies, and he thought he knew where to start to get them filled. He pulled a fresh piece of paper from his rapidly dwindling stack and wrote a quick letter to the Quality Employment Agency. They had been the ones to place him with Lady Sophia when he'd arrived in London after leaving the Queen's Own Hussars, and they would doubtless be a good starting place to fill the duchess's requirements.

A knock on the door, and then she stepped in without waiting for him to call out. What if he had been in a state of undress or something? Although that thought brought other things into his imagination, and he did not want to go there. Not now, not with her standing in his bedroom. Again.

"Mr. Salisbury, I wonder if you would like to go out with me as I conduct some duchess business."

He stood, shaking his head with a wry smile on his face. "There are so many things wrong with what you just said." He chuckled softly. "But you know that, don't you? So you must have some reasons for wanting to go out."

Her expression eased into one of relief. "Yes, thank goodness. There is. If I cannot go outside and move my legs I will have to resort to pacing around the hallways, and we don't want that, do we? Society would disapprove of hallway pacing more than me going outside." She paused. "And I know it isn't done, duchesses transacting their own business. That is precisely why you are here, making sure I don't have to do precisely that. But"—and then her expression got wistful, almost as though she were recalling something pleasant—"I am accustomed to being on my own. I find I do not like being duchessed all the time."

"So you want to be out on your own . . . with me?" he said, allowing a hint of humor to ease into his voice.

She laughed. "Yes, exactly. I wish to be on my own with you." And then her eyes widened, and her cheeks started to turn pink, and he found himself entirely and utterly enchanted.

Which he absolutely should not be.

"That is, I wish to go outside. With you. Alone." And then she rolled her eyes and her mouth twisted up into a grimace. "I cannot say anything properly, which is why you are here. Let us go outside, Mr. Salisbury, and pay visits on people who will no doubt be appalled that I am on my own alone with you."

She shook her head one last time before walking out the door, glancing back to make certain he was following her.

He was. He absolutely was.

"And where are we going?" Archie asked after Chandler shut the door behind them. It was a lovely day, although a bit cold. But the sun was shining, and it appeared people were out and about doing things, and he couldn't imagine somewhere else he'd rather be.

She frowned as she considered it. "Do you know, I haven't figured that out precisely." She shrugged. "I know I should pay a call on the firm that has been handling all of the duchy's assets—I can't even say *my* assets, that's how foreign it is to me still—and I was hoping to pick up some gifts to send to the staff at home." Her face softened. "Cook came to London once when she was small, and she was always telling me about the time she first tasted pear drops. I thought I'd send some to her."

"A bank and a confectioner's, then." He paused at the bottom of the stairs. "Did you want to take the carriage out? I'm sorry, I didn't even think of that. Where is your firm located?"

She withdrew a slip of paper from her pocket and wrinkled her brow as she read it. "I didn't even think of that, either, to be honest." She thrust the paper to him. "And I don't know where this is. Are you familiar with London?"

He took the paper, his chest tightening at her artless question. It wasn't a secret who he was, but he didn't want to be sharing just how familiar with London he was, nor that his family, for all he knew, was currently in residence here, just a few streets away. The thought that he could see them, that more importantly they would see him, cut through him like a knife.

"Ah, yes, we should probably take the carriage," he said quickly, almost without registering just how far the address was from where they were.

If they were enclosed in a carriage there was less chance he would see anyone he knew.

He wished this was all done with so he could return, safely, to Lady Sophia. To his stable, organized life.

He tried not to think of how much duller that would seem now.

The door opened behind them, and the duchess and he turned around at the sound. Chandler's head popped out. "Were you in need of anything, Your Grace?"

"Yes, Chandler, we are. The carriage, please." She accompanied her words with a bright smile, and Archie felt himself flinch inside, wishing it was as simple as just going somewhere rather than trying to avoid family.

Genevieve couldn't stop herself from peering out of the carriage windows even though she knew full well that someone in her position should not be so curious. Engaged. *Interested.*

But there was only so much she could change. Or that she even *wanted* to change. If being a duchess meant she had to lean back against the seat cushions and contemplate her own magnificence, she did not want that. First of all, she didn't want to lean anywhere, not when she could be looking. Secondly, she knew more than anyone that she was not magnificent.

Mr. Salisbury, however, was magnificent. She had been stealing glimpses at him when she wasn't engrossed with what she could see out the window.

He sat opposite her, his hands loosely clasped around his knees, the top of his hat grazing the roof of the carriage because he was so tall. He'd caught her looking a few times, but he hadn't said anything. He had been unusually quiet, actually, while they were inside, merely answering a few of her questions about what she was seeing with tersely uttered replies.

"Mr. Salisbury," she began, because how would she know if she didn't ask? "Are you all right?" She gestured to the window. "Because there is all of London, and it is so exciting, and yet you seem not to be as enthusiastic." She paused, considering. "Perhaps it is because you do know it, so maybe it is not as much of a thrill? But I always find it to be wonderful to share something with somebody; it makes that thing so much more fun in the first place." And then she shrugged, feeling self-conscious. "But you are not me. Although I would like to share Cook's lemon bars with you at some point. Those are worth sharing with everybody."

He didn't answer for a moment; he just regarded her with an odd expression in his eyes. As though she were something he was trying to figure out, just as she was trying to figure out what she was seeing outside the window. But that couldn't be it. "I am sorry, Duchess," he said at last. "I am fine, it is just odd seeing London again after such a long time." And then his mouth pressed together in a firm line, as though he felt he'd said too much. Even though he'd told her nothing.

"Ah," she replied, nodding as though she understood, when she hadn't. Because he hadn't really explained why he was being so quiet, but perhaps that was all part of whatever was making him quiet in the first place.

"I'm from here, you know," he said after a few long minutes of silence.

She turned to look at him. "I assumed you were, since you knew where we were going and everything."

He shook his head, an impatient gesture that seemed directed toward himself. "No, I mean yes, I do, but that's not what I meant. I mean—see, the thing is, I am Mr. Salisbury."

"I know that, *Mr. Salisbury*," she said, stressing his name.

"No, but I should tell you, not that it matters." And then he seemed almost uncertain, and that fact alone startled Genevieve so much her mind started to race in ever-increasing layers of impossibility: He was an escaped felon, he was not Mr. Salisbury (despite multiple assertions of same), someone else had been writing those letters, he wasn't handsome.

Well, scratch that last one; she knew that was not true.

"What is it?" she prompted.

"I am the Viscount Salisbury's son. The third son, as I told you. Everything is as I told you, except that they are likely to be in London, and I don't want to risk running into them." He gestured to the interior of the carriage. "That is why I asked we take the carriage rather than walk." She saw him swallow. "I don't want to mislead you in anything, I wanted you to know."

"Thank you." It wasn't important, at least not to her; he could have been the Prince of Wales, for all she cared, as long as he was able to guide her through her new position. In all honesty, she didn't even know—well, mudpies, and now she was going to ask.

"Why does it matter anyway, who you are?"

He subjected her to a searching look, making her want to squirm or—or something else, and then his expression eased. "You really don't know, do you?"

"No, I really don't." Now she was positively joyous in admitting her ignorance to him. She trusted he knew enough about her to recognize her worth regardless of whatever specific knowledge she might have.

He glanced up at the ceiling, his words coming out slow and measured. "I am—I am from the same world you are. We could—not that it would be at all acceptable, but we could . . ." and he paused, and her mind scrambled again, finally arriving at—

"Oh!" she said at last. "You mean?"

"Yes, if it were known who I was, and who my family was, it might be something that people would gossip about. Rather than if I was just a plain steward from an undistinguished family."

"Oh, well, that won't matter," she said, waving away his concerns with a wave of her hand. Which was, she had to admit, rather dismissive.

But how could anyone gossip about him and her when they didn't know either one of them? And what did it matter who his family was? It wasn't as though they were going to actually become involved. She knew full well that to him she was just a temporary assignment, a burden foisted on him by her aunt Sophia.

But she also knew that it must hurt, somewhere inside, for him to know his family was here and not to be able, or not to want, to see them.

"Do you wish to remain in the carriage while I conduct my business?" she asked.

His eyes snapped to her face, and his expression hardened. "Of course not; that would not be appropriate. You shouldn't even be here with just me, you should have a chaperone and a lady's maid."

"Well, Gran hates going out, and I hate asking her. And I don't have a lady's maid yet," she replied in a reasonable tone. "So you will have to do for me, Mr. Salisbury." She accompanied her words with a smile, and after a long moment, he returned the smile, albeit a forced one.

Dear Mr. Salisbury,

Thank you for trusting me. ~~I am so relieved to find you are not an escaped felon or the Prince of Wales.~~ I also wish to extend my appreciation for accompanying me on my errand today, and I look forward to seeing you at dinner. ~~Yes, I am now writing you, even though we are in the same house.~~

Duchess

Chapter 5

"And how was your day, dear?" Lady Halbard smiled in her granddaughter's general direction.

"It was fine, Gran."

Archie darted a glance over at her, her dispirited tone—far different from her normal voice—making him feel something in his chest. Was it worry?

"What did you do?" her grandmother continued, reaching for a glass of water and drawing it to her mouth for a drink.

"Mr. Salisbury accompanied me to the firm that handles the—that is, my—business affairs." She took a sip from her wineglass, frowned as though she didn't like the taste, and continued. "There are a lot of things to be done, Gran." A pause, during which Archie wondered if he should speak up and remind her that he was there to help. But she knew that, and the footmen were ranged behind their chairs, and he didn't want anyone to start concerning themselves with the relationship between the duchess and her temporary steward.

It was unusual enough that he was dining with her this evening. He did dine with Lady Sophia regularly, but that was out in the country, and Lady Sophia was not a young, lovely, and unmarried lady with remarkable power and position.

But then she spoke again, and he didn't have to say anything. "But I will do them, because there really is no other choice, is there?" Her voice was back to its more cheerful tone, and he felt himself exhale in relief. The thing that had most impressed him was how resilient she was, as well as how sensitive. It seemed as though a person would have to choose one or the other, but she handled both.

"You do have a choice, dear," her grandmother said, her expression mischievous. "You could just refuse to do anything and let the estate and the title crumble. At least then you wouldn't get bothered by so many of your relatives."

Archie felt his eyes widen at the older woman's words. He wasn't accustomed to anybody being so forthright and direct in their comments.

Although now he knew from where the duchess got her humor and directness. And he couldn't help but be pleased that she had; it made things so much simpler, knowing exactly where one stood with her. That she was kind, and honest, and direct.

"Or maybe I should just succumb to one of them and stop worrying my little female head about important things." The duchess's tone was equally mischievous, and Archie found himself marveling that she had survived what sounded like a dreary and lonely childhood. But there had been love, too, she had mentioned; love from the household staff, but love nonetheless.

Archie wasn't familiar with any kind of love, either from family or from servants. His father was a distant, proper man, and his mother was even more distant and proper. He was to have done precisely what his parents wanted him to, which was to marry someone whose breeding and wealth was on par with his. Instead, he joined the army.

He had been fond of his brothers when younger, but his eldest brother got caught up in being groomed for his father's position, and his second brother was determined to join the church, and went through a very long period where he would only respond in biblical verse, which got very tiring.

"Mr. Salisbury?"

Lady Halbard had her head tilted as though in question, and he realized he had allowed his thoughts to drift. Telling the duchess about his family had brought all of those past and best forgotten events to the forefront of his mind.

He was grateful he hadn't seen anyone he knew in the short time he and the duchess had been out. It bothered him how grateful he was. If he were the duchess he would likely just march up to his parents' house and have it all out in the open. But he wasn't, and he didn't like that about himself. But it didn't matter. It couldn't matter, not when he had a duty, a battle strategy, to enact.

"Yes, my lady?"

"What course of action do you advise for my granddaughter? Now that you have been here for a few days."

It was nearly a week, but it felt as though it had only been a few moments.

"Well," Archie began, glancing at the duchess, "I would advise her to prepare for her new role as though she is going into battle."

"Spoken like a captain, retired," he heard the duchess mutter.

"And to be prepared, she needs to have the proper ammunition." He hoped she wouldn't take offense at what he was going to say. But if she did, she would tell him straight out, he knew that. "The proper ammunition being a new wardrobe, knowledge of all the things required of her position and title, and the staff to help her."

"It is excellent that you are here, then." Lady Halbard accompanied her words with a delighted smile. "Because I cannot help her with her wardrobe, for obvious reasons, and I know nothing about any of the other things, either. You might say I am *blind to the problem*." And then she winked.

The duchess threw her head back and laughed, Lady Halbard doing the same, as Archie looked at first one, then the other. He had never been around such . . . exuberance before. He thought he liked it. He wasn't entirely certain, but it definitely made things more lively in general.

* * *

"Your Mr. Salisbury is a nice man," Gran said, raising her teacup to her mouth, her sightless eyes gleaming wickedly.

"He is not my Mr. Salisbury," Genevieve replied in a firm tone. Which would likely only encourage her grandmother to get more outrageous.

"Well, he seems nice." Gran settled the teacup back in the saucer, the clink of the china the only sound in the room, Byron having fallen asleep in Gran's lap after complaining about the ladies coming into the room in the first place. "Tell me, is he as handsome as it seems?"

Genevieve snorted. "As though you don't know full well that he is stunning. Why, the first time you met him you knew. I don't know how, but you did."

Her grandmother smiled in satisfaction. "There is something about the way ladies react to a handsome man. And you, Vievy, I heard how you inhaled when he entered, so I knew he must be something spectacular. Describe him to me."

Genevieve felt her chest tighten. Describe him? How could she describe him without her quite insightful (regardless of her sight) grandmother figuring out that Mr. Salisbury had come to mean more than he should in just a few days?

Fine. She could do this. She just had to keep herself from being too enthusiastic. Something she definitely had difficulties with.

"He is tall," she began in a cautious tone. "He has very dark hair with a curl, he has blue eyes"—as blue as the summer sky—"and he has very strong . . . hands."

Her grandmother nodded in satisfaction. "Strong hands. I should have guessed." And then Gran's eyebrow drew together in concern. "You do know, however, that even though Mr. Salisbury is an excellent gentleman that you cannot . . . ?" and she paused and pressed her lips together.

"I know, Gran." *Believe me, I am well aware of what is allowed for someone in my station, in my position. I am reminded of it every time there is a new problem that I have no idea how to solve. Which is why he is here in the first place, not to do anything so terrible as to marry me.*

"I promise, I will not so forget my place." *How could I?*

Dear Duchess,

You need a new wardrobe. ~~We all agree on that, even your blind grandmother.~~ It is also essential that we find an adequate lady's maid, ~~since the one you have now appears to be crumpling all your drab clothing up into a ball and rolling on it~~. I have already taken the liberty of contacting the Quality Employment Agency for that as well as some of the other positions I deem essential for your household.

Sincerely,
Mr. Archibald Salisbury

Chapter 6

"Where do you suggest I go for a new wardrobe?"

Archie didn't blink anymore when she leaped into his room after the briefest of knocks. He hadn't wanted to have the staff—even though some of them would be leaving—talking about his frequent discussions with the duchess, so he'd taken to working in the room designated as his, but not his bedroom, sending letters when he needed to communicate with her. It suited several of his needs.

But he hadn't counted on her spontaneity; so often her return letter arrived after she did, since it seemed she penned them, sent a footman with them, but couldn't wait to ask the questions herself. So much for not having the staff gossip. She had come by no fewer than five times in the last three days and he didn't even bother getting up anymore. She would just end up gesturing him to sit anyway.

He laid his pen down and ran his hand through

his hair. It was getting longer, and there was one bit that kept falling into his eyes. And each time he smoothed it back, he caught the oddest expression on the duchess's face. So he made sure to smooth it back a lot, since he liked catching that look, even though he didn't know what it meant.

"It is not as though I am an expert in ladies' clothing, Your Grace." He knew where his mother had shopped, many years ago, but he didn't know if those places were still the best to obtain women's clothing. And he certainly didn't have any ladies to ask; the only lady he knew now was standing in his bedroom wearing a gown that looked overwashed and poorly fitting. Like all her clothes.

"Of course you're not, but you have to have a better idea than I do." She gestured down at herself as she spoke, a wry look on her face. "I think the last time I had a new gown was when Gran bought me one. And that must have been at least three years ago. No wonder they are all so horrid." And she glared down at what she was wearing. Not that Archie could blame her; the gown was not at all what a duchess should be seen wearing. "I suppose I could wander up and down Bond Street, announcing who I was, and waiting for a dressmaker to come out and pounce on me." She darted an amused glance at him to let him know she was joking. Even though he wouldn't put it past her. "Or I could attend a party in what I own currently and then ask one of the better-dressed ladies who dresses her." She frowned as she worked through the scenario. "But that would mean my first appearance in public would be in a less than adequate gown, and I don't want to have the immediate reputation that I am not quite what I should be." The last few words she said in a pompous voice, and Archie had to smother his grin. The duchess, he'd found, had quite a delightful sense of humor, but she was also likely to be led astray in conversation just as easily, so if he wanted to keep her on track he had to stay as solemn as possible.

Well, stay solemn and smooth his hair back frequently.

"I know," she said slowly, and he leaned back in his chair, judging by her tone that she had come across the answer. "We will interview some lady's maids, and their first task will be to ensure I am adequately dressed. And I cannot go out in public until I have something that won't cause a commotion." She rolled her eyes. "Even though the thought of judging someone by what one wears, or even what one looks like, seems very facile to me."

"Unfortunately, that is what people in Society often do, Your Grace." Not that Archie had suffered from being judged by how he looked; indeed, he knew some of his success working for Lady Sophia was due to his appearance. He would explain something and he could tell when she wasn't listening and was just—looking at him.

He wondered if he could do the same thing with the duchess. Although that wouldn't be appropriate, and it wasn't as though there was anything he wished to convince her to do.

There was not.

He tried to clear his brain of those thoughts. "That sounds like an excellent plan, Your Grace. In fact," he said, gesturing to the letter she held in her hand, "you'll notice that I have already inquired about a lady's maid."

She beamed at him. "Of course you did! I will send for the carriage now, if that is convenient with you, Mr. Salisbury."

"It is, Your Grace." He resisted the urge to assure her that he could see through her clothing to the woman underneath, but that wouldn't be appropriate. Not at all.

She twisted her mouth up as he spoke, opening it as though to say something, but then just nodded her head.

He wondered what she had been about to say. And again why he was so curious about her.

Mr. Salisbury got no less good-looking the more she spent time with him. And what was worse was that he was not unintelligent, as she had first suspected when they'd met. Instead, he was thorough, processing his thoughts and then saying something that was reasoned and well thought out.

He'd made lists for her, lists that helped to break down and organize what it was she needed to be doing.

Actually, not what she needed to be doing, since it seemed a duchess didn't need to do anything, but things she needed to have taken care of. Chandler was assembling his own list of recommendations for the staff—namely who should stay, who should go, and what positions were required—and Mr. Salisbury had assembled a list of her holdings.

There were a lot of holdings.

She couldn't help but resent her father for leaving her with such a mess. After all, he had been trained to be the duke and he had to have known that having the title meant he had the responsibility. But according to Mr. Salisbury, most everything in the estate was in shambles and needed attention. Even though it hadn't completely fallen apart. Yet.

So not only had her father not prepared for her succeeding him, he'd also thoroughly mucked everything up during his tenure as duke.

She'd resent it more, but it meant she got to spend time with Mr. Salisbury. *Archibald*. He had one piece of hair that kept flopping onto his forehead, and he would brush it back with one strong, long-fingered hand, and for some reason that gesture fascinated her. Plus there was the way he walked into a room—boldly, as though he had every right to be there and expected and demanded attention.

It had to be partially because of his appearance, Lord knew she couldn't be the only person to have found him attractive, but it also must have had something to do with him. With the kind of person who would want to join the military, with all its structure and orders and such.

She admired that, even if she didn't understand it.

"I will just go fetch my wrap," she said, only to stop when he clasped his fingers on her arm.

"Don't go yourself. You should send someone. It is what someone in your position would do," he explained in that low rumble that never failed to send a shiver up her spine. "But you shouldn't do it as though you were asking them for a favor." He stood, so close to her she could see his dark pupils in the field of blue in his eyes. "Practice on me."

She blinked. "Practice? On you?" she stammered, her whole body, it seemed, directing its focus on the part of her wrist he still held. She glanced down at the spot where their bodies touched.

He dropped his fingers abruptly, as though he had been burned.

"Yes," he said in a huskier voice. "Practice on me. Assume that you are correct and superior. Tell me what to do, Your Grace."

Oh dear Lord. Until he said it she hadn't thought just what it was she wanted him to do. But now that he had, she knew very well what it was.

And it was not to fetch her wrap.

She swallowed, and watched his eyes track the movement of her throat. Which just made her mouth all dry again. "I can't do that." *I really can't. Because if I did, you would know what I would want, which is—*

Mudpies. She wanted him to kiss her. To lower his mouth onto hers and do that mashing of lips she'd heard was so popular. She wanted to know what it felt like to be touched by him, and she definitely wanted to know what it was like to touch him.

She'd felt the strength of his arm as he escorted her into dinner. But that did not sate her curiosity as to what it might look like, what it would feel like to be wrapped up in his arms. To have all that strong, male body under her command as she practiced doing what she wanted to.

She had to stop this line of thinking or she would embarrass herself. And him. Of course, he was likely accustomed to having ladies gawk at him, but to actually throw themselves at him?

And her being the unlikely duchess, to boot?

That would not work. Not at all. She knew that perfectly well, and yet his words—his simple words, "Practice on me"—set off a firestorm of want and need and more want.

"Could you get my wrap, please?" Even to her own ears, she sounded hesitant. Nearly squeaky. She couldn't tell him it was because she hadn't said at all what she wanted to, which was "Could you kiss me, please?"

"That won't do." He crossed his arms over his chest, making it appear even broader. Did he know what he was doing to her? "Remember how you felt when you got angry with the first of your demanding relatives? That is how you want to be."

"Angry? I don't want to be angry." She'd spent more hours than she should have being angry— angry that her blood relatives didn't care for her, angry that it seemed she'd been entirely forgotten, except for people who were paid to remember her.

"It's not angry, it's—it's powerful. As you should be." He swept his hand out and down toward her. "Look at you."

She knew he wasn't talking about her hideous gown.

"You're intelligent, powerful, and well-reasoned." *What about beautiful?* a part of her wanted to ask. "You have youth, beauty"—*aha!*—"and wealth. You shouldn't have to ask for anything. It should be given to you."

"So you're saying I should march around and demand things?" She couldn't keep the skepticism from her voice.

He folded his arms over that impressive chest again and nodded. "Yes. That is what I am saying." He tilted his chin toward her. "Try again. I know you can do this." He sounded determined. Implacable. Commanding.

"Fine," she snapped back, feeling the surge of anger within her. Coaxing it to emerge again so she could—of all things—ask for her wrap. No, *demand* her wrap.

"Bring me my wrap, please," she said in what she hoped was a peremptory tone.

He nodded, shifting from side to side. She couldn't help but watch him move, see the harnessed grace and strength of that body.

"Better. But use as few words as possible."

"Wrap!" she blurted out in a loud voice, and then began to laugh as she saw his expression. His eyes had widened, and his mouth had dropped open, and he'd even uncrossed his arms. "Isn't that what you meant?" she said through a torrent of giggles.

He shook his head and that piece of hair fell forward. She clasped her own hands together so she wouldn't push it back for him. "You know what I mean, Your Grace," he said in a stern tone, and then his mouth curled into a smirk, as though he couldn't keep himself from smiling.

"You should call me Genevieve," she said impulsively. He cocked his head as though he hadn't heard her properly. "Since we are working together, and I don't really feel like Your Grace."

"That is why I am here, Your Grace," he said dryly. "It would not be appropriate at all for me to address you as Genevieve. And if anyone were to hear me do so—well, that would be an unfortunate mark on how people viewed you."

"Fine," she said, wishing that things, that *he*, were less stuffy. "But can you just call me Genevieve when we are completely and entirely alone? Where no one even has the possibility of hearing us?"

Which of course brought all sorts of tantalizing scenarios into her mind, where they were alone together somewhere and it was—well, perhaps where they were was incredibly hot, and to prevent heat exhaustion he'd have to remove his jacket. Maybe also his waistcoat. And she would have to take her shoes and stockings off, although her imagination balked at anything more.

Even her imagination was prim, she thought sourly.

"You can call me Archibald, if you want," he said in a resigned tone.

She wrinkled her nose at him. "Archibald is such a thoroughly proper name. You are not thoroughly proper, are you?" she said, stressing "thoroughly." "Perhaps a bit overly organized"— and then she stifled her laughter at his look of outrage—"but that is a benefit in your current situation, so I cannot complain," she added hastily. "But I don't want to call you Archibald," she continued, exaggerating how she said his name so it sounded ridiculous.

"What would you prefer, Your—Genevieve?" he replied, one dark eyebrow rising in what she hoped was amusement.

"Let me think," she said, tapping her lip with her index finger. "It would have to be something that properly conveys your personality but without sounding so—so proper as Archibald."

"My friends call me Archie," he said stiffly.

She beamed at him. "Archie is splendid! I promise, I won't ever say it where anyone can hear us. It'll just be when we are alone together." She paused, then raised her chin and tried to look down her nose at him. Difficult, since he was nearly a foot taller. "Archie, fetch my wrap," she said in a commanding tone.

"Yes, Genevieve," he replied in a strangled voice.

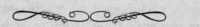

Genevieve:

You can practice on me anytime.

Archie

(NOT SENT)

Chapter 7

Archie walked behind the duchess—Genevieve, he supposed he could refer to her in his mind—as she walked down the stairs, her head held high, and her wrap placed just so on her shoulders.

As he'd arranged it. He had gone to fetch the much-discussed item himself, asking the terrified maid where he might find it in the duchess's bedroom. Of course that would be the subject of talk belowstairs, but he could squelch that with one stern look. And a raised eyebrow. He'd certainly had practice with that in the army.

What he couldn't seem to squelch was his reaction to her. Just now, in his bedroom, of all places, she had told him to call her by her first name. She had laughed at him, and with him, and made the moment between them lighter, simply because it was she. So much of what he'd been feeling lately—a lightness in general—was simply because it was she.

He did not feel this way about Lady Sophia, or any of the ladies he'd met while in her employ, actually. He hadn't minded the attention, since it was something to which he was accustomed, but it wasn't as though he looked forward to seeing any of them in particular. Well, except for Lady Sophia, whose good heart was just irrepressible, if also occasionally irritating.

But Genevieve. She was something special. A person wholly and entirely unique unto herself. It made him feel unsettled. As though his carefully organized life had gotten shifted somehow.

And now, he thought with a grim twist to his mouth, he was thinking about her far more than a steward should be thinking about anyone in the aristocracy, much less a duchess.

If he had met her not as a steward, but as the son of a viscount, he still would not have been worthy to court her. And that alone was reason enough to stop thinking that way, and yet, he couldn't. *Couldn't or wouldn't*, a voice questioned him inside his head.

Never mind that, his mind retorted irritably. *Not just couldn't or wouldn't, but shouldn't.*

But you are here, that same voice pointed out. *And she needs your help. So for now you can be thinking about her. Just not that way.*

"Good luck with that," he muttered, his eyes fixed on her back, on her curves, on how she walked with intent if not confidence.

She stopped and spun around, her gaze wide and curious. "Pardon?" she said, her eyes lingering on his mouth. He felt her so tangibly it was almost as though she was kissing him, and he had to force himself to exhale.

"Nothing," he replied, keeping his voice as neutral as possible. "Just reminding myself of something I need to do later," and then he had to suppress a wince at hearing himself, since what he wanted to do was definitely not what he needed to do. Not at all.

"Oh," she said, nodding as though he'd made any kind of sense. Which he hadn't.

"Please be seated, Your Grace, Mr. Salisbury." Miss Ames didn't seem nearly as nervous as someone in her situation would normally be, attending to a duchess's request, but from what he had heard, dealing with the aristocracy had become a habit for the Quality Employment Agency. A few of the ladies hired had actually ended up married to their employers, not that that would happen now.

It would not.

"Thank you." Genevieve settled herself in the chair and looked over at Archie, who was waiting for Miss Ames to seat herself. "Did Mr. Salisbury inform you as to the purpose of our visit?" She sounded hesitant. It was only in dealing with Miss Ames, but she would have to practice a more peremptory tone.

Is that an excuse to spend more time with her? that same voice asked in his head.

No, she needs this.

As she doesn't need you.

"He did, and I have taken the liberty of asking a few of my applicants to stop by so you can meet with them. The first will be here in ten minutes," Miss Ames said, glancing at the clock atop the messy desk that stood in the far corner of the room.

"That is wonderful," Genevieve said, beaming at Miss Ames. He would have to teach her how to disguise her exuberance. Duchesses didn't beam, they shouldn't show too much emotion, and they definitely shouldn't enthuse.

All of which Genevieve did regularly.

"I am so pleased that meets with your approval," Miss Ames said, returning the smile.

The duchess addressed the last applicant for the day. "And you are available tomorrow? If you need a few more days, that would certainly be acceptable," Genevieve added in a generous tone of voice.

Archie uttered an inward groan. She had a long way to go before she would be able to even enter the ranks of entitled aristocrat. But how much of her natural kindness could he possibly train her to suppress? And was that desirable?

Although it could mean they spent more time together with her . . . practicing on him.

"Oh no, Your Grace, I have been waiting to work again for quite some time," the lady replied. Miss Ames had brought three women to be interviewed, and this Miss Clarkson and Genevieve seemed to have immediately reached an understanding with each other. "Now when you go to see Mrs. Hardwick, do tell her you were sent by me. She was wonderful in dressing Lady Mowlton, and I am certain she will do well by you." Lady Mowlton, Archie had come to understand, was the woman's previous employer, who had accompanied her husband to India, leaving Miss Clarkson behind.

"Thank you, I am certain she will be wonderful," Genevieve replied. She glanced at Archie, a tiny frown drawing her eyebrows together. "If it is convenient, I would like to pay a visit to her now," she said, a questioning note in her voice.

"It is convenient," he replied, wishing they were alone so he could remind her to be more demanding.

"Wonderful," she said, smiling so brightly he was nearly blinded.

"And I will see you tomorrow," Miss Clarkson said, rising. "Thank you for your assistance, Miss Ames," she continued. "I do believe the duchess and I will suit quite well."

"Yes, quite," Genevieve echoed.

"That went well. I thought it would be so difficult to fix on one person, but then Miss Clarkson walked in, and I knew right away." Genevieve settled back against the cushions of the carriage with a contented sigh.

"You should refer to her as simply Clarkson. Not Miss Clarkson."

"Is the purpose of being privileged to speak as few words as possible? First 'wrap,' and then

'Clarkson,' when you could just add a few more words to be polite." She spoke in a grumbling tone of voice that was undeniably entrancing. And he had never found anything entrancing in his life. He wasn't certain he even recognized himself.

She shrugged and continued speaking. "And now we are going to the dress shop. You are certain you do not mind accompanying me? I know Miss Clarkson could have come when she arrives to take up the position, but that would mean delaying things even more. And I don't know her as well as I do you."

"It would be a pleasure," Archie replied, and he found to his surprise that he was not merely being polite.

"Thank you for all your help," she continued, leaning forward to touch his knee. And then she froze, as though realizing what she'd done. As he did, realizing just how welcome the touch was.

"I am so sorry, that was wrong."

No, it was right, that voice clamored in his head. *So right.*

"No need to apologize, Your—Genevieve. Just as long as you do not do such things with . . ." and then he found himself struggling to complete the sentence because just the very thought of her being familiar with another man made his vision blur and his hands clench.

"I like how you say my name," she said in a soft voice. "Not many people have said it in my life. I was always Lady Genevieve when I was growing up." She glanced out the window, but it was clear she was sifting through her memories, not looking at what was actually outside. "Gran calls me Vievy, and now I am Your Grace to most people."

"Well, Genevieve, I am honored that you are permitting me that familiarity."

"Insisted on it, you mean to say," she corrected with a laugh. "Thank you. I didn't know that when I came to London to assume my responsibilities, I would have the benefit of finding a friend. Someone I can talk to, who understands what it is I need and helps me to achieve it."

The reminder—that he was here to help her assume her responsibilities—was a punch to the gut, even though she certainly didn't mean it as such. He relinquished his hold on her hand and folded his arms over his chest so he wouldn't be tempted. And was gut-punched all over again at her expression, which looked hurt and guilty. As though she were the one acting inappropriately when all she had done was be true to herself.

Well. That went horribly, Genevieve thought as the drive continued. She hadn't meant to touch him, to take his hand. It was just—it just felt *right*. She had grown up with touches—fond pats on the head from various servants, her grandmother's holding on to her arm as they walked, so it just felt natural for her to touch him. And now that she had, she wanted to touch him again, only his posture—firmly seated, his arms crossed over his chest in that grim Salisbury pose—was a clear indication that she had transgressed. Done something a lady, never mind a duchess, should never do.

But what was the point of being a duchess if she couldn't do what she wanted? Wasn't that part of being privileged?

But you're a lady first. And as far as she was aware, ladies should not go around holding gentleman's hands, not if they had no indication that the touch was welcome. Although she could ask. And then even the thought of doing that made her blush, and she felt her cheeks burn, and hoped he didn't notice.

But of course he would notice. He was observant, she'd known that from the first time they'd met and he'd caught her rolling her eyes. What's more, he'd probably insist she demand what she wanted.

And what she still wanted was to touch him. So not only was she bright red with embarrassment because she'd thought about asking him if she could touch him, but that hadn't relieved the desire to do so.

But he had said such nice things to her, right before he'd grabbed his hand back. So perhaps he was as conflicted as she was about all of this? Whatever "all of this" was?

With that somewhat comforting (albeit confusing) thought in her head, she began to think on the prospect of new clothing, which was much less confusing and nearly as comforting.

"That one." He nodded in approval, and Genevieve's cheeks turned pink as she felt his gaze on her. All over her.

Mrs. Hardwick nodded in agreement. "That color brings out the richness in your hair, Your Grace. And the other, the green, makes your eyes sparkle quite marvelously."

Genevieve regarded herself in the mirror.

She saw a stranger—a gorgeously gowned, nearly beautiful stranger—gazing back at her. She was used to wearing whatever gowns she had been able to have made by the seamstress who lived in the nearby village. The seamstress usually only had fabrics of a serviceable color, since the rest of her clientele were working women, and Genevieve had never been able to afford more than a serviceable gown.

There would be no mistaking her as anything but a lady now. The gown was a pale blue, the blue of a winter sky. Mrs. Hardwick had pinned it in an approximation of what it would look like, and was holding up and then discarding a variety of trim—ribbons, feathers, and other items, all delightfully useless, designed just to make the gown look better.

They'd all agreed, thankfully, that the unusual circumstances of her inheriting meant that she could eschew the traditional mourning clothes. Mr. Salisbury had delivered the final death knell—so to speak—against wearing all black, since she would have to be seen as being in authority, not in mourning.

Genevieve wondered at that reasoning, but was just as happy not to have to wear black all the time.

"What about this, Your Grace?" Mrs. Hardwick said, seeming to have finally settled on something that met her expectations. It was a flower made of fabric and she held it up against the gown's right shoulder.

"It looks nice," Genevieve ventured. She hadn't minded the other things that Mrs. Hardwick had apparently deemed not good enough, so she wasn't entirely sure what made this fabric flower any better than the myriad things that had not passed muster.

"That one is perfect," Mr. Salisbury said in a definitive tone of voice. Apparently, as in all things, Mr. Salisbury had an opinion. About fabric flowers. "How soon may we have everything?"

Mrs. Hardwick spoke through a mouthful of pins. "I won't have everything that is essential for two weeks. Ten days at the earliest."

Genevieve tried not to be grateful she would have at least another ten days' reprieve from launching herself into Society.

"Ten days." Mr. Salisbury rose, smoothing his coat as he stood. "You will send word when everything is ready."

Mrs. Hardwick nodded. "Yes. And if you could—?" and she gestured toward the desk where the business was done.

"Of course, how much will you require?"

It took Genevieve a few moments to realize that Mrs. Hardwick was asking for money, and that Mr. Salisbury was transacting the business for her. That was not acceptable; he was here to show her what to do, not to do it himself. She stepped off the podium where she'd been standing and went to stand beside Mr. Salisbury. "I will send you a note for half the work, if that is acceptable."

Mrs. Hardwick glanced from Mr. Salisbury to Genevieve and back again. "It is more than acceptable, Your Grace." From the way she spoke, it sounded as though most aristocrats did not pay half up front.

But Genevieve had already decided she would not behave as most aristocrats did.

"If you can just jot the amount down, and I can send a footman back with my check."

"Yes, of course," Mrs. Hardwick replied, beginning to add a long column of numbers.

"If you could help me out of this also—?" Genevieve said, gesturing to the gown she still wore.

"Oh, of course," Mrs. Hardwick put her pencil down and stepped from behind the desk.

"I'll wait for you at the front of the shop," Mr. Salisbury said.

Mrs. Hardwick guided Genevieve back to the fitting room. "Most ladies arrive for their fittings with their lady's maid, but since you've just hired Miss Clarkson, that isn't the case today. I very much appreciate Miss Clarkson recommending my work, and I do hope that the gowns will suit. It is not often I have the honor of dressing a duchess." She undid the pins so Genevieve could step out of the gown, then retrieved her own clothing, which now looked even worse since she'd seen the alternative. She heard herself utter a sigh as Mrs. Hardwick assisted her into the gown.

"I might be able to finish one or two of the things

you've ordered sooner than ten days." Mrs. Hardwick began to do up the buttons. "A day dress or two, nothing that requires too much work."

"That would be lovely," Genevieve replied, grateful the woman seemed to understand. To be able to wear something that was beautiful, just for beauty's sake, rather than practical or long-wearing or any of the other things she'd come to believe were necessary for a proper wardrobe—a part of her felt foolish for caring so much about her appearance, but she knew that the world she was about to enter would care even more, so she had to take pains with it.

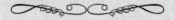

Dear ~~Genevieve~~ Duchess,

I have been going over the statements from the firm that handles your affairs. It appears that some of your estates are in even more dire straits than I'd first thought. ~~I would like to take you to the country~~ I believe it is crucial that we go to the worst one to see what needs to be done in person. With your permission, I will authorize Chandler to make the decisions on the household staff, ~~since you are too soft-hearted to let even the worst employee go~~ since he and I are in basic agreement on what is to be done.

Would you be able to depart tomorrow?
~~I want to spend time alone with you.~~

Mr. Salisbury

Chapter 8

"Oh!" Genevieve exclaimed as she read the letter again.

"Your Grace?" Miss Clarkson inquired.

She waved the letter in the air. "Mr. Salisbury has suggested we go to the country to handle some urgent estate matters. It is not as though there is anything for me to do in town anyway, not without the proper wardrobe." Yes, she was justifying her glee at the prospect of going to the country, alone, with him, but it was also true. Was it justification if it was also accurate?

"Excellent, Your Grace. When are we to leave?"

"Tomorrow. Will that give you enough time to pack?"

Miss Clarkson looked startled to be asked such a question. "Yes, of course."

"Thank you." Miss Clarkson—or Clarkson, as she was supposed to call her—had only arrived the day before, but she'd already managed to put Genevieve's clothing to rights, mending things that Genevieve hadn't gotten around to (mostly because she hated mending), and had also spent a few hours with Genevieve's grandmother.

Gran! She would have to go talk to her grandmother about the trip. She felt guilty for not getting to spend as much time with her as before, but her grandmother didn't seem to mind—she had persuaded Mr. Salisbury to read some poetry to her, and Genevieve had found herself lingering in the room when she should have been off doing duchessy things. Listening to him read in that low, delicious voice.

Not that she yet had a very good idea of what those things were. She just knew she ought to be doing them instead of listening to her altogether far too handsome sort of servant reading poetry.

"Gran, how are you? Where is Byron?"

Her grandmother smiled and raised her cheek for Genevieve to kiss. "I am fine, I did not sleep that well, but it is an old lady's privilege to take naps whenever possible, so I will be doing that later today. Byron is probably napping already somewhere."

Genevieve settled into the chair next to her grandmother. "Have you had tea? Would you like anything?"

Her grandmother shook her head. "No, Mr. Salisbury came in earlier to inquire if I needed anything, and he ordered the tea for me. He is such a thoughtful man," she said, in a warm tone of voice.

"He is very thoughtful, it is so kind for him to leave his position with Aunt Sophia to come help me." She paused. "Speaking of Mr. Salisbury, he has suggested that we go to one of the estates. From what he has indicated, there are some pressing matters that need my attention. We leave tomorrow."

Her grandmother nodded again. "It sounds as though you are doing exactly what you should be, Vievy." As usual, her grandmother didn't ask about the propriety of what she was doing, trusting that Genevieve would make the right decision. Genevieve wished she could be so assured about herself.

"I hope so." Genevieve bit her lip as she thought about the enormity of what needed doing, and how many miscreant relatives would be waiting for her to fail. "Do you want to join us on the trip?"

"No, thank you." She reached over and patted Genevieve's hand. "I like being in one place. It suits me. You'll have your business affairs to concern yourself, and Byron hates traveling."

"I don't know if I hate traveling, I have done it so seldom," Genevieve remarked in a contemplative tone.

Gran smiled. "You're young; you will likely find it invigorating. It sounds as though the end of the journey will have lots of hard work, however."

Leave it to her grandmother to just state the truth. Truth that Genevieve knew she'd have to face.

That unhappy thought was interrupted when there was a knock on the door and Chandler walked in, a displeased expression on his face.

"Your Grace, you have visitors. They say they are your cousins."

More family? "Show them in to the second drawing room, Chandler, thank you. And would you mind asking Mr. Salisbury to come as well?" She was nearly confident of her ability to dismiss her family if they required dismissing, but it wouldn't hurt to have Mr. Salisbury at her side.

Besides which, then she could have the pleasure of looking at him.

Archie walked into the room prepared for the worst. Chandler had told him only that some more of Genevieve's family had come calling, but from what Chandler and Genevieve herself had said, the entire family was worthless.

Except for her. Which he should not be thinking about.

"Mr. Salisbury, thank you for coming." The duchess—Genevieve—gestured to two ladies seated side by side, teacups placed on the table in front of them. "These are my cousins, Miss Lawford and Miss Maria Lawford. They've just arrived in town, and are hoping I could recommend a place for them to stay."

Did she not see through that subterfuge? Of course, she was supposed to offer the two cousins—both of whom were glancing around as though appraising the items in the room—lodging for the duration of their visit.

Archie leaned against the fireplace, his arms

folded over his chest. "Have you considered the Hyland Hotel? I understand it is quite respectable, and caters specifically to ladies such as yourselves."

Miss Lawford squirmed, giving Miss Maria a sidelong glance. As though that wasn't obvious at all. "Well, no, we hadn't yet. We came here first, just to see our cousin." She accompanied her words with an overly sweet smile toward Genevieve, who smiled back.

"I would offer that you could stay here," she began.

"That would be wonderful!" Miss Maria interjected.

"Only I am about to leave town, so that is not possible." Again, she smiled, but the smile didn't reach her eyes. But Archie imagined only he knew that it was a false expression. The two ladies were far too self-absorbed by the ruin of their plans to pay the duchess much attention.

"Oh." The elder sister took a sip of tea. "Well, then, we will make our way to the High Hotel?" she said, with an inquiring look toward Archie.

"Hyland," he corrected.

The duchess placed her cup back in the saucer. "Do let me send you there in my carriage. It is the least I can do."

Judging by the sisters' expressions, it was the least she could do. The very least.

"Thank you," one of them said at last. They glanced at each other again, then both rose from their seats. Archie bowed as they rose, feeling proud of Genevieve for having deflected her relatives so deftly.

"I will be out of town for some time, but I am so delighted you were able to find me," Genevieve said as the ladies made their way to the door.

She turned to him as the door shut behind the two ladies. "Another set of relatives dispatched. Do you suppose I could just invite them all in and tell them to go away and leave me alone in one big meeting? It would certainly save a lot of time." Her expression was rueful, and he squelched the indignant anger he felt on her behalf.

"I thought you might have been exaggerating about them, but it appears you are not," he replied. He gestured to the sofa.

She settled down on the sofa with a contented sigh. A sigh that made him wonder what he could do to engender it himself.

He should not be thinking about those things, he reminded himself.

"They truly are dreadful," she admitted. "I do wish my brother had survived, and he would have been the one to deal with all of them."

"What happened to him? If it is not too painful," he added quickly.

She shook her head, that rueful expression intensifying. "Charles was similar to our father. Not that I knew either one of them well." He felt his throat constrict at her momentarily sad expression. "From what I understand, there was some sort of wager and a ridiculous amount of port involved." She glanced up, clearly trying to regain her composure. "Thank goodness that the title was allowed to come to me. Even though it was—unusual, to say the least." That was putting it mildly.

He was grateful as well—but he couldn't say that to her. Because if she hadn't inherited, and hadn't needed assistance, they would never have met.

"Did you have a chance to review my letter?"

Even though there was so much in it he didn't say. But knew he couldn't.

He'd never had so many things he wished to say before. It felt chaotic, not at all like him. And yet it didn't feel wrong.

Her expression eased. "Yes, it sounds like a wonderful idea. I am so pleased you thought of it—being away from London for a while will give me the opportunity to . . . practice doing what I have to," and she accompanied her words with a glance up at him that went straight to his groin.

Not where it should be going at all.

"Yes," he replied in a strangled tone of voice. "We can ensure things are running properly, and you can work under my guidance," which sounded horribly and wonderfully wrong, given where his thoughts were, "so you will be able to handle things yourself."

"Yes, you will have to return to Aunt Sophia eventually." She wrinkled her nose. "And I suppose eventually this will all get easier as I learn it, because I have no plans to get married to someone who will just take it over."

His hands gripped his knees. The idea of her marrying anyone—even though her comment made it clear she had no thoughts in that direction—made his gut churn with jealousy.

"I will not leave until you are confident in your

own abilities." He sounded clipped and formal, as he did when he'd first arrived.

She reached over and took his hand. "I cannot thank you enough, Mr. Salisbury. Archie," she corrected with a laugh. Apparently she didn't think he sounded unfriendly. Should he be pleased about that or not? "Is it wrong to admit that I am excited about going to the country, even though I am certain there are far more problems for me to solve?"

It was wrong, but Archie had to admit to himself—if not to her—that he felt the same way.

He squeezed her fingers, then let go of her hand, knowing how easy it would be to go from holding her hand to holding her.

Dear Genevieve,

I know you think ~~I'm foolish idiotic overly organized~~ it's ridiculous for me to write you when we will be leaving in an hour, but I wanted to let you know I've written to Lady Sophia and informed her I might be away from my position for longer than I first thought. I will remain until ~~I no longer feel this pull toward you, no longer feel this palpable urge to touch you~~ all of your immediate concerns are properly addressed.

Archie

Dear ~~Archie~~ Mr. Salisbury,

In order that ~~I can spend more time with you~~ we can go over what might be required, I would like you to join me in my carriage for the journey. ~~Miss~~ Clarkson will ride in the other carriage with our luggage. Please ensure you have whatever paperwork might be needed.

~~Genevieve~~ Duchess

Chapter 9

"Well," Genevieve said, glancing out the window with a bright smile, "we are off!"

"Yes," he said in his low rumble. "And a good thing, too. There is much to be done."

"Yes, much," she echoed. She looked down at her hands, which she seemed to have clasped tightly in her lap, her right thumb rubbing on the back of her left hand.

He reached out and took both her hands in his one larger one. The warmth of it, the intimacy, made her want to melt all over the cushions.

"Don't be anxious," he said in that low, resonant tone. "You have me to help you, Genevieve," he replied, the way he spoke her name washing over her like a warm rain.

"Thank you."

He let go of her hand after she spoke, only this time it didn't feel like a rebuke. "I have made a list of what needs to be done," he began.

"Of course you have," she interjected.

He scowled at her, but didn't say anything

in response. He was learning as well. "As I was saying." He withdrew a sheaf of papers from the bag that sat on the cushion beside him. "While I would likely wish to address the expenditures on the estate," he said, looking down at the paper, his eyebrows drawing together over his strong nose, "I believe you would want to first hear the concerns of your tenants." He looked up suddenly, and she was caught by the directness of his gaze.

A moment. Two, as they continued to look at each other, the sound of the carriage wheels— *thump, thump, thump*—the only sound.

"Yes, you are correct." She shouldn't be so breathless. Or at least she shouldn't sound as though she were breathless. She was fairly certain duchesses were not breathless, even if they occasionally squeaked.

His mouth curled up in a half smile. "I know I am." She had to admit she liked how confident he sounded. "We can settle in when we arrive, and then we can head to the village and locate someone in charge."

"That is very military of you," she said with a grin.

"It is, isn't it? I was in the army for five years; I suppose I learned more than I thought when I was there." His gaze went dark. "There were times I never wanted to remember it, that I tried to blot it out from my mind. But I suppose there were some benefits." He gestured ruefully toward the papers in his lap. "The ability to organize things, and make lists, and lead people into battle. Not that I have cause to do that anymore."

She doubted he'd learned all of that in the army. It had to have been born into him. "But you do have cause to do that, don't you see?" She hadn't realized until now that he was just as out of place as she was, albeit in a much less obvious way. "You're leading me into battle, the fight to prove I am worthy of my position so I can effect some sort of change. Like you, I want to do the right thing, and banish the wrong things."

He smiled more warmly, his eyes holding an appreciative gleam that did something to her insides. "You would see it that way." He leaned forward, clasping his hands between his knees, holding her gaze. "I admire you, Your Grace. Genevieve. You're so—so honorable." He leaned back against the cushions, his voice musing. "I don't know that I've ever heard a woman described that way."

"Hmph," she murmured. She appreciated the compliment, but would also have appreciated *You're so lovely* or—no, *You're so lovely* would just about cover it.

He held his hand up, forestalling whatever else she might say. "And I don't want you to misunderstand me, it's not that I don't think women should be described as honorable. They should be. They *are*. But it's only when a woman occupies a position that is usually held by a man that anybody tosses that word around."

"So what you're saying is there would be more honor if more women were in charge? If one had been your general, say?" She spoke with humor in her voice, but a part of her wanted him to confirm what she'd said. She had never thought of herself as a particularly progressive thinker before, but now that she was in charge of all these people, this land, and wealth, she had to be. She had to keep looking forward, to see what kind of progress she could make, to try to stem the tide of neglect and mismanagement her father had left as his legacy.

She wished she had known her father well enough to be able to curse at him. Unfortunately, she didn't even have that much of a memory of him. The only memory he'd left her was all the work ahead of her.

That pressure made it even more imperative that she not succumb to any of Archie's charms. Not that he had indicated he was in danger of succumbing to hers.

And that was a lowering thought, even though it was precisely what was appropriate. What was *right*.

"If a woman had been my general," he mused, and she was happily surprised that he didn't immediately scoff at the idea. "If a woman had been my general. Well, I think the battles would have been shorter, for one thing."

"Why?"

He turned his head to look out the window. Only Genevieve could tell he wasn't seeing anything but his memories.

"It is probably not right to say that women are softer," he began, "because they can be hard when they want to be." His lips thinned, and she felt a stab of jealousy at whatever female had given him such an impression. "But they are far more reasonable when honor is involved." He met her gaze, a hint of laughter in his eyes. "Back to honor again," he said. "Now that I am no longer in it, I have to say that there is very little honor in battle. There is courage, and strength, and forethought. But when it comes down to it"—and he shook his head almost mournfully—"the only honor is the false honor paraded around to puff up the people who are determined to lead men to their deaths."

Her heart hurt. Because he hurt.

"That's a harsh view of it, Archie," she said softly, but loud enough for him to hear. His mouth twisted into a rueful grimace. "What about what you said before? About making certain that the right things stay right, and the wrong things are dismissed?"

"How can mere mortals know what is right and wrong?" he asked, his expression haunted.

"How can we not?" she replied, in a forceful tone. "What else do we have if not our determination to stay on the right path? Should I just allow my various cousins to march into my life and take what they want, even though it isn't right? It would be easier, wouldn't it?" She paused. "That is what my father did," she said in a quieter voice.

"Your father—what kind of man was he?"

He hadn't responded to her question, but then again, he hadn't dismissed her.

She shook her head. "I have no idea. I mean, I have some idea, since he left the estate in such a shambles, but I don't know what kind of man he was. Besides an irresponsible one. I only saw him a few times, my mother died when I was very young, and even before then, from what I understand, he was more often in London than at any of the estates with us. My brother was much older than I; he knew him better." Although she doubted he'd known how to be a duke any better than she.

"Your father missed out on knowing his daughter, then," he said in a fierce tone. He captured her hand again, but his gaze didn't waver from her face. "Because she is a strong woman, an honorable woman, and it is my pleasure to know her."

Oh. Could her insides melt into a puddle any faster? Nobody—with the possible exception of her grandmother, who was admittedly biased—had ever expressed such an opinion of her.

"Thank you," she said, so low she wasn't certain he had heard her. But it appeared he had, since he smiled that warm smile that made her heart thud a little faster in her chest.

He needed to focus on the work. Not the work of getting to know her, either. The work of doing the job he had sent himself here to do, the one that would mean she was presentable to her world, a world he had only barely ever belonged in, and didn't belong in at all now. And now that he thought more about it, it wasn't just that she needed help in knowing how to behave; she also needed help in knowing what to do. From what she'd said, her father hadn't known what to do, and so the duchy was suffering. It was important that she know, and that he help her.

But it was difficult to keep that in mind when faced with her and how she managed to maintain her optimism and cheer despite everything being thrown at her.

And then there was the way she was. Earnest, and passionate, and opinionated, even if she hesitated to express her opinions. He wanted to capture some of that passion for himself, spark the fire he knew burned within her.

He couldn't help but imagine how earnest and passionate and opinionated she'd be in bed. And she wouldn't be wearing one of those horrid gowns, either; she'd be gloriously naked, all that fine, smooth skin exposed to his touch. To his hand.

But even though he was attracted to her, and had all sorts of thoughts about her, it wasn't her body he admired as much as her mind. That was a first for him; he was handsome enough, he supposed, to attract more than his fair share of feminine interest, and many of those women had been beautiful. But he hadn't wanted to delve further, to find out what made them happy, or sad, or what their dreams or goals were.

Unfortunately for his own dreams, her goals did not, and could not, include a disinherited viscount's son whose only attribute was his knack for organization. No title, no wealth, no status.

He glanced at her again, only to find her regarding him as well.

"What if I can't—?" she began, then shook her head.

"You can." He didn't even know to what she was referring, he just knew she could. She would.

"But there are so many people who will say I shouldn't be."

That sentiment could apply to so many things. But only one he could politely address.

"You have the title, you have the wealth, the land, everything associated with the duchy." He paused. "You have me."

She gave a half smile. "And they say, 'Possession is nine points in the law,' don't they?"

Damn it. Now he was thinking about her possessing him, practicing on him as he'd told her to do before.

"Precisely." He deliberately kept his tone neutral and managed to force his gaze away from her face to look out the window. The late afternoon was easing into darkness, and he glanced up at the sky and the scudding clouds. "I think it might rain soon. How long is this trip supposed to take?"

"You're the one who plans and organizes," she pointed out. "I believe we have been traveling for five hours, though? So perhaps just another hour or so."

Archie glanced up as a streak of lightning zagged through the clouds. He didn't think the rain would hold off for an hour, and the roads in this area—no doubt thanks to the duchess's father—were horrendous already, the coach pitching and swaying as it rolled along.

She followed his gaze and her expression immediately got concerned. "I do hope it doesn't pour so much that the coachman is made too uncomfortable."

Of course. She wasn't worried about whether she would get wet, or that anything would happen on the journey; she was just concerned that the coachman, her servant, not be made uncomfortable.

Another streak of lightning, this one sounding as though it landed closer than the first. She jumped in her seat, her eyes wide as she looked at him. "That was awfully close, wasn't it?" she said, her voice in a higher tone than usual.

He was seated beside her almost before he realized he'd moved, taking her hand in his, resting both of their hands on his thigh. "It is fine. Only a spring storm."

"I am—not fond of this kind of weather," she admitted. As though he couldn't tell from the way she was shaking. "The servants learned to come check in on me when it was raining at night."

Servants? Checking in on a frightened girl?

From what she'd said, they loved her nearly as much as a family member could, but he still wished he could go back in time and pummel her father.

"You're safe now." He heard the promise in his voice, the commitment he was making to her. Hopefully she wouldn't hear it as well, wouldn't think her temporary employee was overstepping his bounds.

Even though he absolutely was.

"It would be just our luck if the carriage overturned." He could tell she was working herself into a panicked state. He withdrew his hand from hers, instead wrapping his arm around her shoulders and drawing her into him. She needed this, damn the impropriety. "You must think I am silly to be scared of a storm," she said in the vicinity of his waistcoat. He smiled over her head, willing himself not to kiss her head.

"Not at all. You'd be surprised at what can frighten people."

She tilted her head and looked up at him. He could see the tension around her mouth. "I can't imagine anything frightening you, Archie."

He grinned down at her. "Imagine this: a group of soldiers camping in a field, the distant sound of guns and cannon blazing."

"Well, of course battle is frightening," she interrupted.

"Shh, I'm not done."

She smiled and clamped her mouth shut.

"As I was saying, the guns were blazing,"

"The *cannon* was blazing. It was the *sound* of guns."

He huffed a sigh. "Are you going to let me finish, Duchess?"

He got only a tiny chuckle in reply. "There was all this noise, and we were accustomed to it. It didn't frighten us anymore."

And wasn't that the worst truth about war? But he was trying to cheer her up, not lower his own spirits. "And then there was this screech that interrupted all of it, and we all froze, terrified that it was ghosts, or a sudden attack, or something."

"What was it?"

He lowered his mouth to her ear. "It was a group of owls, out hunting."

"That's called a parliament."

He drew back, his eyebrows raised. "Is it? That makes more sense than it should, doesn't it? Screeching hungry birds out searching for innocent mice to eat."

She laughed, as he meant her to. "I'll have to take my place there, eventually. In Parliament, not amongst the owls," she clarified.

He squeezed her shoulder. "Since that night I swear most of the men were scared of owls. Not me, of course," he added.

"Of course," she echoed, a mocking tone in her voice.

The carriage lurched more, and her hands tightened around his waist.

He tried not to think of how good it felt, how right it felt. It wasn't right. He wouldn't go so far as to say it was wrong—they hadn't done anything yet, precisely—but this was as far as it could go. He needed to remind himself of that. And also remind himself that he could not and should not react to her touch. Even though he wanted nothing more than to lose himself in her taste.

Archie:

> ~~Thank you for listening to my concerns on the journey.~~
> ~~More importantly, thank~~ for listening.

~~*Genevieve*~~

(NOT SENT — YET)

Chapter 10

"I should let you go," Genevieve said after a few minutes. She didn't think the thunder sounded that bad anymore. Although perhaps it was because her heart was thundering now.

He didn't reply, just rubbed her shoulder with his hand. Which felt substantially different from when Gran touched her. Probably because Gran was not the handsomest man she'd ever seen, for one thing. Nor was she tall and broad, conveying power and safety all at once.

"The storm is receding," he assured her, his hand still moving in slow circles on her shoulder. "It seems as though your coachman should be retained; he has done a very good job of getting us through the storm."

Genevieve smiled in the depths of his waistcoat. Another servant who would be allowed to stay in the duchess's employ. She did hate to have to let them go just because her father had been a terrible master, not guiding them in the way they should be doing their jobs.

"I can hear you smiling, you know," he said in a rumble, the deep notes of his voice palpable in her body.

She withdrew from his comfort, wishing she didn't immediately want to dive back into his arms. "It feels as though we are here," she said as she felt the carriage slow. She looked out the window, but couldn't make out anything but the shape of a large house, thanks to the rain and the trees and the darkness.

Darkness. A candle burned in only one of the windows. "Did you inform the staff we were coming?" she said, visions of huddling in a dark, cold house suddenly haunting her.

Although they would have to stay warm . . .

Stop that, Genevieve, she admonished herself.

"I did. I sent a letter that should have already arrived." He leaned over her to peer out the window. "I did not have high hopes that they would be able to put things to rights in such a short time, but I would have expected more than one meager candle." He drew back and met her gaze, an amused look in his eyes. "At least the candle indicates someone is within, so there is that, at least."

The coach came to a stop as Genevieve's eyes widened. "You're enjoying this, aren't you?" she said in an accusing voice. "All of this means you get to plan and organize and be useful."

She spoke in humor, but his reply was serious. "Yes, Duchess. All I want is to be useful."

It was true. He did want to be useful. But now he knew he wanted more than that, wanted things he couldn't get. Things he shouldn't even be thinking about.

He pushed all that away as he helped her down from the carriage, steadying her as she faltered on the muddy ground.

"Mudpies," she said, looking down at her feet. "There's another reason I hate storms. Wet feet."

"Mudpies?" he asked.

"Not literally. It's just something I say. So I don't say anything worse." She glanced up at him with an amused look that turned serious as she looked searchingly at his face. "Are you all right?" she asked, smoothing a piece of hair away from her face. She glanced down the road, not waiting for his reply. "I hope the second carriage arrives soon. I would not want Miss—that is, Clarkson to have suffered any kind of mishap due to the storm. Yet another reason to hate storms," she said grumpily.

"Clarkson is able to take care of herself," Archie assured her, trying to hide the amusement in his voice.

Apparently not well enough, since she glared at him and made a *hmph* noise that was both damning and adorable.

"Let us go inside and see what awaits us," Archie said, taking her elbow and guiding her toward the front door. "Unload the luggage and stable the horses," he directed the coachman, who had dismounted and was at the horses' heads. The man nodded in reply.

Archie didn't bother with knocking; it was raining, there was only one candle inside, and besides, she owned the house and everything surrounding it.

The door swung open, a loud creak of warped wood announcing their presence. He put his arm in front of her as she was about to step inside. "Let me go first," he ordered, not waiting for her reply as he stepped over the threshold into the gloomy foyer.

He felt her behind him, so close that if he turned around, she'd be—well. He shouldn't be thinking of that. "Anyone here?" he called, his voice echoing around the empty room. He walked to where the candle was on the ledge and snatched it up, holding it over his head.

What he saw was as he'd imagined—a clearly neglected house, a few odd pieces of furniture scattered about, nothing to give the impression that the house had been cared for or even had people residing in it.

"There has to be someone here, though," he muttered.

Just as he spoke, he heard a shuffling as a person walked into the room.

"Good evening!" a cheery voice rang out, completely at odds with the overall gloom of the house.

"Good evening," Genevieve replied, as friendly as if they were meeting on the street, not in the hallway of her own poorly treated possession.

A man made his way toward them slowly, an obvious limp hampering his progress. "Your Grace, I assume?" He didn't wait for her affirmation. "I knew you would come, I left the candle burning just in case it was this evening. Terrible storm, isn't it?" He came close enough for Archie to see him. An older man, perhaps in his fifties, he had a welcoming smile on his face, with no hint that things were not as they should be here. "I am Wickes, the caretaker here. And the butler, the groundskeeper, the gardener, and whatever else needs to be done."

He spoke with glee as he recited his various positions, and Archie could only gawk at the man. Did he not see what was—and more specifically wasn't—happening here?

"Thank you for your service, Wickes," Genevieve said. "Perhaps you would be able to make us some tea? Or is there a cook?"

"No cook," Wickes said, beaming. "I do all the cooking here."

"It is just you, then?" Archie couldn't take it anymore, his words sounding as though they were shot out of a cannon. He could feel the disorganization flowing around him like a tangible thing.

"Well, there are a few maids that come in to air out the house every so often. And of course the overseer," and then his face did lose some of its cheery charm.

The overseer. Of course, Archie thought. Put someone in charge and they were as likely to overstep their authority and look out solely for themselves, not do what was actually good.

Except, he had to amend, for her. She was in power and yet she was neither shirking her duty nor taking advantage of it.

He thought he could include himself in that as well—he wanted to do what was best and right for his men. And now for her.

"The overseer, where is he?" Archie tried to keep himself from sounding as though he were barking orders, but judging from her indrawn breath, he was not successful.

"Why, he's in to town, as usual," Wilkes replied, apparently not bothered by being barked at. Perhaps that explained his friendly countenance. Maybe he didn't know when he was being taken advantage of, or if things were not as they should be.

"In town?"

Wilkes nodded. "That's right. He goes to town most every night to the pub. The Golden Stars, it is," as though the name of the pub was important.

"Does this overseer—what is his name?"

"Leonards."

"This Leonards, what are his duties? Since it sounds as though you do everything." Poorly, Archie wanted to add, but that was hardly the man's fault—the estate, from what he'd read in the duchess's documents, was enormous, and it would take twenty Wilkeses to keep it up.

"He collects the rents, deals with the tenants, makes improvements."

"Ah. Thank you."

"Mr. Salisbury?" Genevieve's voice was soft, but no less commanding. To him, at least.

"Yes, Your Grace?"

"Perhaps we can save the discussion of what Mr. Leonards does until after we have had tea and gotten a chance to sit down."

Archie wanted to punch himself in the nose for his thoughtlessness. "I am so sorry, Your Grace. Wilkes, could you see about that tea? And perhaps direct us to one of the sitting rooms?"

"Certainly," Wilkes agreed. He picked up the candle from the window and frowned at it as though trying to figure out what to do.

Archie emitted an exasperated sigh and strode over to a side table at the far end of the room where he could just barely discern some candles there. He walked back and held his unlit candle out so Wickes could light it.

"Just so," Wickes enthused as the candle's flame got larger for a moment. "Go on in through there, that is what we call the Owl Room, on account of what it has a stuffed owl in there."

"The Owl Room, hm?" Genevieve said in an amused tone.

"And I'll be back as soon as I can with your tea. Can't account for if the milk is entirely fresh, though. I'll take a sniff."

"You do that," Archie said as he took Genevieve's arm, guiding her toward the coincidentally named Owl Room. "When is Leonards likely to return?"

Wilkes pondered. "In a storm like this, he'll probably stay overnight at the inn. So maybe tomorrow mid-morning?"

"Mid-morning," Archie repeated. The missing Leonards seemed to be so bad at his job, likely even the duchess would agree he should be let go.

The thought that he could take Leonards's position—that he could work here, organize what needed to be done, that he could work for her, but not be with her so he was tempted—it was very appealing.

Although for right now his only concern could be making sure she was comfortable. Not made uncomfortable by anything he said or did.

~~Dear Genevieve,~~

~~I want to be useful. To you. In so many ways, with
only a few of them appropriate to our respective positions.
I need to stop this way of thinking immediately, I need to
do what needs to be done, I cannot jeopardize your position and your reputation with my own wants and desires.
I tell myself that, and yet it is as though there is another
voice in my head urging me to forget duty, for once. Forget
listening to what I should do. For once, do something that
feels right rather than what is actually right.~~
~~This way of thinking, it's dangerous. It's wrong.~~
~~And yet it makes me burn.~~

Archie

(NOT SENT)

Chapter 11

Archie led her into the Owl Room, holding the lit candle in one hand and her arm in the other. Her skirts felt as though they were picking things up as she walked, and she shuddered at the thought of what might be swept up in there.

"Are you cold?" he asked in a concerned tone.

"No, thank you. I am fine," she said, using a more emphatic tone than was necessary so as to convince herself as well as him. If she were cold, he would want to warm her up, and—well, she shouldn't be thinking about that.

"Sit here," he said, withdrawing a handkerchief from his pocket and whacking at a chair that was pulled up to the fireplace—even though there was no fire.

Genevieve coughed as dust went down her throat. "Are you certain?" she said, eyeing the chair skeptically. "I can just as well stand."

He looked at the chair for a moment, and Genevieve could practically hear the wheels of his thoughts spinning in his head. Then he took his jacket off and laid it down on top of the seat cushion before she could object.

"No, you can't—you'll ruin your jacket!" she expostulated.

"Too late. It's already ruined, if it is to be ruined," he said with a shrug. "If you don't sit, my sacrifice will be for naught. You don't want my sacrifice to be for naught, do you? That would be completely illogical." He had crossed his arms over his chest as he spoke, and looked so thoroughly in command it managed to both annoy her and intrigue her.

As he had done from the first time they'd corresponded. Although the balance was far less annoying than it had been originally.

She plopped down on the seat, wondering if the ability to lower oneself gracefully into a chair was something normal aristocrats knew how to do. He unfolded his arms and leaned over her, so close she wondered if he was going to—

"Hold on, there's a spider in your hair," he said, so calmly that at first it didn't register. But then—

"Ack!" She leaped up so quickly she catapulted into his arms, feeling him enfold her as she froze.

"You are afraid of spiders as well as lightning, Your Grace?" His tone was amused.

She was not.

She scowled in the confines of his waistcoat. Then drew back and tilted her head so she could look at him. Even in the flickering light of the dodgy candle, he was stunning. It didn't make her any less angry, but it was a more pleasant anger, she had to admit.

"It is not as though those two fears are completely unreasonable," she said in as haughty a tone as she could muster. Given that she was currently being held by her temporary steward in a house that had seen many better days as some sort of eight-legged creature went on its way after making merry in her hair. "Spiders, lightning. Some people are even frightened of owls," she added, emphasizing the word. "There are plenty of fears, reasonable and unreasonable. Is there a limit to how many things may frighten one? Besides, I am not frightened of spiders as much as not wishing them to take up residence anywhere near me."

"No disrespect meant," he said, his tone still amused, damn him.

"Just you wait," she said with a *hmph*. "I'll find out what terrifies you and I'll—I'll go and sneak it into your bed when you're not looking."

"You terrify me, Duchess," he murmured, only to stop speaking as they heard Wilkes's return. She withdrew, but slowly, just in case the spider was still about hoping to return to the place of its former triumph.

"Tea, Your Grace, Mr.—what was your name?"

"Salisbury."

"Mr. Salisbury. Well, if you could just move those thingamabobs I can place the tea down." Wickes nodded to the table next to the chair with the coat.

"Of course," Archie said, removing all the whatever-they-weres off the table. "Please go ahead."

"Well, I don't have much, I knew you were arriving, but I wasn't certain when, and Mr. Leonards controls the funds for the estate."

"I would imagine he does," Archie said in a low voice that promised some sort of reckoning with Mr. Leonards.

She'd have to tell him it was important that *she* be the one to deal with the man. If she was to have any authority at all, to know what she was doing, and to have people respect her—well, she'd have to do it herself.

Even though people in her position seldom did things themselves. But then again, people in her position were even more seldom unmarried females. So she would be rewriting the rules.

"But I did manage to find some eggs, so I've soft-boiled them with a bit of toast and some tea. The milk hadn't gone off, and there was a wee bit of sugar."

He clapped his hands together and looked from one to the other. "If there's not anything else, it's time for Mr. Wickes to head to bed! I have an early day tomorrow, now that you've arrived you'll want to see Blakesley Estate at its best!"

Genevieve smiled back at him. He was clearly a dear soul, and he likely couldn't help it that the house was in such poor shape. Or maybe he hadn't noticed. "Thank you, Mr. Wickes, we will be fine. That is—could you just show Mr. Salisbury where our bedrooms are? And the linens, of course."

"Took care of that when I heard you were on your way. Here, let me show you," he said, walking out of the room followed by Archie.

Leaving her alone with a half-burned candle, a full array of tea, and a dangerously homeless spider.

She brushed at her skirts and walked to one of the windows that overlooked the front of the house. It was too dark to get any more than a vague idea of the property, of course, but she could see a large row of trees flanking the driveway they'd driven up. The window itself was large, running from floor to ceiling, and there were more windows along the length of the room. It was probably a lovely, impressive room at one point, before the dust and the spiders and the general dilapidated state of the entire house.

This was a big job. And how many more ducal estates were in as poor shape, thanks to her father's mismanagement? It was daunting, it made her anxious, but it was also the most fun she'd had in her entire life. Most importantly, it was *her* fun.

"What are you looking at?"

She jumped at his voice. "Nothing. There's nothing to see out there. Only . . ." and then she paused, since she felt foolish. But if she was to consider him a friend, she should treat him as one, shouldn't she?

"Only there's so much to do." She turned around to face him. He was so very large, it struck her anew each time she saw him. "And it's not as though I think I can't do it—I know I can. It is that there is so much to do, and so many people are going to want to see me fail, and—"

"And just as many are going to want to see you succeed," he interrupted.

"Yes, of course." She waved her hand to brush that aside. "Those people, however, are people like me. That is, not precisely like me, I am the woman in charge, but I am a *woman*. I don't have any intrinsic power. If it weren't for this external thing that has happened to me, I would be as powerless as any of the people who depend on the duchy for their livelihoods. It's unnerving."

He stayed motionless. That unnerved her also. When he did speak, however, it was as though he'd actually heard her. "I have never thought about that. Coming at it from that perspective." He drew closer, and she could make out the fierce lines of concentration in his expression. "I have always accepted that people in power have more power than the people who don't. And yet—and yet why is that? It's just something we accept. Which is why your estates are in such a tangle. Because no one told your father, or he didn't recognize it, that his title was more than just power. It takes a lot of bravery to be the person in power who comprehends that their power is a responsibility, not a right."

"So you're saying that by being concerned that I am actually brave?" She put her hands on her hips and raised an eyebrow. "That is an equation I am not certain I can sort out." She walked forward to stand in front of him, putting her hands on his forearms. Looking up at him in the dark, feeling the piercing light of his eyes focused on her. "I do know I don't think I could be brave without you."

He looked at her, not speaking, and she saw

how his throat moved as he swallowed. And felt
the muscles in his forearms shift, as though he
were about to move. And then he grasped her
elbows and drew her into his body, lowering his
head to place his mouth on hers.

~~Genevieve:~~

~~I couldn't help myself.~~

Archie

(NOT SENT)

Chapter 12

He hadn't meant to kiss her. But as soon as she spoke, he couldn't help himself. And when he did?

Well, when he did he had to wonder why he hadn't done it before.

Because she tasted delicious. Not that he knew precisely what she tasted of; it wasn't as though she had just been eating strawberries, and so her lips were berry-flavored. It was that her mouth was warm, and soft, and tasted sweet.

He licked her mouth and she sighed. He could feel how she leaned into him, her exhalation making something unbend within her. Toward him.

Her hands were working their way up his arm, her fingers gripping as they slid up, toward his shoulders. He heard her make a small sound in the back of her throat, and he felt his cock harden in response. She twined her fingers at the nape of his neck and he could feel how she stretched up, her mouth pressing as much against his as he was pressing his mouth against hers.

He licked her mouth again, this time pressing in, hoping she would widen her lips so he could thrust his tongue inside. Taste her even more thoroughly.

She did, and he felt her start of surprise and how her fingers tightened in his hair as his tongue entered. She had never been kissed. At least not properly.

There was something so primal and male about being proud that one was the first one to kiss a lady, but he couldn't deny how it made him feel— like he should go beat his chest and proclaim her his. Even though she was absolutely her own woman, and what was more, she had infinitely more social standing than he.

But he wouldn't spend time thinking about that, not now, not when she was melting in his arms, a palpable warmth licking between them, her tongue now chasing his as she learned— quickly—the proper way to kiss.

He had decided to come here to ensure she was doing things properly, hadn't he?

Although he couldn't have anticipated this.

This was chaos, but it was a delicious, welcome chaos.

Now she was leaning more into him, so close he could feel how her breasts pressed against his lower chest, how her body was moving insistently toward him.

His hands had found their way to her waist, and he spread his fingers so his fingertips were at the small of her back. It took everything in his wavering willpower not to reach lower, to caress the curves of her arse, to slide his hand around to the place he longed to bury himself. He couldn't do that, though. A kiss was one thing, but all of that? Given that he was likely the first gentleman of her approximate age that she had ever met? He could not take advantage of her. If he did, he would be as reprehensible as all those grasping relatives he was trying to keep away from her.

Although the experience would be far more pleasant for both of them than just doling out money and power.

Instead, he reached his hand up to cup her cheek, caressing the soft skin of her face, burying his fingers in her thick hair as he continued to kiss her. Plundering her mouth with his tongue as she reciprocated, a delightfully equal balance of power that made him want to cede control to her, to see what she'd do with him.

The thought made him even harder, the image of her practicing on him, only instead of asking for her wrap, it would be for more. So much more. Which he would be pleased to give to her.

"Mm," she murmured, and her fingers began to travel down his back, toward his—

At which point he broke the kiss, stumbling back from the contact. From their contact.

She looked steadily at him, not shrieking, or pouting, or doing anything but just standing there, an intense look in her eyes. The weak candlelight sent flickers of shadow over her face, and he caught his breath at how beautiful and mysterious she looked.

Before, when he'd just met her, he'd thought her

pretty. But now? Now he was entirely fascinated by her looks, from the dark hair that was coming undone because of his fingers, to her dark eyes and kiss-swollen mouth. She looked gloriously undone, and he had made her that way. He'd disheveled her, he'd untidied her, and he couldn't regret it.

"That was . . ." she began, and then he felt relief, because she sounded as shaky and confused and chaotic as he felt. "That was . . ." she started again, then shook her head in clear frustration. "I should go to bed." And then she clapped her hand over her mouth, her eyes wide, her eyebrows raised. "I didn't mean—mudpies," she said, sounding entirely embarrassed.

"I will show you to your bedroom," Archie replied, stressing the "your." He kept his tone as calm and measured as he could, given that all he wanted to do was claim her mouth again and thrust his cock into her, all warm and willing.

"Yes, please." She walked past him to the chair with his coat, picking it up and holding it out to him. "You should take this; Clarkson can likely do something to set it to rights. Once she arrives, that is," she added, another reminder that they were essentially alone. In a large house. With bedrooms that were not too far from each other.

Stop it, Archie, he warned himself. *She is not for you, and you are not for her.* No matter that kissing her felt like home. Or that he had never felt the layered emotions of protection, and desire, and a sympathy that made him want to be a better man.

He'd be a worse man if he acted on his emotions. More than he had done already, he noted ruefully to himself.

"As for this," he said, gesturing to the space between them, a space that hadn't existed when they'd been kissing, "I do apologize, it was entirely my fault. I should not have . . ." and he paused, the frustration at not being able to do or say what he wanted—to kiss her and to tell her he wanted to take her to bed, respectively—making his breath short and his chest tight. "I should not have, and if you would like me to leave, I would understand."

"No!" she burst out, almost before he was done speaking. She advanced toward him, his coat over one arm. "No," she repeated in a softer tone. She held his coat out to him. "You cannot leave, not just because of a kiss. It didn't—it doesn't mean anything, I need your help."

It doesn't mean anything? Had she experienced the same kiss he had?

Suddenly he wasn't so certain about the warm and willing part. Perhaps it was just another experience she had yet to have that she could now cross off her list. It was his duty to help her do things she had no experience with, after all.

Perhaps she just saw the kiss as another extension of his duties.

He took the coat from her, not speaking, then gestured for her to leave the room, picking the candle up as she began to walk. She didn't turn around, didn't even seem to notice that he was directly behind her. That he could step forward and enfold her in his arms again.

Damn it.

She paused in the hallway and then she did look at him, her head tilted questioningly.

"Just up here," he muttered, walking up the stairs. He held the candle aloft so she could see her way up, a coiled tension moving through his body.

Doesn't mean anything. He was tempted to just stop right there on the stairs and give her a kiss that would mean something, but that wouldn't be right. And besides, he wasn't confident he could kiss any better than he just had—he'd felt more connected and engaged than he had ever felt with a woman before, but if she thought it didn't mean anything? Was just another experience?

His masculine pride, he had to admit, was shaken. Which absolutely meant he should pretend it didn't mean anything, either, just continue to advise her and try to forget how her mouth felt, how she moaned and stroked his hair.

All of that.

"Here is your bedroom," he said as they reached the next floor. Wickes had flung the door open and had managed to build a small fire in the fireplace. It was otherwise dreary, but at least she wouldn't be cold. At least he wouldn't have to worry about her in a cold bed, wondering if he should—

"Thank you, Mr. Salisbury," she said in a low voice. "I hope Clarkson and the second carriage has not suffered an accident. Please do wake me if they arrive in the middle of the night?"

She didn't have a night rail with her. All of her

clothing was in the second carriage, and she was still wearing one of her old, drab gowns.

But he couldn't inquire about that, could he, since that would be inappropriate even if he hadn't kissed her. But more so because he had.

He nodded, unable to find the right words. All the wrong words buzzed around in his brain— *what do you mean it doesn't mean anything? Were you just being kind, as you are to all the servants?*— although he knew that wasn't the case.

Were you just being kind, as you would to a friend? Is this how you think friends behave with each other?

"Good night, Mr. Salisbury," she said at last. "Sleep well."

And she walked into the bedroom without another word. Without another glance back at him.

Leaving him alone with his chaotic thoughts.

~~Dear Archie,~~

~~That was by far the most wonderful experience I have ever had, kissing you (as though you didn't know to what I was referring). I am shaken. I am shook. I want to storm down the hallway and demand you kiss me some more, only that is not at all what I can possibly do.~~

~~If I hadn't become a duchess, and needed help, I would never have met you. But because I am a duchess, I can never—well, you know. That. Again.~~

~~I wish it were possible to both be yourself and be some= one else. What would it have been like if I had been just a governess? Meeting the steward of a nearby estate?~~

~~Would you have wanted to kiss me as much then? Would you have kissed me at all?~~

~~Sincerely,~~
~~Genevieve~~

(NOT SENT)

Chapter 13

Genevieve leaned against the door, her heart still pounding from the kiss. The kiss. Her first and likely the best she would ever have. Because how could anything be any better?

Her fingers still tingled from where she had touched him. She raised her hand to her mouth and touched her lips. They still tingled also.

From where his mouth had touched hers.

She still couldn't quite believe it had happened. That he had wanted to kiss her, even though she was frightened of lightning, and spiders, and needed help with almost everything she had to do.

She wished she had a friend—well, a friend besides him—with whom she could discuss all these feelings. It felt, in fact, as though the feelings were almost too much for her body; it felt as though they were going to burst out of her and land on the floor in a profusion of feelingness.

A wry grin curled her mouth when she thought about his reaction to her words after—so obviously piqued that she hadn't said it was the best thing ever. But she couldn't, not without meaning to take the next logical step, and she knew she was unable to take that step—marriage, and everything that went with it—with a man who worked for a living, who wasn't one of the lofty few upon whom she could bestow her hand.

That he was a viscount's son wouldn't matter if he had sullied his hands with any kind of work.

She walked to the enormous bed, glancing around at the room. It—obviously—appeared as though it hadn't been used in some time, but it didn't look neglected. The furniture was light and elegant, typical of the style in previous decades, and she thought she preferred that to the heavy stuff that decorated her London home.

The bed's covers were pulled back invitingly, and she got onto the end of the bed, entirely forgetting she was a duchess and should be more regal about it.

And then stopped short as she realized she did not have anything to sleep in, and more to the point, couldn't get out of the gown she was wearing.

Mudpies. Either sleep in her gown, which was the gown she had for tomorrow, or she'd have to go down the hallway and ask Archie—Mr. Salisbury—to undo her buttons.

Neither choice was good.

She weighed her options.

And came to the inevitable conclusion.

"Drat," she said, picking the candle up and stepping back out into the hall and toward his room.

The door swung open quicker than she would have thought. She shouldn't have been surprised that he had opened the door—it was his door, after all—but she jumped nonetheless.

Or perhaps that was because of his appearance.

He'd taken off his coat, and rolled his shirt-sleeves up. Not to mention removed the cravat at his neck so she was presented with a tremendous amount of skin. Salisbury skin. All exposed, with some intriguing black hair on parts of it, and she heard herself inhale rather suddenly.

"Are you all right?" he asked, his eyebrows drawing together in concern.

"Fine," she managed to gasp out, trying to keep her eyes fixed on his face. Not on his strong throat, or bare forearms, or the hint of where his chest began.

Now she wished she could summon a stronger expletive than "mudpies." But she couldn't think of anything at the moment. Her whole vision was filled with him, with his height and his skin and how his eyes showed concern, yes, but also a hint of what she thought was interest. In her.

"What are you doing here?" he said at last.

"Uh," she began, wondering if it was too late to scurry back to her room and just sleep upright so she wouldn't wrinkle her gown, "I can't . . ." and she raised her arm and pointed down at her back, hoping she wouldn't have to ask him.

"Can't what?" His eyebrows were no longer pulled together in a concerned vee, but now he just looked confused.

She would have to ask him.

"Can you undo the buttons in back here so I can remove my gown?" She felt her face get hot.

And watched as his cheeks started to turn pink. It only made him look better, whereas she was willing to bet she looked like she had stuck her face into a fire.

He made a gesture that indicated she should turn around, accompanied with some inarticulate murmurings. At least it seemed he was affected as well.

His fingers brushed the nape of her neck, and she shivered. He undid the buttons swiftly, faster than her previous terror-stricken maid. Not as fast as Clarkson, of course, but it wasn't his profession.

"Uh—that is done," he said in a low voice. "Unless you need more undone?" The last part of that sentence emerged as a croak.

"It should be fine," she replied. She turned back to face him, acutely conscious that his fingers had been undoing her buttons and now her gown was partially undone, and here they were, just the two of them. "Good night," she said, nearly sprinting down the hall back to her room.

Because if she had stood there any longer she might have said something she would regret. Well, not she, but the duchess part of her. The only reason she was here at this forgotten estate in the first place.

She slammed the door behind her, wincing as she heard just how loud it was. And now she had embarrassed herself yet again in front of him.

Although he had seemed just as embarrassed, so perhaps they had that in common.

* * *

Genevieve would have thought she'd be awake all night, reliving each second of that kiss—her first, but hopefully not her last—but no, apparently her body was far too pragmatic to stay awake when it could be sleeping.

She woke very early, feeling supremely comfortable, blinking as she glanced around the unfamiliar room. In the early morning light the room was even prettier, with a pleasant floral wallpaper covering the walls, a few delicate-looking pieces of furniture, including a lady's writing desk, and a scattering of pictures on some of the surfaces and on the walls.

She sat up, pushing her hair away from her face, glancing out the window to the outside. If the inside was lovely, the outside was spectacular. This was all hers?

The driveway was wide as well as long, and there was a row of bushes on either side. Bushes that didn't appear to have been trimmed recently, but impressive for their multitude nonetheless. Beyond the bushes were enormous trees that were probably planted long before there was even the suggestion that a woman would someday become duchess. The lawn in between was lush and green although also clearly not maintained, and there were a few square beds of flowers that made Genevieve itch to go investigate.

And then she heard the voices. At first she couldn't discern the tone, but then she heard the voices rise in anger, and she leaped out of bed, rushing to the window to open it—only to realize she was wearing her chemise. And that was all.

It wouldn't matter how decisive and duchesslike she could be if she did it in her undergarments.

So instead she picked up her gown from where she'd laid it and tossed it over her head, doing up what buttons she could. Hopefully Clarkson would be here soon, if she wasn't already, and she wouldn't have to back away from anybody she met so they wouldn't see her shocking state of undress.

"Now see here, how do I know you're with the duchess?"

Mr. Leonards was, as Archie suspected, not a pleasant man. He was large, though not as large as Archie, and broad, and appeared to have a habit of using his loud voice to intimidate people. At least that was what Archie gathered seeing him speak with Mr. Wickes, but it would take a lot more than a bully with a hearty voice box to frighten him. He'd been in the Queen's Own Hussars, after all, and he'd met men of Mr. Leonards's ilk before; all bluster, shouting at people to go on and get in the thick of danger while remaining behind nursing a drink and a poor attitude.

"I am with the duchess," Archie said through clenched teeth, "because I say I am. Mr. Wickes says he received the letter informing you of her impending arrival. Unless you think it is a remarkable coincidence that the Duchess of Blakesley sent you a letter and then an impostor suddenly appeared claiming to be the duchess, I believe you should accept that we have arrived. And that things are not as the duchess would wish."

"Oh? And what is it that the duchess finds fault with?" It seemed Mr. Leonards was not going to back down. Archie glanced around the area they stood in, assessing the ground in case there was to be a fight. He would not want to pitch over into the grass because of negligent gardening. He had no doubt he could best Mr. Leonards in a fight, but he wasn't so certain about the horticulture.

"Well, for one thing, that you seem to have only Mr. Wickes to maintain this entire estate while you—what do you do exactly?"

Mr. Leonards puffed up his chest, which just made him look more like a rooster. "I oversee the tenants, take the rents, oversee the repairs, overs—"

"Yes, you oversee things. Since you are the overseer. But what do you *do*?"

Mr. Leonards began to sputter, then his expression changed as he looked past Archie. Judging by the mixed look of trepidation and pugnaciousness, the duchess was there. Hopefully she'd managed to get herself somewhat dressed, since he didn't think Mr. Leonards would respect a duchess who appeared in—well, whatever she'd figured out to sleep in.

Images of which were merely distracting him from the matter at hand.

"Good morning, Mr. Salisbury." Her tone was cold and correct. As it should be. As though she were the duchess and he was the steward. As it should be.

So why did he feel so unsettled?

"Good morning, Your Grace." She came alongside him and he saw she was holding her gown closed in the back with one hand, the other wrapped around her waist. He stepped forward so as to shield more of her back from view, and she cast him a quick grateful look.

"Your Grace, I didn't know it really was you. And may I say what a pleasure it is to welcome you to the Blakesley Estate?" Now Mr. Leonards had turned to the obsequious portion of this morning's performance. Archie wanted to roll his eyes at the man's obvious pandering.

"Thank you, Mr. Leonards." She squirmed as though she were about to let go of the back of her gown, and Archie held his breath, his own hand tensing as he considered whether it would be less shocking for her gown to show a gap or for him to put his hand on her back.

Thankfully, she got herself under control before Mr. Leonards could do more than regard her with a bit more suspicion than a moment ago. And Archie wouldn't have to touch her.

Never mind, now he was regretting her not having difficulty with her clothing.

"I couldn't help but overhear," Genevieve continued, using the stern tone of voice Archie had first commended her on, "that you and my employee were discussing the validity of my arrival? Is that correct?"

A long silence, which Archie tried not to break with a cheer resembling what would follow a particularly successful ambush on the enemy.

"Uh, well, that is, Your Grace . . ." and then Mr. Leonards stopped speaking. Since he couldn't really come up with anything that wouldn't make him sound worse than he already did.

"Yes?"

Go, Duchess!

"Uh . . ."

"Thank you, Mr. Leonards. If you will be so kind as to take Mr. Salisbury to your office and allow him to examine the books." She turned toward him, but not so much that her back was exposed. "Mr. Salisbury, would you also be so kind?" and then she stopped, and tilted her head in what was most definitely a duchesslike gesture.

"Certainly, Your Grace," Archie replied, bowing. He rose and addressed Mr. Leonards. "If you would—?"

"Hmph," Mr. Leonards replied, striding back to the house, Archie keeping up easily.

Dear Bob,

I am, as you know, assisting the Duchess of Blakesley with her new duties. ~~I am also keenly aware of her as a woman. A lovely, intelligent, lonely woman.~~ She has requested that I find no fewer than twenty men to fill various positions at the Blakesley Estate. The positions include a stable master and grooms, a butler, footmen, a gardener, and ~~a steward~~ a steward. Please direct the men to write to me c/o the duchess's estate, address, etc.

Archie

Chapter 14

"It was as we might have known."

It was a few hours after the Intimidating Men Incident. Genevieve was grateful Mr. Salisbury was with her, not just because he was nice to look at.

She could, and would, do what had to be done in terms of managing things, but it was so much more helpful and easy that she had him as her advance guard, so to speak. She glanced up at him, her breath catching—as usual—at his overall handsomeness.

She did not look terrible herself; Clarkson had come just after the Incident, and had clucked her tongue and put her to rights, including dressing her in one of the new gowns that had arrived.

But she did not start with the raw materials Mr. Salisbury did. She was not tall, not muscular, not almost savagely beautiful. Nor did she exude a kind of raw power that made her all fluttery inside.

"What might we have known?" she asked, realizing she should be speaking with him, not just viewing him. That is, she could do both, provided she could remember to speak, and not just to tell him how much she enjoyed his appearance.

"Mr. Leonards is a scoundrel."

She leaned back in her chair and regarded him, glad she had an excuse to do so. "In what way?" She shrugged. "I assume he has been skimming whatever funds come into the estate. I also assume he has allowed things to fall to ruin because nobody was here to object. Has he done more than that?" And her words faltered as she thought about what else he could have done—a powerful man out here in the country with people, especially women, who were less powerful than he.

"Not that," Mr. Salisbury returned quickly, obviously sensing her concern. "He did put people on the payroll, other people whose last names are Leonards, doing jobs that as far as I can tell have not actually been done."

"You fired him, I presume."

He nodded. "Yes. I did not want him to stay here a moment longer than necessary, for fear he would do more damage."

Genevieve rose and walked to look out the window. It was still a gorgeous sight, but there was just so much of it. So much land, so many lives out there depending on what she decided. "So now we just have Wickes and—?"

He walked to stand beside her. "With your permission, Your Grace, I will send word to my former comrades-in-arms. I know there are many who are still out of work, and if it suits, we can hire some of them. I know they would be happy to work in such a tranquil place."

She turned and looked at him, hearing something in his tone. "And you? Do you find it a tranquil place? Is it a place where you think you could be happy?"

He met her gaze, and what she saw there made her heart race. There was something so poignant and wanting in his eyes, and it seemed as though she could feel his hurt, feel whatever pain he carried inside. And yet nothing he had said would suggest he was in pain, it was just—it was just that she felt it. Felt a connection to him far more than simple friendship and one kiss would suggest.

Far more than what should be between a duchess and her temporary steward, that was for certain.

"I like the tranquillity. One of the things I like about working for your Aunt Sophia." He looked as though he were lost in memories. "The one thing that they never mention about going to war is the noise. From the sound of the guns, to the men the night before, singing or talking or getting into fights. To the time after, when the battle has ended, but some men's agony has just begun, and they're screaming, and you can't help them."

Her throat tightened as she listened, really listened to him. It felt as though she heard not only what he was saying, but what he wasn't saying also.

"I don't mean to try to steal you away from Aunt Sophia, that is not why I asked," she continued hurriedly, before she could ask something really inappropriate, far worse than seeming to want to hire him: *Are you lonely? I am, too. Can we be less lonely together?* "But there is work to be done here, good, honest work that is very different from the noise and rumpus of London. I am not sure I will ever adjust entirely to London. I don't know if it will make me happy," she said in a softer voice, now almost speaking to herself.

"I do like it here. But as for happiness?" He paused, and Genevieve saw how his shoulders lifted as he drew in a deep breath. "I am not sure that is possible. I would settle for contentment. Peace." His lips twisted into a rueful smile. "Peace isn't the same as happiness, but I would take peace over anything at this point. The obvious peace between nations, but also peace within myself. Not just order, although you know I value that." He turned his head to look out the window, and she followed his gaze. What did he see when he looked out? Did he see opportunity? Did he just see grass, trees, and a driveway? Did he see the future?

"But speaking of work, we do have plenty of it," he continued. He gestured toward the door. "We can begin in what was Mr. Leonards's office going through the books. We can make a list of the positions we need to fill here, and then I will send word 'round to my second at Lady Sophia's, a Mr. McCready. He has all the men's addresses, and can contact them to see about their coming to work here."

"Yes, let's begin." She had never been asked to work before. She hadn't even ever been consulted about work before. It felt wonderful, as though this was what she should be doing. To be useful, to try to find—what had he said?—peace through this effort.

Mr. Salisbury:

~~Would it be possible for you to tone down your attrac-~~
~~tiveness? It is quite distracting. First I think I am concen-~~
~~trating on one thing, something related to my duties, and~~
~~then I realize I have actually been thinking about your~~
~~blue eyes for nearly fifteen minutes.~~
~~Thank you for attending to this matter.~~

~~Sincerely,~~
~~Duchess~~

(NOT SENT)

Chapter 15

Had she actually looked forward to working? She knew she had never worked so hard in her life, but since she had never worked before, it wasn't that hard to top.

"Try it again," he said, leaning back in his chair. She glowered at him, but picked the pen up nonetheless, ticking off each number as she checked it against the second set of books.

"Why did I want to do this again?" she asked.

"Because if you want to have authority, true authority, you need to know every single thing about your estates. All of them, in specific detail.

She exhaled, pausing to look over at him. "You're right. I know that. I just didn't think there would be so many details about being a duchess."

"You didn't know anything," he retorted.

She laughed. "True enough. And I couldn't respect myself if I didn't know what I had to know in order to do the right thing by the position. Unlike my father," she murmured. "How could he not have seen that Leonards was stealing? It was so blatant, even I could see it without any kind of training!" She shook her head and drew another paper toward her. "Thank goodness I have your help or I would never get through this."

"You'd do just fine," he replied in a quiet tone. Quiet, but it felt as though he'd shouted from how his words spread warmth throughout her body.

"I suppose I would," she said after a moment. She would. She was glad he was here, of course, but she would have figured it out. Eventually.

It was enlightening, doing the accounts. It horrified her that the cost of one of her gowns would pay for feed for the flocks of sheep on the estate for close to six months. But if she weren't dressed as befit a duchess, she wouldn't have people's respect, and that went a long way toward being able to help them.

So she might as well wear her lovely gowns since the duchy was paying for them.

But musing about the relative cost of a gown and sheep feed wasn't solving the estate's problems. After only three muttered "mudpies," and one broken pen, she finished, and handed what she'd done over to Archie, who reviewed it as she waited, hoping she'd done it correctly. At last he nodded. "It's good, only one minor mistake, which I've marked here." He showed her where she'd neglected to check off one of the many budget items against the proposed budget. "Oh," he said, "I've heard from my friend Bob—Mr. McCready. He says there will be a few men arriving within the next few days, with more on the way after that." He paused and cleared his throat. "I haven't thanked you for giving them this chance."

She felt her cheeks get hot. "Don't thank me, thank yourself. It was your idea, after all," she said, with a wave of her hand.

"My idea, yes, but your money."

Of course. Her money. Her power, her influence, her position. Her gowns. Her everything. It continued to weigh on her, all that responsibility, the knowledge that there were likely people, never mind her own relatives, who would argue she had no right to hold the position she did. That was why she absolutely had to show them, to prove to them, that she could do this, that a female was just as good as a male in the role. Better, given that the last male was her father.

"And speaking of my money," she said, her cheeks still burning, "I suppose I should venture into town and spend some of it. To show the people here, my tenants, specifically, that I am committed to restoring the estate and the lands to whatever former glory they had. Clarkson has also heard that there is to be an assembly, and I thought perhaps I would attend. Would you—could you possibly accompany me, Mr. Salisbury?"

His hand stilled on the book, which he still held. "Are you certain that would be appropriate?" He didn't say "Your Grace," but then again he didn't say "Genevieve," either. Was he thinking about that kiss as much as she was?

Impossible. Because when she wasn't thinking about ways to improve the duchy and the possibility of rain—not to mention when she would next get tea—she was thinking about that kiss. Which meant she thought about it nearly ninety percent of her waking hours.

Far more than she should be, she knew that.

"I think it would be less appropriate for me to attend on my own," she said after a moment. "Plus if I did go on my own, and I entered the ballroom, and I was entirely on my own, and I am already not of them, and they will turn and stare, and then someone will introduce me, and I will feel like . . ." and then to her horror she couldn't catch a breath. Which was probably just as well, because if she continued to speak, she would end up squeaking.

He got up out of his chair and came to kneel beside hers, taking her hand in both of his. "It will be fine. I would love to come with you." And he smiled up at her, a smile that reached his eyes, making the corners crinkle up, and she knew she had been breathless before, but this made her feel as though she had had the wind knocked out of her. By him.

"Only if you promise to dance with me. You have to practice, don't you?" he asked, his mouth curling up into a lazy grin. A smile that revealed a shared joke between them, that made her insides get all squirmy and her skin feel as though it was on fire.

"I do. And I would like to continue practicing on you."

And then she just stopped speaking, too lost in his gaze to form a coherent thought. Well, she amended to herself, an appropriate coherent thought. Because she had plenty of inappropriate thoughts she could cohere.

I would like to continue practicing on you.

The words rang through Archie's head like a claxon, reminding him of everything that had happened, everything that couldn't happen, everything that should happen.

None of which were the same everythings.

He had found himself enjoying the past few days, even though they were filled with work. And not work that was enjoyable at all; it was paperwork, drudgery, the kind of work that made you cranky and tired at the end of the day, not exulting in sore muscles and a job well done. Because the next day there was always more work, and he spent far too much time just sitting in a chair or hunched over a desk looking at infinitesimally small figures written in cramped hands.

But it was work he was doing with her. The her who greeted him in the morning with a warm smile, the her who sat opposite him when they dined, the her who wielded a massive amount of power and influence, even though she wasn't quite certain how to wield anything more than a pen at the moment.

The her whom he'd kissed that first night they were there.

He was in his bedroom preparing for the assembly. She was getting fussed over by Clarkson for her first official appearance as duchess—albeit in a small village, not a London ballroom, thank

God—but he was a servant, so he didn't warrant a valet. He had to get dressed on his own. Which meant that he had a lot of time to get lost in thought.

And he couldn't stop thinking about her.

He'd replayed that kiss a thousand times since. What might have happened if she wasn't so innocent and wasn't so much of a duchess?

The thoughts kept him up at night, kept him on the edge of—

A knock interrupted what was sure to be an inappropriate thought or several.

"Enter," Archie called, stuffing his shirt into his trousers.

Mr. Wickes popped his head in, his usual smile firmly in place. "There's a couple of people waiting to see the duchess, say they're her cousins, and since Her Grace is busy, I thought I'd ask you."

"Oh." More cousins? He'd thought they would be rid of them when they left London. "I'll come down straightaway." So much for thinking about what might have happened after that kiss; now he was about to be forcibly reminded that the duchess seemed to have relatives who would like nothing more than to take advantage of her. Like he could be accused of doing after kissing her.

The thought was sobering.

"My goodness," Genevieve breathed as she gazed in the mirror. She looked at Miss Clarkson, who stood behind her. "You have worked a miracle," she said.

Miss Clarkson shook her head. "Miracles are only made when there is nothing there in the first place, Your Grace." She patted a curl down on the back of Genevieve's head. "Mrs. Hardwick is an excellent dressmaker, to be certain, but her gowns are only as lovely as the woman wearing them."

Genevieve grinned. "It sounds as though you are spouting some kind of feminist philosophy, Clarkson. Be careful or you will be accused of sedition." Clarkson laughed in reply; she and Genevieve had discovered they both loved to read, although Miss Clarkson preferred reading essays on humanity, while Genevieve couldn't resist the allure of a good novel.

She and Miss Clarkson—whom she had finally gotten comfortable with calling just plain Clarkson—also appreciated the comfort of a good, strong cup of tea, and the two women had gotten into the habit of meeting in Genevieve's office at four o'clock. Clarkson was, Genevieve realized, her second adult friend.

Although not as bewitchingly handsome as the first.

And she and the first were about to attend a party together. Only a small gathering, Genevieve assumed, since the town itself was small, but still. Her first official outing as duchess, and she was wearing this new gown and would arrive escorted by Mr. Salisbury and all his Salisburyness.

The gown really was lovely. Not worth its weight in feed, but still lovely. It had arrived only a few hours earlier, along with a few of the men

Mr. Salisbury—Archie—had recruited to join the staff.

It was made of a stiff purple satin, the color that of the darkest possible grape. It came in tight at the waist, then flowed out over Genevieve's hips in a wide swath of fabric, which had rows of black ribbon on it. The sleeves were small, little frills of lavender lace, a tiny bow of black ribbon on each one.

It was tasteful, reminded people seeing her she was in mourning, but also that she was a lady in power. Clarkson had swept her hair back into a low chignon, pulling a few strands out to curl around Genevieve's face. She hadn't thought to see what ducal jewels might be available to her, so Clarkson had devised a choker made from the same black ribbon with a cameo that Gran had given her attached to it.

She didn't look anything like herself. And yet this was who she was now.

A knock at the door interrupted her contemplation of her own magnificence.

"Enter," she said after glancing toward Clarkson.

The door opened and Mr. Salisbury stepped inside, a disgruntled look on his face.

"Oh dear. What is it?" Genevieve asked. Was he going to refuse to come to the assembly with her? And why was that the first thing that worried her, rather than if something was on fire or there was some sort of duchess emergency?

Because you have been looking forward to this since you first thought of it, a voice reminded her inside her head. *Because you are trying very hard not to anticipate what it will feel like as he holds you in his arms.*

"It's more relatives." He said it as though he'd said, *It's more vermin*, or *It's more unpleasant items in bookkeeping*.

"More of my relatives?" she began, only to catch herself. "Of course it is, why would you say 'more' when you haven't even had one of your own yet? And your family . . ." and then she paused, since she didn't know if Clarkson knew about Archie's estrangement with his family, and she didn't think he would want to share the information this way if she didn't.

"Right," he said, although she wasn't sure what he was confirming.

"Downstairs?" she asked, even though she thought she knew the answer. Unfortunately.

"Yes."

"It isn't to be helped, then," she said in resignation. "Clarkson, am I presentable?" She turned in a circle, her arms spread wide.

"Absolutely, Your Grace. Mr. Salisbury, what do you think?"

Clarkson, the wretch, had an expression on her face that indicated she knew just how much Genevieve wanted his answer.

"The duchess looks lovely." His voice sounded raw, and Genevieve felt her insides tremble.

"Thank you, Mr. Salisbury." She took the gloves—black, of course—Clarkson was holding out for her and put them on. "Now let us go dispatch my relatives in some speedy way. If we can," she muttered.

* * *

Archie's throat was still tight with the things he wished he could say in answer to Miss Clarkson's question—*You look gorgeous, but no less pretty than when you are in your drab duchess attire.* Maybe *You are beautiful, but much less approachable, because now you truly look like who you are. And yet I wish I could approach you as a man approaches a woman, not as a steward approaches a duchess.* That was far too complicated, and yet not nearly enough of what he wanted to say.

Instead, he kept his mouth shut as they descended the stairs together. She kept pace with him down the stairs, so he deliberately let her go ahead to make it clear to whoever was waiting below that she was most definitely in charge, never mind that it was the usual thing for a man to do for a woman. That she had kept pace with him spoke volumes about how they saw their relationship—if he was reading into it, which of course he was.

He had to stop reading into it, had to stop looking for signs that this could be more than what it was, which was already more than it should be. A friend. A trusted advisor. Not anything else, no matter how intoxicating he found her presence, nor how much he wished he could kiss her again.

Two people, a man and a woman, waited for them at the foot of the stairs, plus two others who were clearly servants, delineated by their clothing and posture.

The gentleman stepped forward, removing his hat as he smiled at the duchess and spoke. "Your Grace, thank you for receiving us." His teeth were white and even and Archie loathed him on sight. "We are your cousins from your mother's side. We are your great-aunt Millicent's second husband's grandchildren from his first marriage." He gestured to include the young woman standing at his side. "You met my sister years ago when our parents visited your father's country house."

Genevieve peered at the gentleman's sister, then her expression brightened.

"Of course! It's Miss Garry, isn't it? I remember spending an afternoon having tea in the garden while your parents . . ." and she trailed off, the gentleman chuckling as she made a vague gesture in the air.

"While our parents likely tried to coerce someone into something." He grinned ruefully. "But we are not our parents, and Evelyn had such a strong memory, so when we heard you had inherited, we had to come see you. I am Sir William Garry."

"It is a pleasure to meet you," Genevieve replied, holding her hand out for the man to shake. "And to see you again, Miss Garry."

Archie stood behind her, his hands clasped behind his back as he assessed the situation. Was it possible these relatives were not entirely grasping?

The gentleman was good-looking enough, if one liked blond hair and too broad a grin. He looked to be about Genevieve's age and had a softness Archie associated with men who hadn't quite grown up yet.

The woman was even younger, probably about nineteen years old, a little sprite of a thing with light brown hair and a matching broad smile.

He didn't dislike her as much as he did her brother.

"This is my—this is Mr. Salisbury, my temporary steward," Genevieve said, sweeping her arm out to indicate Archie's presence. He nodded. "Mr. Salisbury," she continued, "would you ask Mr. Wickes, or whomever, really, to serve us tea in the sitting room? My cousins have likely had a long journey."

Archie nodded again, still not speaking. Of course she invited them to tea. Possibly she would invite Sir William later to relieve her of her spinsterhood.

He strode off toward the kitchens, throwing a backward glance toward her as he went.

She was not looking at him.

Duchess,

I wish to update you on the hiring process. Three of my former soldiers have arrived, and I have tasked them with the jobs of footman, cook, and groom.

Mr. Donnelly, your new cook, made all the meals for us in the army, and I can assure you as to his skill. I am hopeful Mr. Norris will learn his duties quickly, and might therefore be a suitable person to eventually serve as your butler. Mr. Madden is an expert on horses, and with your permission, will acquire a few for your stable.

~~Don't trust those people.~~

Sincerely,
Mr. Salisbury

Chapter 16

Genevieve didn't miss Archie's skeptical look as he went in search of Wickes and tea. But she did recall that afternoon so long ago, and Miss Evelyn seemed very sweet, while she appreciated Sir William's frankness about their parents.

Not to mention the siblings were close in age, and appeared not to be horrible relatives, at least at first blush. She had to give them every opportunity, didn't she? She couldn't go through life mistrusting every single member of her family. She had wanted to feel part of a family for so long.

"Do come through here," Genevieve said, leading them to the sitting room. Sir William walked in front of his sister, which would have seemed rude if the girl hadn't seemed so shy.

"This is a lovely home," Miss Evelyn said in a small voice.

"It will be, I hope," Genevieve said, laughter in her tone. "It is in need of a lot of work, work that Mr. Salisbury is helping me with." She gestured toward the seats for the two to sit down, then sat herself on the sofa.

Sir William didn't take the proffered seat, instead sitting next to her. He had an easy smile, and she found herself smiling back. He was good-looking, she realized. Of course, not approaching Archie's splendor, but he had a certain approachability that Archie lacked. Being so frighteningly attractive and all.

"You must be wondering why we are here," he began, crossing his legs at the knee. "I know your inheriting came as a surprise"—*to me as much as anyone*, Genevieve thought—"and no doubt you have many people clamoring for your attention."

"Indeed." She couldn't help but allow a rueful smile to curl her mouth up.

He held his hand up as though to forestall her objections. "But we are here simply to wish you the best of luck in your new position, and to offer assistance, should you need it. We had heard that you had taken residence here with only your lady's maid, and we thought—or Evelyn thought, actually—that there would be less talk if there was another female, one of your world, in residence."

Oh. Well, she hadn't really thought all that out before, had she? She'd never had to consider whether it was appropriate for her to be somewhere. Nobody had expected her to be anybody worth noticing, so they hadn't told her that people would talk.

"Are people talking? That is, you said there would be less talk, which intimates that there has been talk at all. Is there?" She knew she was likely squeaking, but she couldn't help herself.

"Not very much, Your Grace," Sir William said in what he likely thought was a reassuring tone, but wasn't reassuring at all to Genevieve.

"Well, thank you for your thought on my behalf. Yes, and in fact, I am attending an assembly this evening. Mr. Salisbury will be accompanying me."

"Your steward?" Sir William said. Genevieve immediately felt defensive, even though there was nothing to defend. Was there?

"Yes, he is a—well, he is a gentleman as well as a steward," since there was no need to acquaint her cousins with Archie's history, especially if she hadn't even wanted to share it with Miss Clarkson, "and we thought it would be best if I didn't go alone."

"That is perfect, then. If it is a public assembly, we can accompany you as well." And then Sir William beamed at her, as though it would be a great pleasure.

Something in her warmed at the sight. "Oh yes. That would be lovely. And you two will stay here, of course, for the reasons you've mentioned."

Except that Sir William was male, and so everyone would speculate about what she and her young relative were doing together. But that talk was probably better than the alternative—that Genevieve was engaged in something untoward with her temporary steward.

"Thank you, that would be splendid," Miss Evelyn said in a quiet voice.

"Yes, thank you. I would not want anyone to

speak ill of you, merely because you might not know what is expected." Sir William spoke in an earnest tone, one that conveyed a fervency that she appreciated. Especially since it seemed he was fervent in his desire to protect her reputation.

The door swung open to reveal Mr. Wickes. Not Mr. Salisbury. "Mr. Salisbury said as how you would like some tea, Your Grace," Mr. Wickes said as he lowered the tray to the table. "And I brought it," he said with a triumphant flourish of his hand.

"Thank you, Mr. Wickes." Genevieve waited as he arranged the tea things.

"Anything else, Your Grace?"

"No thank you," Genevieve replied.

He bowed, then walked toward the door.

"Mr. Wickes," Genevieve called, "could you ask Mr. Salisbury if he would mind coming in?" Because if she had to guess, she would say he was waiting for her to dispatch these two as handily as she had the other beseeching relatives. And now she had to tell him they were all to attend the assembly together. Although he would have to accede to her wishes, wouldn't he? Because of who she was?

Mudpies. Now she was doing it herself, lording (so to speak) her consequence and position over someone else.

"She wants you in there," Mr. Wickes said as he tromped back into the kitchen. Archie started guiltily, caught in the act of sneaking a freshly baked biscuit in his mouth. Mr. Donnelly had wasted no time in his new position, and Archie was testing out the results.

"Delicious, as always, Will," he said, getting to his feet. He brushed a few crumbs off his evening wear.

"Thanks again, Captain—Mr. Salisbury," Will replied, his face even redder than usual from the heat of the ovens. "Mr. Wickes has already made me feel right at home, and I'm happy to be back cooking again." Will had returned home, like so many of the men, without a definite occupation, and with family to take care of. From what Archie understood, there was a younger sister who had several children and a husband who wasn't able to provide for them all.

"You're welcome. I'm just glad I won't have to keep eating shepherd's pie seven nights a week," he said, winking at Mr. Wickes.

Mr. Wickes thrust his chest out. "I challenge you to find a better shepherd's pie anywhere, Mr. Salisbury," he said.

"It is delicious; there is no arguing with that. But not every night, surely."

It was apparently the only thing—besides tea— that Mr. Wickes could make. Archie never wished to see another cooked carrot in his life.

"While you're nattering on about my cooking, the duchess is waiting to see you," Mr. Wickes reminded him.

"Thank you." Archie snatched another biscuit from the tray and popped it in his mouth. "I will see you gentlemen later."

* * *

"You sent for me, Your Grace?"

The two relatives were still seated, both of them looking nearly comfortable. Even the lingering flavor of the biscuit couldn't banish the bad taste in his mouth at the sight of them. He couldn't explain, or wouldn't, why he felt so protective of her. But if these two did anything to break her fragile trust—well, he would have to do something.

She looked up at him with an expression that verged on defiant. If he weren't so contrary, he'd be delighted she had learned the lessons so well. "Yes, Sir William and Miss Evelyn will be staying here for a while. And both of them have agreed to attend the assembly this evening. Will you ask Mr. Wickes to ask the new groom to bring the carriage around in forty-five minutes?" She looked over at the new residents of the house. "You would probably like a chance to settle in, and you will both need time to make yourselves ready for the assembly. Mr. Salisbury can show you to your rooms." She looked back at him. "Mr. Salisbury, the two rooms at the opposite end of the corridor from mine, if you please. I believe those are the cleanest of the ones available."

Miss Evelyn had already risen, and Sir William followed soon thereafter as Archie nodded to indicate he'd understood Genevieve's expectations. Or, more appropriately, the duchess's orders.

"Follow me, please," Archie said through a clenched jaw.

"Mr. Salisbury, do stop back here when you have shown my guests to their rooms."

It was so clear, crystal clear, that she was in

charge. He would have to remember that whenever he thought about how sweet she tasted or how much he liked getting to know her.

Genevieve watched the door shut behind them, and then sank back down onto the sofa. It would be wonderful to have a friend close in age, to have family she could, perhaps, depend on.

And having her relatives here would reduce the allure of Mr. Salisbury. Or reduce the chances of her finding Mr. Salisbury both alluring and alone so she could kiss him again. That was a benefit she couldn't explain to him, because to discuss it would be to acknowledge it had happened, and she didn't think she could do that without either wanting to do it again right away or bursting into flame. Or both simultaneously.

She was trying very hard not to think about that when the door opened and the object of her thoughts walked in.

"Your guests are settled into their rooms." He did not sound pleased, and she tried not to be delighted that he was so protective of her.

"I know you suspect they are yet another set of people who want something from me," she said, gesturing for him to sit. "But they seem pleasant enough, and it appears less odd if there are others in residence here besides you, me, Clarkson, and the rest of the staff."

"Ah," he said, his expression easing as he sat down, "I hadn't thought of that. I should have." He stood again, and began to pace. "With Lady

Sophia it is not an issue because . . ." and then he paused as he seemed to search for what words to say.

"Because my godmother is so old?" Genevieve supplied, then winced as she realized she had, basically, just alluded to the whole kissing scenario.

"Yes."

"Right."

They sat in silence as Genevieve felt herself get more and more uncomfortable. In a pleasant, want-to-kiss-him sort of way.

That could not happen.

"Mr. Salisbury," she said abruptly. She rose from the sofa as she spoke, and he stopped his pacing to look at her. "Mr. Salisbury, since we have time as my guests get ready, could we—that is, could we practice my dancing?" She gestured down at her feet. "I was taught, but I have never actually danced with a partner. Or a partner that wasn't Cook. When she lands on your feet, you feel it," she said with a laugh.

"Of course." He sounded as though she had just ordered him to do something. Not as though he actually wanted to. But that was to be expected, wasn't it? The other—the intimacy, the friendship—that was the anomaly. This was how it should be. She'd learned his lessons well, it seemed.

"Then let's go into the ballroom. It's just behind the dining room, isn't it?" She had gone on a tour of the house when she'd first arrived, but hadn't had occasion to return to any of the larger rooms, being concentrated on the paperwork and getting the estate to rights before doing anything so rash as throwing a ball.

"It is," he said, pushing the door open and holding it for her. To get out of the room she had to duck underneath his arm, and she wished she could just stop right there, to see what he'd do. Would he kiss her again? Would he remind her that she was not acting duchess-appropriate?

Would he just look down at her and curl his lip?

But she didn't stop, she just kept walking, feeling his presence at her back, wishing things were different.

"I will place my hand at your waist, and hold your other hand in mine," Archie explained. She stood opposite him, dressed in that gorgeous purple gown, looking as sumptuous as he had ever seen her.

He did find her attractive and definitely more approachable in her normal clothing, but he had to admit that this gown did a lot more for her than her others.

The dark purple fabric made the whiteness of her skin nearly sparkle, while the black choker made her delicate neck much more appealing. He wished he could just untie the ribbon and put his mouth where it had been.

She put her hand on his shoulder and held her other hand out for him to take. "Like this?"

He placed his palm at her waist, his fingers prickling with the sensation of wanting to touch her, to gather her into his arms and kiss her senseless.

"Yes. Exactly." He swallowed after he spoke, wondering just how he had come to this state. This chaotic, disheveled, wanting-to-kiss-her state. When he'd first met her, he had assumed she was blundering along with some sense of her own importance. And then as he got to know her, he was struck by her humor, her intelligence, and, yes, he had to say, her face and body.

And now he wished he could toss his mission aside.

"We don't have any music," she said after a moment of standing in his arms.

"Right. No, we don't. We can count—what did Cook do, anyway?"

She grinned at him. Clearly she was not in the same thinking-constantly-about-the-other-person state as he was. "She would sing songs she'd learned when she was little. Her father owned a pub, and she knew all the songs the sailors sang. They were not very proper," and then she laughed at the memory.

He arched an eyebrow. "Can you hum something then? I don't want you to offend my delicate sensibilities with your ribald songs."

"I think you should hum. I will be too busy trying to figure out where my feet should go. I have no idea if Cook was actually a good dancer."

"That makes sense." He ran through his memories of having attended balls with his older brothers, long before he'd joined up and lost his family. Thankfully, he was able to recall a few tunes, and he began to hum, moving her as he did.

She nodded in time to the music and then began

counting—"one, two, three, one, two, three"—as they danced.

It was wonderful. She made up in joy what she lacked in skill, and he found himself holding his breath a few times, which definitely made his humming worse.

It was just that—she was so lively, and graceful, and clearly delighted with what they were doing. He wished he could capture this moment with her, place it in a jar, and bring it out to savor when he was back with Lady Sophia and fielding all the questions from the interested ladies.

He stopped humming after a few minutes but they didn't stop dancing—her counting continued, only now she peeked up at him from under her lashes as though they were in on an enormous joke with each other.

"And done," she said at last, dropping his hand to lower herself into a curtsey. "Thank you for the dance, Mr. Salisbury. I will need to give Cook a raise; it seems she did very well in instructing me."

"You need to be less . . ." *Less you*, he wanted to say, only he didn't want to make it seem as though he was criticizing her. "Just less," he finished, spreading his hands out as though that would explain things.

"What do you mean?"

He drew a deep breath. "A duchess, even more than a lesser member of the aristocracy, can't be seen as being too enthusiastic. About anything."

Her eyebrows drew together as she wrinkled her brow in thought. "Is this like the other time, when I had to be more abrupt?"

"Yes, precisely. You should demand things. You should assume that things will be done for you because it is you who wishes it. You should be above it all."

As you are above me in rank, in station, in everything.

"Above happiness?" she asked, her eyes widening. "Above common courtesy?" She shook her head. "I can be many things. I can, and will, be a good duchess, one who cares for the people under her. Who leaves the estate to the next person to inherit in much better shape than it was when I inherited it myself. But I cannot and will not be rude to people just because it increases my consequence."

She spoke sharply, and it felt as though she'd walked up and punched him in the chest. But that could be just because every part of him wanted to keep her the way she was, keep every joyful fragment of her, and he hated having to remind her that who she was had to adhere more closely to what she was.

"I don't want you to be rude," he said in a quiet voice. "I don't think you could be, even if I asked you to. What I want," he said, placing his hand on her arm, even though he should not be touching her at all, not if they weren't dancing, or he wasn't assisting her into a carriage, "is for you to be you, but to keep yourself close." He wasn't explaining himself properly. It was frustrating; in the army, he just told people to do things, and they did it. Even Lady Sophia normally did as he asked without too much fussing.

He stroked her arm. He couldn't help himself. "What I mean is that you are too rare and too special a person to allow people who aren't worthy of it to see you. You . . ." and then he paused, not sure he should be saying this, knowing he probably shouldn't, but unable to stop. "You are far more than your title. But your title is all that people will see when they look at you. Most people, that is. People like me and your grandmother, and the staff who raised you. Those people know who you are. Some of us might even deserve to know you, but most of the rest of them," he said, throwing his arm out in exasperation, "they don't. They don't deserve you."

She looked up at him and bit her lip, her eyes moist with unshed tears. "That is the nicest thing anyone has ever said to me," she said in a soft voice. "I—I am so glad you are here to help me through this. As though this being a duchess thing is the worst fate to happen to anybody," she added with a rueful laugh. "But it wouldn't be half as fun as it is—and it is fun, I am having fun going through paperwork and solving problems and doing things I never thought I would— without you. Thank you." And then she leaned up and kissed him on the cheek, steadying herself by putting her hand on his arm.

He froze. He wanted nothing more than to turn his face, press their mouths together as they had before, but that wasn't what this was about. This was about being a friend, being someone she could depend on. Who wouldn't take advantage of her.

Who meant every word he said. And who wanted her to be able to succeed without the impediment of complications, like being inappropriately entangled with her temporary steward, the disowned third son of a viscount.

"You're welcome." He took a deep breath and stepped away from her, took his hand off her arm, allowed her hand to fall away from him. "It is probably time to go to the assembly. Where you will raise your nose and allow people to be honored by your presence."

She did just that, only her raised nose was also accompanied by a sly grin and a laugh.

"We're going to have to practice," he muttered as he took her elbow and led her out of the ballroom.

Dear Mr. Salisbury,

Practice. I want to practice ~~kissing dancing~~ being properly duchesslike with you. Will you rate me on my superciliousness? I will settle for nothing less than a perfect rating. It will take lots of practice ~~thank goodness~~.

I believe we should consider returning to London soon as well. It seems that you have solved the employee problem, and Mr. Wickes is more than capable of being my steward, given his knowledge of the estate. I need to face what is to be my future soon ~~or I will never be able to~~.

~~Will you want to return there with me? With the chance you might see your family?~~ I am hoping that Aunt Sophia can spare you for a bit longer, just to make certain I am settled in London properly and able to navigate in Society.

Duchess

Chapter 17

"Your Grace, might I have this dance?"

Genevieve smiled at Sir William, who was bending over her hand. "Certainly, sir. It would be my pleasure."

He straightened and took her hand, leading her out onto the dance floor. The assembly was very crowded, people who were obviously some of her tenants elbow to elbow with landed squires and other people who were clearly gentlefolk. It was very democratic, and Genevieve wished she had thought to bring along Clarkson, who would no doubt have enjoyed the mingling of the classes.

She stood out in the crowd, not just because of her gown, which likely cost more than some of these people made in a year, but also because of the deference shown to her no matter where she turned. When they arrived, the entire room stilled, all the heads swiveling toward them at the entrance to the room. She kept herself as distant as she possibly could, given that she just wanted to rush over to everyone in the room and assure them she was not at all the toplofty person one might assume, given her title.

But that would be the exact opposite of what she was supposed to do.

The music began, and Genevieve had to push aside all those concerns to focus on the dancing. She did her counting inside her head, relieved she had yet to step on his toes. She did not allow herself the luxury of glancing around to see if Archie was watching, and could assess her skill. Perhaps he was dancing with Miss Evelyn.

"This is," Sir William began as they moved together in the dance, "quite pleasant." He sounded surprised, and it immediately made Genevieve feel defensive. After all, it was more than pleasant, it was wonderful, but that could also be because this was the first such event she'd ever gone to.

Maybe this was only mediocre, and she had no way of knowing? But the people here all looked so happy, and the music was fine, and the room wasn't over-stuffy. Really, what else did he require?

"Evelyn and I have so little experience with country events, you understand," he said, as though hearing what she'd been thinking. "We have only been to a few dances in Lon—"

And then they parted, Genevieve continuing the steps of the dance without stepping on anybody else's toes as well.

"—don," he finished.

"This is my first such dance," Genevieve said, hoping the words wouldn't cause her to lose count.

"Truly? Why, then you and I have a lot in common," Sir William replied, his easy grin making her dismiss the thought that he was being condescending.

"It seems we do," she replied, making him smile even more broadly. He wasn't as good-looking as Archie, but then again, he was far more eligible, should she even be thinking about that possibility. Which she should, given that everyone she would meet now that she was duchess would be thinking about it.

But she couldn't keep herself from glancing over to where she spotted Archie. He was impossible to miss, even if she wanted to, what with being taller than any other gentleman in the room and twice as handsome, even including Sir William, who would be quite good-looking if he weren't being compared to Mr. Salisbury.

But she couldn't help but compare them. Probably only natural, given that these two now numbered the two gentlemen she knew at all.

They finished the rest of the dance in silence, for which Genevieve was exceedingly grateful, not certain she could continue to keep up conversation and continue not stepping on anyone's feet.

"Thank you for the dance," Sir William said, bending over her hand.

"Thank you," Genevieve replied. "I see your sister over there; shall we go to her?"

Miss Evelyn herself had just finished dancing with a ruddy young man whose eyes twinkled as he gazed at his partner.

Sir William's eyes narrowed as he saw his sister. "Yes, that is an excellent idea."

Genevieve could tell from how he stiffened

up that he was not pleased about something his sister had done. Was it dancing in general? Or dancing with that gentleman? Whatever it was, he did not look pleased at the moment, and she felt something surge up in her to protect Miss Evelyn from her brother. A ridiculous notion, given that she had no idea of their circumstances. But still. She didn't like how he was striding through the crowd toward his sister, nor how Miss Evelyn's eyes widened as she saw her brother approach.

Although there was something to be lauded, as well, in that kind of protectiveness. She had only met Miss Evelyn years ago, and she had no idea what kind of person she'd turned into. Perhaps her brother was watching out for her.

It would be nice to be watched out for like that.

"Might I have this dance?" Mr. Salisbury's low tone pulled her out of what seemed to be sliding into a morose mood, despite being at her first dance.

She turned to him, suppressing a gasp at seeing just how magnificent he was up close. He was just as distinctive as she in this crowd, dressed in evening clothes that revealed how intensely masculine he was, all broad chest and shoulders, his hair lacking that curl she found irresistible, but brushed back and tamed even though the look in his eyes said he was not tamed. Would never be tamed, in fact.

"Yes, please," she said, holding her hand out. His hand was warm and solid, and he drew her to him as closely as he could without drawing comment, or at least it felt that way to Genevieve. Her skin felt prickly, and her fingers tingled where they touched him.

The music started and Genevieve was delighted to hear they were dancing to a waltz—a less complicated dance, and one where they wouldn't have to separate.

He didn't say anything, just gazed down at her. Her chest felt tight, as though her bosom was suddenly too large for her gown. But it didn't feel wrong or unpleasant; it felt as though she wished she could squirm out of her clothing and into him, which was probably wrong on the face of it, but didn't feel that way to her.

Her mouth felt dry, and she licked her lips. His eyes dropped down to her mouth, and it felt as though he'd touched her there, his stare was so intense. So visceral.

"Are you—are you enjoying the assembly?" she said in what she absolutely had to describe as a squeak.

"Immensely," he replied, his gaze not leaving her mouth.

"I am as well."

His eyes met hers, and he smiled. A real smile, one that reached his eyes. And she felt warm all over, as though he'd enfolded her entirely in his arms, holding that large body against hers.

She wasn't just alone in this feeling, was she? Not that she could ask, especially not when they were in public and dancing together. But she wished she could, if only to know she wasn't alone. In this, and in so many other things.

The thought struck her, again, that eventually

he would leave, he would return to his life at Aunt Sophia's, and she would have to do this all on her own.

"What is wrong?" he said, the smile leaving his face.

Oh, and he was so very perceptive.

She sighed and shook her head. "It's nothing."

His lips tightened, as though he wanted to argue with her, but he didn't, just twirled her around the dance floor, she resolutely putting everything besides the present moment out of her mind.

There was something bothering her, he could tell, but he also knew it wouldn't do to pursue it here. She wore her heart on her sleeve, but most times it felt as though only he could see it.

He tightened his hold on her hand unconsciously, then released it as she gazed up at him with a questioning look in her eyes. He shook his head, now angry at himself for denying what he was feeling, just as he was—was it angry as well?—angry at her for not expressing herself.

Even though he had just told her that was exactly what she had to do in order to maintain her position. He should have been delighted she danced with Sir William, a presumably not horrible relative who would offer her more respectability and credence than he could.

Should have, but most definitely was not.

The music ended, and he withdrew from her, bowing low, which only put him in the unfortunate position of being close to her breasts, which were as revealed as he had ever seen them. He wished he could just lean forward and lick one of those exposed curves, but that would be far more scandalous than her being exuberant.

He felt his mouth twist up into a rueful smile at the thought.

"Thank you for the dance." She sounded breathless. The dance itself hadn't been that lively—it was a waltz, after all—and he had to wonder if she was feeling a fraction of what he was. If she was thinking about that one kiss, the one that burned in his mind, especially late at night. If she was wondering what would happen if they were all alone, were dancing, were touching.

He felt his cock twitch in his trousers, and he clamped his lips together, willing himself to stop thinking. About her.

Easier said than done, of course.

"I am getting tired," she said. He snapped out of his useless images of sexual abandon with her and peered down at her face. She did look weary, a tightness around her mouth, her eyes not as sparkling as when they had been dancing, when they had looked brighter than the stars on a cold, clear night.

"I will let Sir William and Miss Evelyn know you wish to depart," he said, only to pause when she put her hand on his sleeve. His arm tensed where she touched it.

"No, I don't want to ruin their enjoyment of the night simply because I am tired. The carriage can take me home, then return to pick you and them up."

"I am not sending you home alone."

Her lips tilted up into a half smile, one that felt as though it reached into his chest and tugged. "I thought you might say that. But I do not wish to have anyone else there." A moment as she bit her lip. "Is that wrong of me? It is just that I am not accustomed to being around so many people all at once. I always thought I wanted this, but it is just so much, all of a sudden. Too much." And she glanced up at him with a look of near panic. He wished he could just hoist her up into his arms and run all the way back to the estate.

"If you will wait here for a moment, I will let your guests know of the plan." He left before she could object some more—he knew she was likely berating herself for being so selfish, even though she was merely being self-preserving.

Sir William voiced his objections, naturally, but Archie squashed him in a few brief sentences, too intent on returning to Genevieve to adhere to strict politeness.

"Tell the duchess we will see her in the morning," Miss Evelyn said, a concerned expression on her face. He did like her, despite his antipathy toward her brother.

"Thank you Miss Evelyn, Sir William," Archie said as he bowed. He strode off in search of Genevieve, wishing there was a way he could protect her from all this. From relatives, to small assemblies, to being overwhelmed in her position.

But there wasn't. And he knew she would conquer it, he had faith in her, but still he hurt for her. In a way he had never hurt for anyone before.

"How do you feel?"

They were in the carriage, and with the exception of the wheels churning over the road, it was blessedly quiet. And dark. She could barely make out his face opposite; she could just see an enormous black shape, as she had when he had first arrived in her London house.

"Fine, I suppose." She took a deep breath. "It is fine. I am fine. I feel foolish, because I don't feel ill, just—overwhelmed."

"It's not surprising," he said in that low, rich voice that flowed over her and seemed to seep into her bones. "You are doing so many things that you're not familiar with, and having to do them under intense scrutiny."

"Yes." That was true, only—"Only I should have been familiar with these things. If my father had held any kind of loyalty to the position, he would have at least thought to teach me so I wouldn't be absolutely lost here."

"You're angry with him." He didn't say it as a question, but as a statement.

"I suppose I am," she said after a few moments. "I didn't know him well enough to be truly angry with him, not as a person. But as someone who knew just what he was doing when he didn't do anything to set me right on this course? Yes. I'm angry. I'm furious." She was startled to discover she was, so furious she was shaking with it.

"You should be."

They sat in silence, Genevieve's hands holding on to the seat on either side of her legs, gripping the leather so tightly she knew there was likely to be a mark on the palm of her hand. "Is this the anger you were trying to get me to exhibit before? When you were teaching me how to be . . . me?"

That might make her even madder, to think he had manipulated her into this moment so she would make a better duchess. So his responsibility to her would be over quicker, so she would be on her own again.

"No," he said, laughter in his voice. "That would have been clever of me, wouldn't it?"

"Oh."

"I like working here with you. I have said that before." His voice was still amused, and she felt herself softening, unbending, feeling not so . . . stifled as she had at the assembly.

She could hear the movement as he leaned forward, uncurling her hand from the leather of the carriage seat. His fingers were strong and firm around hers. "I wish you weren't the duchess, either," he said, and now it sounded as though his voice had dropped into an entirely different register, one only she could hear. "If you weren't, I . . ." and then he paused.

Genevieve's mouth went dry, and she licked her lips. "If I wasn't, you . . . ?" she prompted, but she didn't wait for his reply; she drew herself up and over to his side of the carriage, both of them facing backward. "You would what?" she said, bringing her hand up to his cheek. Feeling him still in the darkness.

"Imagine you were just Archie, and I was just Genevieve." His stubble prickled her skin. She could just barely see the gleam of his eyes. He reached up and grabbed her hand, turning his head to kiss her palm. "If I was just Archie," he said, then drew her into his arms and placed his mouth on hers.

Oh. For just a moment it felt that there was nothing but them in the world. And the world was dark, warm because of his lips, perfect because nothing else existed.

She slid her hand around to cup the nape of his neck, her fingers reaching into his hair. It was thick, and she found herself tugging on it to draw him closer.

His mouth was so warm. Her breasts felt heavy, too full constricting against her gown and the cloak she had on over it. She pulled her hand out of his hair and went to the strings on her cloak, undoing the tie with one graceless pull.

His hands slid up to her shoulders and pushed the cloak down, and he accompanied the movement with a groan that made parts of Genevieve feel ablaze. Not just warm, but on fire. She opened her mouth and licked his lips and he opened to her, their tongues tangling together. All she heard was their rapid breathing, felt how their noses bumped as they devoured each other.

My God. This was—this was everything. How

had she gone so long without having it again? This warm, moist licking and sucking, the feel of his bare hand on her shoulder, the slide of his work-roughened fingers on her skin.

She wished she could just have him touch her everywhere. Yes, there, too, where she could feel herself getting wetter. There where it felt it burned the most, where she felt a sense of urgency about something.

She wasn't so naïve she didn't know what that something was, either. But if she had to think about it—and she couldn't now, not with what his mouth was doing, and how he was holding her tightly up against his lovely, massive chest—she would have to say, on balance, that she would prefer not having her first time in a moving carriage. That seemed as though it had a degree of difficulty even Archie couldn't surmount. So to speak.

But she could keep kissing him, and she brought her hand back up to his neck, sliding her fingers down his back, raising up his jacket so she could flatten her palm against his back. His strong back that shifted and flexed under her touch.

She couldn't miss how he was moving, as well. As though he wished to press himself up entirely against her, his hands frantically moving on her skin, caressing her, until he was trailing his fingers against the neck of her bodice, her whole self wanting to just have him touch her breasts to make the ache go away. Or intensify.

She didn't wait for him, instead she reached down and placed his palm right on her breast, pushing into his palm almost—actually never mind almost, certainly—wanton, but she didn't care.

Because for now it was just them. Genevieve and Archie. Not the duchess and her steward, or anything like that. Not just friends, either, but not yet lovers. Stuck in a kind of purgatory between the two, filled with sighs and aching, and want, and more kisses until she didn't even remember her own name.

But she did know his. "Archie," she moaned against his mouth, pressing into him. His fingers had found her nipple, and were rubbing it through the fabric of her gown.

"That feels good, doesn't it?" he murmured. "Me touching your gorgeous breasts. If I could, I would lean down and run my tongue over your stiff nipple. Suck it into my mouth and kiss it as I caress your curves."

Oh. Well. She hadn't known those words in that order existed, much less what it would do to her to hear him say them.

She squirmed even closer, her hands at his narrow waist, her face lifted to his, his mouth taking hers with a fierce, savage possession that rendered her breathless.

He withdrew from the kiss, breathing raggedly, his fingers still dancing on her skin, reaching down into her gown to stroke over her nipple, sliding across her shoulder to cup her neck, to hold her in what Genevieve wished was a moment that could last forever.

Even though it couldn't. Even though now it seemed as though she could feel the slowing of the carriage, the wheels less noisy than they had been before.

Their breathing still as labored.

He gave her one last kiss, as though he couldn't help himself, and drew away, his eyes seeming to spark in the darkness.

"Genevieve and Archie," he said at last. "Just us."

Her mouth felt bruised. Her heart did, too. She wished she could just tell the coachman to keep driving, to take them away together so they could forget who they were, and who they were supposed to be.

But she had duties. And so did he. And neither one of them would be allowed to be just them for much longer.

~~Dear Genevieve,~~

~~I want you. I want you so much it burns. I don't know
what is worse—having kissed you and knowing what
your mouth tastes like, knowing I can never be able to
savor the rest of you, or having kissed you and imagining
what it would be like if I could taste you. Everywhere.~~

~~Archie~~

(NOT SENT)

Chapter 18

"Ye need nothing else then?" Mr. Wickes said, glancing between them. Sir William and Miss Evelyn's servants were waiting in the kitchen for their master and mistress, while Archie and Genevieve stood in the hallway, Wickes having taken her cloak.

Thank goodness the man was not only remarkably unobservant, but also that it was relatively dark; Archie could feel how his breathing, still, was labored, his chest going up and down as he tried to calm himself.

Tried to keep himself from going to her and pleasuring her until she screamed his name.

"We are fine, thank you, Mr. Wickes." Her voice trembled. Did Wickes hear it?

"Good night then," Wickes replied, handing the candle in its holder to Archie. "Mind that third step, it's been creaking. I'll be taking a look at it tomorrow."

"You take such excellent care of the estate," she said, her tone approving.

Even in the dark, Archie could see how Wickes's cheeks started to turn red. "It's worth it, Your Grace, when there is something like you to take care of." He turned and walked to the hallway leading to the kitchen.

Leaving them here alone.

"Well," she said, her voice higher than usual, "we should be getting to bed." And then she emitted—was it a squeak?—as she realized what she'd said. "I mean," she began, sounding breathless and excited and anxious all at once.

They'd had this exact conversation before, he wanted to remind her. He didn't, but he did take her hand in his. "I know what you mean." He drew her arm into his. "Let me guide you up to your bedroom. I will see you safely there where Clarkson is no doubt waiting to hear all about the assembly."

"Yes," she replied, sounding grateful and disappointed. It was remarkable how nuanced one person's voice could be.

Or perhaps that was just because he was attuned to her as he had never been attuned to anyone before.

They made their way up the stairs, Archie acutely conscious of her beside him, how her skin glowed in the flickering of the candlelight, how she kept pace with him as they walked.

He led her to her door—mercifully, a few doors down the hall from his, too far away for him to risk discovery, but close enough that he could imagine what might happen if he did—and stopped just outside, gazing down into her face. Her mouth was full and red, and he felt a fierce, triumphant joy that he had done that. He had branded her with his kiss, he had made her eyes get half lidded with a sensual gaze, he had said those words to her, words that had made her breathe faster, and grow more excited under his touch.

"Thank you," she said, a glimmer of humor in her voice.

"For what?" he said in a whisper. "For kissing you? For touching your skin?" He leaned in to speak right into her ear. "For reaching down into your gown and finding your nipple, stroking your breast with my fingers, wishing it was my tongue?"

She clutched his arm and turned her face up to his, her eyes gleaming bright as stars. "Yes," she said in a fierce tone. "For all of that. Because"—and he saw her expression falter—"because I might not ever feel anything like that again."

He tried not to show how her words impacted him, even though they were words he'd told himself. *Never again.* That moment was only because they had been in a carriage by themselves, on the way home from an event where she'd gotten overwhelmed. Where their mutual attraction had overwhelmed both of them, to the point where they'd done something so foolish, so risky. Something that, if it were to happen again, would put everything she was working so hard to accomplish at stake.

"I might never feel anything like that again,

either," he admitted at last, his hand dropping away from her, turning to walk back down the hallway to his room.

Feeling her standing there staring after him.

Genevieve waited until she heard the door close behind him, then turned to enter her own room. The firelight cast a warm, golden glow over the room, and Clarkson rose, placing a book on the table beside her.

"You're home early," Clarkson said, glancing at the clock in the corner. "Did you have a pleasant evening?"

Pleasant was one way to describe it. The best and the most disappointing evening she'd ever had—or likely ever would have—was another way.

"Yes, thank you." Genevieve turned her back to Clarkson, who began to undo the buttons on the back of her gown. "I came home early, I don't think I was prepared for such an enormity of people all under one roof."

Miss Clarkson made some sort of clucking sound, her fingers working diligently. "I would imagine so, that kind of thing is intimidating if one isn't used to it. And I don't think you would be, from what you've said of how you were raised."

"No." A moment. "I'm not."

Was that why she had turned so readily to Archie? Why it felt so good to be held by him? She couldn't help but think it was more than that, far more, which made it only too dangerous to think on.

"Let me slide your sleeves off," Clarkson said, oblivious—thank God—to the turmoil inside Genevieve's mind. The fabric slid over Genevieve's breasts, and she shuddered, recalling his fingers. His touch.

She had had no idea that the simple act of a man touching a woman there would be so powerful. And imagine if he put his fingers elsewhere. Did men put their fingers there? She had to think so. At least, she could see Archie doing just that, sliding his fingers down her arm, to her waist, then lower down.

"Are you cold?" Clarkson said in a concerned voice. "Because it seems like you're shivering."

No, I'm burning up, Genevieve wanted to retort, only of course she couldn't.

"I am fine."

Clarkson placed the back of her hand to Genevieve's forehead. "I hope you're not getting sick."

If only it were that simple, Genevieve thought. She stepped out of her gown and waited as Clarkson picked it up and shook it out. "I feel fine, I cannot get sick, there is too much to do." And there was—there were more workers arriving tomorrow, and she had to go over more paperwork with Archie—Mr. Salisbury, that is—and now she had houseguests, of all things, and she also had to plan when to return to London.

She should return soon, she knew that. Not just because she was dreading it so much that she knew it was something she should face. She should ask Archie as to the best way to approach it—to devise some sort of strategy for it, so she wouldn't be caught unawares, and so she had the best chance of facing it all without feeling panicky, or having to leave early.

Although if she had to leave early, he would leave with her, which would mean—no. She couldn't think like that. Gran would be with her, would be chaperoning her. Even though Gran was blind. What if they—?

No, that wasn't right, either.

She had to pretend none of it had happened.

Ha. As though she could forget any of it. She had the feeling she'd be reliving those moments in the carriage for a very long time. She could just see herself—a spinster duchess hiding out in one of her numerous estates—thinking about that one time that she had been treated as a woman, not as a duchess, or really as a lady.

When she had done something, acted on her desires, and reveled in the consequences.

"Now your chemise," Clarkson said, gesturing to Genevieve.

"Oh yes, of course," Genevieve replied, undoing the ties at the neck. Clarkson bent down to draw the garment over her head, then held her night rail out to her, her eyes averted.

"Thank you," Genevieve replied. "Clarkson," she said from the depths of the gown, "do you think it is wrong for me not to wish I had to do all these things I apparently have to do?"

She emerged from the gown, her hair coming entirely undone. She blinked at Clarkson, who was regarding her with a raised eyebrow.

"What?" she asked. Did she look ridiculous? Well, of course she did. She'd been thoroughly kissed in a carriage, was entirely in a muddle about it, and her hair was untidy. Again.

Clarkson didn't say any of those things, however. "I would have to be concerned about your intelligence if you felt any differently." She adjusted Genevieve's night rail, then stepped back and nodded. "I believe the remainder of your gowns should be on their way here soon, likely arriving within a few days. Mrs. Hardwick included a note with this one saying as much."

More gowns. More duties. Less time to be able to spend with him.

At least she'd be dressed gorgeously as she slid toward the inexorable twin terrors of panic and responsibility. So she had that in her corner.

"Good morning, Your Grace." Miss Evelyn glanced shyly up at Genevieve, a teacup in her hand. She looked very pretty, dressed in a morning gown made of light-colored fabric and stamped all over with tiny flowers. "I hope you are feeling better this morning?"

"Yes, thank you," Genevieve replied, gesturing to the footman—one of the new gentlemen—that she would like some tea. "Did you stay at the assembly for much longer?"

Miss Evelyn shook her head, sending a cascade of curls dancing about her shoulders. "My brother didn't see what the point was if you—that is," she corrected, blushing furiously, "we had traveled a long way yesterday and we were both tired as well."

Genevieve hid her smile as she drank her tea. Sir William was going to have to find a way to keep his sister from making artless comments once they were in proper London society. And she did have to admit she was flattered he was so intent on the possibility of wooing her. Not that she could even think about such a thing, not with what had happened in the carriage.

Maybe that was an indication that she wasn't as susceptible to gentlemen as she had worried? Since she had never met any, she had thought that when she did meet some, she would be swept away by their general . . . gentlemanliness.

No, it turned out she could be swept away, but only by one gentleman in particular. At least one out of the two in her current acquaintance.

She should probably test out the gentleman waters more thoroughly before she made a decision about how susceptible she was. So there might be hope for Sir William after all.

"Your Grace, would you be so kind as to show me around the gardens this afternoon?" Miss Evelyn took a bite of toast after she spoke, a dab of butter landing on top of her lip.

"That would be lovely," Genevieve replied. She gestured to Miss Evelyn's mouth. "You've got a bit of . . ." she began, then Miss Evelyn turned an even deeper shade of red as she wiped at her mouth with a napkin.

It was good to know that there was someone in

the world who blushed as furiously and deeply as Genevieve did.

The door to the dining room swung open to allow Sir William to enter.

"Good morning," he said, allowing the footman to draw his chair out for him. "Your Grace, I trust you are feeling well this morning?" His brows were drawn together in an expression of concern.

"Yes, thank you. Your sister and I will be touring the gardens this afternoon, if you would care to join us?"

He leaned back in his chair as the footman placed a plate of food in front of him. "Yes, that would be pleasant," he said as he put marmalade on his toast.

Genevieve drummed her fingers on her thigh under the table. Was this what life was going to be? Was this what it should be? Tea and blushing and marmalade and gardens and talk of things being pleasant? It all just felt so dull. Not at all what she'd hoped for when she'd thought about what it would be like to have friends or be an adult, never mind be a duchess.

She stifled a yawn and drank more tea. At least the tea was delicious, even if everything else was bland.

Dear Mr. Salisbury,

We should begin discussing plans to return to London much as I don't wish to enter Society. Then again, I don't seem to want to do anything but spend time with you. Sir William and Miss Evelyn have expressed that they wish to accompany us, since Miss Evelyn has a particular friend she wishes to see is desirous of renewing her acquaintance in town.

Sir William is no doubt trying to secure me as a wife.

Do you suppose we will be able to return within a week? We should endeavor to spend time alone together practicing what I will face upon entering Society.

Duchess

Chapter 19

"What do you want to practice first?" Archie clenched his jaw as he tried to keep his voice neutral. Not the voice of someone who'd been thinking about an event for the last five days.

The estate was on its way to not being the worst of the duchess's holdings; more former soldiers had arrived, and Mr. Wickes had been officially appointed as the steward, despite his protestations that he wasn't worthy. Archie retorted that the only thing he wasn't worthy of was being the sole cook, for the aforementioned shepherd's pie reason.

Sir William and Miss Evelyn were still in residence, but Sir William seemed to have recognized his earlier misstep with the duchess, and was now being more discreet in his pursuit of her.

If the sight of him didn't enrage Archie, he might even admit the gentleman was going about his courtship the right way—asking her for her opinions, complimenting her gently on her appearance. Being there when she needed it, but not stepping in to take care of things. Allowing her to ask for help rather than just assuming she couldn't handle it herself.

"We should practice my interacting with people." She sounded anxious, and he wished he could just step toward her and take her in his arms.

It wouldn't reduce her anxiety, but it would make him feel better.

It was a feeling he'd had most of the past few days, when he hadn't been engrossed in reviewing accounts, calculating potential expenses, and instructing the new employees as to their positions. He'd also heard troubling news that Mr. Leonards had been hanging around the village, making pointed comments about what the duchess and her temporary steward were doing together so often.

Not what Archie wished they were doing, that was for certain.

This was one of the first times they'd been alone together since that evening in the carriage. It was early afternoon, and he'd seized on the chance to be with her after he'd received her letter.

"Interactions like social interactions? With people you have just met?" He hadn't realized the impact her isolated childhood had had on her, not until he'd seen how she'd come close to panic that evening at the assembly. She was so much more comfortable among the servants, with people who weren't constantly assessing her importance versus theirs. That distinction existed, of course, but she was so much more comfortable that she was able to put everyone— including herself—at ease.

"That would be best." She bit her lip, keeping her gaze fixed past his shoulder. As she did when she was thinking of something that made her feel awkward. That he had gotten to know her so well to recognize that sign was—well, he was grateful for it, but he also already missed her in his life. Even though she was directly in front of him.

"We will start slowly," Archie replied. "How about I am a debutante who has just made your acquaintance? We can move up to the Queen."

She laughed, as he'd meant her to. "I will have much in common with a debutante," she replied. "Not as much the Queen."

"Although you are both powerful women."

She grimaced. "Don't remind me. The Queen, at least, knew she might be Queen someday. And she has a mother who is there to help her, even if that help might be unwelcome." She shook her head as she flapped her hands in the air. "But never mind that. You are a debutante. Excellent." She drew herself up to her full height and arched one eyebrow. "It is a pleasure to meet you, my lady," she said in a voice nearly befitting the Queen, to be honest.

Archie took her hand in his and did his best version of a curtsey. Which was not very good. "The pleasure is mine, Your Grace." He edged the tone of his voice higher, but apparently he sounded ridiculous, since she couldn't help but start to smile.

"No smiling," he said in a mock-serious tone. "No humor at all; we are having a conversation. There is no room for enjoyment."

She rolled her eyes at his comment, but then

resumed her serious mien. "Are you enjoying the party, my lady?" She wrinkled her nose. "What is your name in this scenario anyway? It feels odd speaking to someone when you don't know their name."

"Uh"—he wasn't very good at this, he hadn't even thought about what his name might be. "How about Lady Arch?"

She closed her eyes in an exaggerated horrified response. "I think you should be Lady Anne. That is a real name."

"Fine," Archie replied in a terse tone. "Lady Anne." He spread his arms out. "May we begin, please?"

And then she smiled, a real smile, and tilted her head to him. "Yes, we may. Lady Anne, are you enjoying the party?"

Archie tried to imagine how a young girl would feel when conversing with a duchess. Certainly not like she wanted to kiss the duchess in question, which was unfortunately how Archie himself felt. He clasped his hands in front of him and tried to slump down so as not to be towering over her. "It is lovely." He glanced around, as though absorbing the room—the candles, the people, the music. "I have never been to such a grand event before."

Her smile turned even warmer, if such a thing were possible. "I am just recently from the country myself. It is all rather grand, isn't it?" she said, lowering her voice as though she were confiding a secret.

Archie paused.

"Did I do something wrong?" Once again, her voice was higher, almost squeaky, and he felt the impact of her stress right in his chest, which suddenly felt tight.

"No." *You were merely yourself.* "I just want you to keep in mind that you should maintain a certain distance from the people to whom you're speaking."

The thought occurred to him, as he was talking, that in fact he did know more about being a duchess than she did. Lady Sophia had been right to send him, even though he knew from her ever-increasingly strident letters that his employer was eager to have him return.

Apparently she was lonely since fewer of the town's ladies came to visit once word of his absence became known.

He tried not to grin at how Lady Sophia was likely complaining to Bob about it all.

She stepped back from him, her eyes sparkling. "A certain distance? Should I carry a measuring tape and make sure I remain remote and unapproachable at all times?" And then her eyes widened, as though recalling—as he couldn't seem to stop recalling himself—the times when she had not been remote and unapproachable at all. When she had been the opposite; approachable and, perhaps, *mote.* Even though he didn't think that was an actual word.

"A measuring tape is not required, Your Grace," he said, allowing his lips to curl into a smile. "You can just judge the metaphorical duchess distance." He glanced down at the space between them. "This is the approximate space I would suggest keeping between yourself and another individual."

She glanced down as well. "How far is that? I am not certain I can gauge it."

He put one foot directly in front of the other, then again, until he was nearly touching her. "It is three of my footsteps, Your Grace, so perhaps three feet apart?"

His measuring tactic had worked, yes, but now he stood in front of her. Where he'd been longing to be, and yet should not be at all.

"Three feet is the duchess distance?" Now she sounded less squeaky and more—breathless.

He knew how she felt. He was having difficulty breathing as well.

He was right here. Standing in front of her, so close she could make out the tiny lines that spread out from the corners of his eyes, so close she could see the blackness of his pupils against the deep blue of his eyes.

She tried to take a deep breath, only to stop when she realized that that motion would put her chest in even closer contact with his. So she stopped, mid-breath, swallowing as she exhaled through her nose.

Who knew that her prurient interest in him would affect the way she breathed?

Well, likely anyone who'd had the experience before. But she hadn't, and so she hadn't known.

"Archie," she began, just as he stepped back away into the required duchess distance space.

"Your Grace," he replied. His jaw was clenched, and his hands were as well, the whites of his knuckles indicating his emotion.

That shouldn't make her glad, to see how affected he was, but she couldn't help but feel delighted that this whatever it was wasn't entirely on her side. He felt it, too, felt it so much he was holding himself back, was using her honorific rather than her name. As though using her name would be too intimate for him.

"Let us practice again," he continued, the words coming out in one low order. As though enunciating enough to make the words less monotone would open him up for—for something.

It did thrill her, even though she regretted that he had so much self-control.

"Yes," she said, "let us practice." She allowed some of what she was feeling to seep into her voice, suppressing a smile as she saw his eyes widen. And his fingers flex.

"My lady, this is a lovely party." She gazed off into the distance as though assessing the people and the refreshments and finding them adequate, but still wanting. He regarded her intently. "I do so enjoy meeting such . . . unexceptionable individuals," she continued, keeping her voice as autocratic as she could.

She ruined the effect by turning to him with a wide smile. "That was good, wasn't it?"

He folded his arms over his chest and raised an

eyebrow. "It was, Your Grace." He uncrossed his arms and gestured toward her. "But you'll have to maintain your duchess demeanor for longer than a few seconds."

She regarded him for a moment, then tilted her head back and placed her hands on her hips as though in challenge. Which it was, wasn't it? A challenge for her to be worthy of the position she had, a challenge to meet people and to handle their disdain and possible dismissal of her with grace and no small amount of haughtiness.

A challenge not to give in to the feelings she had now, concurrent with the feelings of being a duchess. Of being a woman, someone who wanted and felt things that she had never felt before. Specifically, wanted to feel *him*.

Her father had been able to indulge in his desires because he was a man, even though he had been a terrible duke. But even if she was a terrible duchess—which she knew she would not be— she could not be a wonderful woman, not with how she imagined a wonderful woman would be. A wonderful woman would be one who loved where she wanted to, who was happy. Who was loved in return.

At most, she could likely manage not being a miserable, inappropriate duchess. It was a goal.

With that in mind, she drew her duchess demeanor over her like a cloak and nodded to Archie. She had to stop thinking about who she wished she could be and start being who she really was. "This time, I would like you to pretend to be a man." And she had to suppress a laugh, since of course he was a man; that was the problem in the first place. "I would like you to pretend to be someone I will be dealing with in business matters," she clarified. "Someone who doesn't think I should be in my position"—in other words, likely everybody—"who makes his opinion known by his attitude."

He narrowed his gaze. "Are you certain you want that?" It looked as though he was about to move closer to her, to bridge the duchess distance, but then he paused and clamped his lips together. She saw a muscle tic at his jaw.

"I do want that." She paused, then took one step forward herself. Closer to him, but not as close as she'd like to be. "That is, of course I don't want that. I'd be foolish to actually *want* that, but I need to know how it will feel, and to prepare myself for it. It's an eventuality," she said in a rueful tone of voice.

He kept his eyes on her for a long moment, and she felt her breath hitch inside her chest, quickening as it seemed she felt the impact of his scrutiny all over her body.

"Let us begin, then." He straightened up to his full height and widened his stance, folding his arms over his chest. "I am someone who deals with your estate in some form of business." His eyes narrowed and his lip curled, and now the impact of his scrutiny was much different. It felt as though his scorn was a physical thing, something that was traveling over her body.

"Your Grace, you need not concern yourself with these matters," he said, his voice cold. If she didn't know he was pretending, she would have felt as though he truly disliked her. As it was, she couldn't help a shiver run through her at how terrible he sounded. But the truth of it was, she was going to encounter these people in actuality. It would be better if she learned how to react now.

What had he said before? *Assume that you are correct and superior.* She could do this.

"You are mistaken, Mr.—?" and then she paused, tilting her head as she waited for his reply.

He quickly smothered the grin as he heard her speak. "Mr. BetterThanYou."

She bit her lip to keep from laughing. "Well, Mr. BetterThanYou, these matters are my matters. All matters relating to the duchy are my purview. Unless you disagree—?" and again she let the words hang there, lingering in the silence as she felt her position gathering strength in the pause.

"It is just that I am not accustomed to dealing with a lady in such things," Archie said, shrugging dismissively. "Surely there is a gentleman with whom I may have this conversation?"

"No." The word was out before she even realized she'd spoken. Sharp, peremptory, decisive.

She resisted giving a triumphant yell.

"No, there is no gentleman with whom you may have this conversation. I am the person to whom you should be speaking. And will be speaking. Unless you wish me to take my business elsewhere?" And this time she accompanied her words with a raise of her chin and an arch of her eyebrow, feeling as though she was the duchess in truth for the first time.

Granted, in a room with just her temporary steward who was playacting to build her confidence, but still.

"No, no, of course not, Your Grace." Now Archie's tone had changed to one that was bordering on obsequiousness. "I did not realize just who I was dealing with. If you will allow me to show you what we've been doing on your behalf," and then he unfolded his arms and smiled broadly at her. "That was excellent. Remarkable. You found your tactic and made it work for you. Dealing with people is a strategy, every bit as much of a battle strategy as actually being in battle." His brows drew together in thought. "I had never realized that before." His eyes widened, and his next words came out all in a rush. "If only more battles and business meetings had you at their helm the world would be a far more prosperous and peaceful place."

She could only blink at him in shock. "I—that—thank you," she said at last. How could you tell someone that they had just paid you the best possible compliment ever? "So you don't believe as Mr. BetterThanYou does, that these things should be best left to the gentlemen?" She retreated to a teasing tone, unable to say what she was really feeling. Mostly because so much of what she was feeling was—was so much.

He snorted. "Of course not. While I admit that at first I found it unusual that you had inherited your position as you had."

"You're not alone in that," she muttered.

"It seems ridiculous that men are given this power simply because of their gender. Was your father a better duke than you are a duchess?" He nodded at her eye roll. "Of course not. But far fewer people will dispute his right to be the duke simply because of what he was. Not who he was." And now he had somehow moved closer to her, his gaze intense. And then he placed his hands on her shoulders, grasping her in place. Not that she was planning on moving. "You are magnificent, Genevieve. You will be wonderful in this position."

She nodded. "I will." It wasn't an affirmation of what he'd said. It was a statement.

The pads of his fingers caressed her skin. "You can do it."

And now she was finding it hard to breathe for some reason. As though she didn't know why.

"Your Grace," he said, his voice showing concern, "are you all right? We can do this another time."

Apparently her breathlessness had crossed over into asphyxia when she hadn't noticed. Or breathed.

"I am fine, thank you." She glanced up at him. Struck, as always, by how large and handsome he was. But more than that now—now she knew he was a caring man, one who took his duties seriously. As she did.

"Should we ask for tea?"

She snorted. She couldn't help it, and what was more, she didn't want to help it. "I am not feeling so poorly that you have to ask for tea, your most loathed beverage."

"It is not that I hate tea," he retorted, removing his hands from her shoulders. "It is just that the act of tea itself can camouflage the lack of so many other acts. When people sit around and drink tea they are not doing things. They are just . . . sitting."

"And you prefer to be in motion? To be accomplishing things?" Now that he'd explained it, it made so much sense. And there was also—"Your family. Did they sit around and drink tea rather than do things?"

His expression froze at her words. She wished she could take it back, could pretend she didn't know about his family, nor about how she could see how they affected him. But she couldn't. To pretend otherwise would be disingenuous, and he would know it for a lie. He would think she pitied him, when really she just wanted him to be happy.

"I am sorry. I shouldn't have asked that."

"No, no, it is fine." He held his hand out to her and she took it, allowing him to guide her to one of the chairs at the edge of the room. She sat down and waited as he dragged another chair opposite her, his long legs nearly touching hers.

They both turned as they heard the door open. "Pardon me, Your Grace?"

Sir William stepped into the room as he spoke, and Genevieve resisted the urge to shriek at him to leave.

"Yes, sir?" she said instead, using the cold duchess voice she seemed to have mastered within the past ten minutes. She saw Archie smother a grin out of the corner of her eye.

"Your Grace, my sister was hoping to ask your opinion on a few things before tea is served." Now it took a concentrated effort not to laugh, which would be incredibly rude. "We expect to return to London in time for her to enter Society, but she is very anxious about it all. I told her you would be able to ease her mind."

Before she would have wondered how she could possibly ease anybody's mind, given how disheveled hers was. But now? Now she knew she could.

"Of course. Tell your sister I will be up momentarily."

Sir William waited as she stood, holding the door open for her. Was he being polite, or just ensuring she and Archie were no longer alone together?

"I will see you for tea, Mr. Salisbury," Genevieve said over her shoulder as she walked out.

She wasn't sure, but she thought she heard him mutter some sort of curse.

~~Dear Genevieve,~~

~~You asked me about my family. I never thought I missed them until I met you and have seen how you collect people around you who become your family—people like Clarkson, and Wickes, and even me.~~

~~I wish they held as strong a feeling about the importance of family as you do. Maybe then I wouldn't be dreading and anticipating our return to London.~~

~~Archie~~

(NOT SENT)

Chapter 20

"Miss Evelyn," Genevieve said, handing the younger woman a cup of tea, "would you like to go to town with me later today?" The thought made her stomach get all fluttery, an after-effect of having felt so unsettled at the assembly, but she had to enter Society eventually—probably as soon as a few days—and this would be dipping a toe into the vast waters. The very vast waters filled with potential derision and doubt.

"I think it would be good for me to do some shopping, to show myself so my tenants know what I look like, and that I am just another person. Like them." She only wished that were so, but going to the village would show that she was striving to be an approachable owner. Not someone who collected rents via an intermediary, who didn't care.

She cared. Perhaps too much.

"That would be wonderful." Miss Evelyn sounded honestly thrilled, and Genevieve found herself smiling in reply.

"Thank you for seeing to my sister's comfort." Sir William lifted his teacup toward Genevieve in a toast. "You are a most gracious hostess." He settled the cup back down in the saucer. "When are you returning to London? Evelyn and I have taken a house, and we will certainly wish to see you as often as we can." He glanced at Miss Evelyn. "I know my sister will be overjoyed to have a friend, especially as she enters Society."

Miss Evelyn's expression turned bright and hopeful.

"Yes, well, Mr. Salisbury and I were discussing that very thing," via letter, oddly enough, although typical for them, "and I was saying that I should return soon. It is past time for me to show myself." Would she suffer a return of the anxiety she'd had at the assembly? But Miss Evelyn and Sir William would be there. Mr. Salisbury would be there as long as he could withstand Aunt Sophia's entreaties to return.

She could do this. She could.

"Excellent!" Sir William replied in an enthusiastic tone. "Perhaps we can travel together."

"Yes, that would be perfect," Genevieve said, wishing she wasn't already regretting the fact that she would not be alone with Archie. *Mr. Salisbury*. Although that also meant there wouldn't be a repeat of their earlier encounter.

Whether that was in the positive or the negative column, she couldn't say. Or wouldn't, more precisely. She nodded to Miss Evelyn. "Would you be free to depart to the village in about an hour?"

Miss Evelyn nodded enthusiastically as Genevieve finished her tea. Swallowing down all her feelings along with the liquid.

"Going to town?" Clarkson said, adjusting Genevieve's gown.

"Yes, I thought it would be a good thing to show my people, the people in the village, that I am a real person. Not someone who just takes the rents and forgets about them the rest of the time."

Clarkson's face grew concerned. "Are you certain that is wise?"

Genevieve had told Clarkson some of how she'd felt during the assembly—she had not confided what she had done in the carriage ride on the way home because she wasn't entirely foolish, but she'd said enough to make her maid worried.

"Do I have a choice?" Genevieve swallowed against the tightness in her throat. "I mean I do have a choice, but I choose not to be an absentee duchess. To be someone unknown to my people." She shook her head in disbelief. "That I have people at all is remarkable. But they need to know I am not any of my relatives," not even Sir William and Miss Evelyn, who thus far had been the best relatives she'd met yet.

Clarkson made a disapproving noise. "I know that I am the first to want a woman to have as much responsibility as a man, but it depends on the woman."

Genevieve raised an eyebrow. "And you think I am not the right woman for the job?"

Clarkson shook her head. "No, not that. I can't

imagine anyone better for what you have to do. It is just that I worry about the toll it will take on you." She patted a ribbon on Genevieve's gown, a movement that Genevieve had come to recognize as a soothing measure for her maid, regardless of the ribbons' need to be smoothed. Clarkson cleared her throat. "And I've seen how you've come to rely on Mr. Salisbury, and I don't . . ." and then she stopped speaking.

"Don't want me to fall in love with him?" It might be too late for that, Genevieve thought.

Clarkson blanched. "No, that is not what I was going to say at all." She peered at Genevieve. "Is that what is happening? Are you falling in love with him?"

"Uh, no, not at all." Genevieve felt herself start to color up. Apparently blushing was not restricted to when she was with Archie; it also applied to when she was talking about him. Or even just thinking about him. "It is just that is what everyone assumes, because I am a—well, me, and he is . . ." and then she twirled her hand in the air, not quite sure what she should say since she really shouldn't say he was possibly the handsomest man of her very limited acquaintance, not to mention the best kisser out of a field of one. None of that.

Now Clarkson looked both shocked and appalled. Genevieve wanted to ask specifically what was causing that response, but she didn't want her maid to think things were happening when they—when they absolutely were.

"But he is working for you. He is certainly not

a peer, and besides, he is dependent on you for a good name." Clarkson frowned in thought. "I know his being with you is only temporary"— *unfortunately*, Genevieve added inside her head— "but while he is working for you," and she stressed the last two words, "he is vulnerable."

Genevieve felt a bubble of hysterical laughter welling up inside her, but knew she had to contain herself. But still. "*He* is vulnerable? I am the unmarried duchess whom no one thinks should have inherited."

Clarkson came as close to snorting as Genevieve had ever seen her. "Yes, and you also have the position, the wealth, and the leverage to ruin his life, should you wish to." She clasped her hands in front of her and narrowed her gaze at Genevieve. Was this how it would have felt if she'd had a mother?

"I don't wish to," Genevieve replied in a low voice.

"Of course you don't," Clarkson said. "I just—it is just that you don't have anyone taking care of you, and I wanted to remind you that . . ."

"That I am a duchess, and therefore able to ruin people's lives with one sweep of my hand," Genevieve finished. She tried not to sound bitter, but she knew she failed. What else would she fail at?

"I am not expressing myself well." Clarkson shook her head in obvious frustration. "I don't wish to put more pressure on you. It is . . ." and then she reached out and took Genevieve's hands in hers, "I know it is difficult. It would be difficult no matter who was in the position." She squeezed gently. "But it is you, and you are so kind and thoughtful and caring."

Genevieve felt her eyes start to prickle. She couldn't speak for a moment. She looked at the older woman, still smiling down at her, and returned the smile, a few tears spilling down her face. "Thank you," she said in a soft voice. "I never thought that when I inherited that I would also find friends." She'd said the same thing to Archie, hadn't she? And now she had two friends. Perhaps three, if Miss Evelyn could be coaxed out of her shell.

"But I am keeping Miss Evelyn waiting," she continued, withdrawing her hand and wiping her face. Clarkson made that clucking noise and pulled a handkerchief from somewhere to dry Genevieve's face properly. "Thank you," she repeated. Clarkson nodded in reply, patting another ribbon on Genevieve's gown.

"I will be joining you, if that is acceptable," Sir William said, in a tone that assumed it would be. Mr. Salisbury would likely compliment Sir William on his confidence.

Genevieve smiled. "Of course, you are welcome. Although I will warn you, I have my heart set on purchasing a new bonnet." No more ribbons, at least—Clarkson's attentions to them would likely ensure she would never be without perfect ribbons for the rest of her life.

Clarkson held her cloak out and Genevieve slid her arms through the sleeves, waiting as Clarkson tied it around her neck. She had gotten accustomed to someone doing something she had always done herself; the privilege of being a duchess, apparently, was never having to lift a finger when someone lower in the hierarchy could do it.

Genevieve hoped she was never alone with the Queen, or she would be forced to relearn everything she had likely forgotten in her duchess tenure.

"Mr. Salisbury, we are going into the village." He could see, even if nobody else would notice, the tension in her expression. He gritted his teeth as he stopped himself from going up to her, from touching her to reassure her it would be all right.

"I have errands to take care of as well," he said, nodding to Norris, who stood at attention in the hallway. Norris nodded and left, presumably to retrieve Archie's coat. He couldn't touch her, not without causing inappropriate notice, but he could be there for her, physically.

"Oh, excellent," she replied, giving him a smile that warmed his heart, even though he would have to warn her against showing that kind of exuberance when next they had Duchess Practice. Norris returned, holding Archie's coat. "Shall we go?" She looked at her guests and then at Archie, then nodded at Norris, who leaped to the door to open it.

"Miss Evelyn, you must let me know if the hat I've chosen looks hideous on me. I have so little experience choosing garments." Genevieve took

Miss Evelyn's arm as they walked outside, Archie and Sir William trailing behind.

"Oh, I am certain you have excellent taste, Your Grace," Miss Evelyn replied. She sounded pleased to have been asked, and Archie silently applauded the duchess.

The ride into the village was a short one, no longer than fifteen minutes, but to Archie it felt like a lifetime. Mostly because Sir William was doing his best to be charming, which he was succeeding at, drawing Genevieve out in conversation without badgering her. Including his sister and Archie in the discussion as well so he wouldn't seem to be monopolizing her.

Archie had to admit he was jealous. Of something he could never have himself. That made no sense at all, and yet it was the truth. He wished he could be the one having the right to ask her questions, to embark on what was clearly a courtship. But he couldn't. He could kiss her—or more accurately in their recent encounter, she could kiss him—but he couldn't be open in his admiration of her, as Sir William could be.

"Oh, it looks busy." Genevieve was looking out the window, a flush staining her cheeks. Was it excitement? Nerves? Both? She glanced over at him and bit her lip.

Nerves, then.

Damn it, why couldn't he just hold her when she needed it?

Because it would be entirely inappropriate.

Because it would likely lead to even more inappropriate action.

Because he wasn't sure who needed it more—him or her.

Sir William looked out the window as well. He was sitting facing Genevieve, beside Archie. "It is. But you will be able to get whatever you require, Your Grace, due to your position."

Panic flashed across her expression. "That is—well, yes. That is a good point." She had been about to say something else, likely something that would reveal how she truly felt, but she didn't. Was it wrong that Archie was pleased she didn't feel comfortable enough with her relatives to share how she felt with them?

Perhaps. Wrong but true.

"Mr. Salisbury, what business do you have to conduct?" Her voice was strained. Did anyone else hear it?

"I wanted to review what types of farming supplies might be available before I send off to get what I believe the estate needs. Mr. Wickes will need someone to help him with the tenants' property, but until that person arrives, he has me."

"You're a steward for Lady Sophia Waterstone, I believe?" Sir William asked. Archie heard the implied dismissal in the other man's voice. As though reminding him he was essentially a servant would tarnish him in the duchess's eyes. And yet from what he knew about the duchess, he thought that she likely found more in common with servants than with people of Sir William's rank.

Something the other man obviously did not recognize.

"Yes, Aunt Sophia—I call her aunt, even though she is not of our family—was kind enough to send him when I had some questions."

"How kind of her," Miss Evelyn said, her tone revealing none of her brother's implication.

"Yes, and he has been so helpful."

"Mm," Sir William murmured. Archie shot a quick glance at him, meeting his gaze, resisting the urge to punch him.

That was odd. He'd never had that urge before, not since he'd begun to tower over people so thoroughly that he had to restrain any of his baser impulses. Until they had become second nature.

And yet here he was, pondering violence. In a way that was so unlike him he had to wonder what was happening to him.

Thankfully, the carriage slowed before Archie had to think too hard about who he was becoming.

Dear ~~Archie~~ Mr. Salisbury,

Clarkson worries that I am too fragile to do what I have to do. I don't think I am ~~(do you?)~~, but I do know I am too ignorant still of my duties and responsibilities. It's terrifying to think that in just a few days I will be announced to the world as the Duchess of Blakesley. My life is changing. My life has changed.

I always wanted it to be different, but not this way.

Duchess

Chapter 21

"Welcome, Your Grace, please do come in." The shopkeeper curtseyed so low Genevieve was immediately concerned about the woman's knees.

"Thank you." She stepped inside the small shop, pleased to see how tidy and clean it was. Not that she wouldn't patronize the only millinery shop in the village if it had been less than tidy and clean, but it certainly made it easier to imagine wearing one of the shop's products.

"This is lovely," Miss Evelyn enthused behind her. Genevieve turned and smiled at the girl. She was, if possible, even more naïve than Genevieve thought she had ever been. Somehow it was reassuring to know that there were Society ladies who had that in common with her.

Even if the Society lady in question had yet to enter Society, like Genevieve herself.

"What may I help you with?" the shopkeeper said, a tension around her mouth indicating just how anxious she was.

That makes two of us, Genevieve thought.

"The duchess is in search of a new hat or two," Sir William answered.

"Yes, I would like to purchase a hat. Perhaps also some ribbons," she added, just to show she knew her own mind.

Although buying more ribbons would mean Clarkson had more ribbons to smooth, and she wasn't sure her maid would be able to deal with the pressure.

"Allow me to show you some right over here," the woman began, gesturing to a table with, indeed, a large variety of hats.

Genevieve was engrossed in her appraisal of the hats when the bell at the door rang, and she heard someone walking in. It was only when he spoke that she realized who it was.

"The duchess come here to roam among the common people," Mr. Leonards said with a sneer in his voice. She turned and looked at him, her eyes widening as she took in his disheveled appearance, so much worse than just a week or so earlier when he'd been dismissed.

She saw both Sir William and Archie step toward him, just as he lunged forward. "Who are you to tell me I don't have a position?"

Sir William moved to stand beside her, but she gestured him to the side. She would not rely on anyone, no matter how male, to solve all her problems. This very moment was the purpose of all her Duchess Practice, after all.

"Allow me to address your concerns, Mr. Leonards." She was pleased, but not surprised, to find her voice was calm. "You stole consistently from the estate." She held her hand up when he opened his mouth to speak. "I could almost forgive that if you did good work. But you didn't. You harassed my tenants, you kept urgent repairs from happening, and because of you"—*and my father*—"the Blakesley name is derided."

He did speak then, bellowing into her face, making her want to step back. Only she didn't. This was but the first test of her new position, of how she needed to be seen as being in authority. Even though this first test was accompanied with the strong scent of alcohol and too-long-unwashed man.

"I saw how you and he were talking," Mr. Leonards said, pointing at Archie. "You think no one's going to notice? That you can't do anything without a beast at your back?"

It said too much about what she had done that she was relieved he hadn't mentioned how close they seemed to be in an entirely different way.

"I am no beast," Archie said, in a low voice that made Genevieve shiver. Whether it was because of the implied threat, how protective he sounded, or both, she didn't know.

No, scratch that. She knew. It was both. She just didn't want to admit it to herself.

And he did seem quite beastlike at the moment, she had to admit.

"The duchess is more than capable of taking care of herself, but she shouldn't have to waste her time on someone like you," he continued, his tone one of seething disdain.

"You should leave," Sir William said, striding forward and pushing Mr. Leonards in the chest.

She saw how Archie winced, and then how his hand clamped on to Mr. Leonards's arm as the former overseer was about to throw a punch.

And how Sir William turned pale.

Archie kept hold of Mr. Leonards and drew him backward through the shop, his clear strength making it appear that the other man was going willingly. Only Genevieve saw how Mr. Leonards was pushing back, trying to wrest himself from Archie's hold. But he wasn't strong enough.

"Your Grace, are you all right?" Sir William spoke as the two men stepped through the door, his hand reaching up to touch her, then falling away as he realized the impropriety of what he was about to do.

"Yes, thank you," Genevieve replied. She watched through the shop window as Archie spoke to Mr. Leonards, very close to him, an intense look on his face.

"Would you like to return home?" Sir William continued, not seeming to notice all her attention was focused outside. But then that meant his attention was focused on her. Wasn't that a welcome thing?

She did wish she could go home, that was what she wanted to do most of all, even before she'd been accosted at the milliner's. But that wouldn't be doing her job, and that was why she was here in the first place. To do her job, to live up to whatever low expectations anyone had of a female duchess.

"I wish to stay." She looked over to the shopkeeper and offered up a semblance of a smile. "I apologize for the interruption. Perhaps you can show me what you would recommend?"

The woman froze for a moment, then nodded vigorously. "Yes, Your Grace, if you would just step over here."

She nodded, walking to where the woman had gestured, Sir William following closely behind.

Archie fumed with the need to stay calm, not to do what he wanted, which was to first punch Mr. Leonards in the face, then haul Genevieve away from anyone but him.

Efficient, but not practical.

Instead, he watched as she chose a hat, one with some sort of fruit hanging askew on the top, as Miss Evelyn stayed close by, rather like a duckling following its mother around.

And Sir William was the rooster, strutting about as though he had been the one to deal with Mr. Leonards. And not exacerbated the situation.

It was irksome. And he knew he was mixing up his bird species, but he was a soldier, not a farmer.

"Mr. Salisbury, do you need to go do . . . whatever it is you were planning to do?"

And now he had to add Sir William to the list of men he wanted to punch in the face.

"Yes, I do." He glanced at Genevieve, who was already looking at him. "Your Grace, I will return within fifteen minutes." *Don't get accosted during that time*, his look said. *I won't, you foolish man*, her expression seemed to say.

His errands took even less time than fifteen

minutes, likely because he was rushing through what he had to say and showing clear impatience when the people he was talking to took too long to say anything.

Still, he arrived just in time to watch as Sir William assisted her into the carriage. The other man turned and offered up a satisfied smile, as though knowing precisely what was going through Archie's head at the moment.

Which he didn't, because if he did, he wouldn't be smiling.

The ride back home was no less torturous, but this time it was because everyone was silent. Although that allowed Archie to imagine various ways he could hurt Mr. Leonards, which wasn't very helpful, but did make him feel better.

Archie broke the silence. "Your Grace, if I might speak to you for a moment?" They had disembarked from the carriage, Sir William lingering behind to shepherd the duchess into the house.

Her expression eased, and he felt an answering ease in his chest. "Yes, of course, Mr. Salisbury. I will join you in the office in five minutes."

Archie couldn't resist shooting a look of triumph at the other man, who appeared disgruntled.

"That was awful," she said as she walked in. He stood near to the door, putting one hand on her shoulder to draw her close while shutting the door firmly behind them with the other.

"Are you all right?" he asked, peering into her face.

She looked up at him, only the faint trace of strain showing on her face. "I am fine. A bit shaky at first, but fine."

He wished she were less than fine, if only for his own selfish reasons. Then he could pull her completely into his arms, hold her, protect her from anyone who would harm her.

But he couldn't. That wasn't his place, it wasn't even within his scope of duties for his actual employer, Lady Sophia.

"Thank you," she said, breaking the contact with him to go sit down on the chair. The one he'd thrown his coat on that first night, when he'd kissed her.

And now he was becoming the type of person who looked at things, things like chairs, and carriages, and buttons, and remembered the moments that happened with them. He had never been so sentimental, so romantic in his entire life. And yet here he was, getting reminded of something because of a chair.

He would be disgusted with himself if it also didn't feel so right.

"I want to return to London," she declared. "Tomorrow." Her tone allowed for no argument. And there wasn't an argument he could muster anyway, not a reasonable one.

He had given her as much instruction as he could, and she was well on her way to being a superb duchess. She didn't need him anymore, and they could part, him back to his country life, and her to guiding the duchy in the way she was born to, if not trained for.

"Fine. I will tell the staff. Wickes will hire for the remainder of the vacant positions; he knows what is required now."

"Yes, thank you." He heard the movement as she rose, the soft scrape of the legs of the chair on the plush rug. "Mr. Salisb—Archie—am I . . ." and then she stopped speaking, and he felt her hands on his back, sliding over his ribs to clasp together over his chest. "I wish I weren't so anxious about it all."

She placed her head on his back and they just stood there, him barely daring to breathe. She was here. Holding him, as though he was the one who needed comfort when she—well, damn it, he needed comforting, too.

Because he had to admit he didn't want to leave her.

"You are prepared for this, Your Grace," he said, deliberately using her title. "You have practiced, and you know what is expected of you." He shrugged, knowing she would feel the gesture as well. "You are going to be wonderful."

She squeezed him in response. "Thank you," she murmured. "I feel so much more confident because of you."

I feel more feelings because of you, he wished he could reply. But he couldn't. It wouldn't be right to burden her with knowing he wanted her when it wasn't right for him to have her.

~~Dear Duchess,~~

~~Tonight when you walked down the staircase you were~~
~~so beautiful it hurt. Although it wasn't your gown, which~~
~~was admittedly nicer than the things you used to wear, it~~
~~was you.~~
~~I think I've fallen in love with you.~~

~~Mr. Salisbury~~

(NOT SENT)

Chapter 22

"This is my favorite, Your Grace." Clarkson stepped back and viewed Genevieve with an appraising eye. She made a sweeping gesture that encompassed the entire gown. And Genevieve, one presumed.

"The color makes your eyes get all golden," she continued. And then, because it seemed she couldn't help herself, she smoothed one of the ribbons that fluttered at Genevieve's waist. "I would suggest you wear this color green all the time, only that would be to deny the other colors in your wardrobe," she said, glancing back at the item in question.

It was full to bursting with new gowns, all in a riot of color that indicated that Genevieve was most definitely an important personage who did not need to hew to convention and that she was most definitely not in mourning.

The gown she wore for her first official evening out in London was an olive green, trimmed with gold ribbon and lace. When she had first seen it, she had worried the gown was too much for her; after all, she had never thought of herself as particularly striking. Merely adequate on an attractiveness meter. But now that Clarkson had assisted her into it, and she was gazing at herself in the glass—well, now she could say she was close to stunning, even though the gown had a lot to do with that. But since the gown wouldn't comprehend compliments, Genevieve would receive them in its stead.

What would Archie think of her now?

The thought plagued her, even though she knew she should not be thinking of him. Miss Evelyn and Sir William were likely waiting downstairs for her to go to the party. Mr. Salisbury was not one of the group. He hadn't been invited, as much because nobody knew who he was and that he was here in the first place, but also because he was technically Genevieve's servant, and therefore it wouldn't be appropriate for him to be in attendance.

She had arrived in London only a few days earlier to find that Chandler had made drastic changes to her staff, letting go the servants he deemed incompetent and staffing up from the same agency that had supplied Mr. Salisbury to Aunt Sophia.

The house had likewise been dramatically altered, cleaned within an inch of its life; the old furnishings seeming to gleam with a newfound glory that made Genevieve smile when she saw them.

Gran had welcomed her back heartily, and even Byron had seemed pleased to see her.

She was here, she was a duchess, and she was on her way to her first party. Ever.

That the first party she was ever to go to was as an incredibly powerful, wealthy woman whom everyone would be gossiping about did not make her concerns about the evening lessen, of course. It was only the thought that Miss Evelyn—who did indeed seem to be even shyer than Genevieve— and to a lesser extent her brother would be there that made her heart race a little less fast.

So it was more of a trot than a gallop, but still racing nonetheless.

"You will be fine," Clarkson said, interrupting her thoughts.

"Thank you, Clarkson." Genevieve smiled at her maid. "What is the worst that happens?" Thoughts of tripping down the stairs as she was announced, spilling red wine all over her olive gown, and squeaking when she should absolutely not squeak rushed through her mind, and she flapped her hands to try to dismiss all those images. "Never mind," she continued hastily. She did not want Clarkson supplying her with even more horrible things that might happen tonight.

"I'll find your cloak as you go downstairs," Clarkson said in an understanding voice.

"Thank you." Genevieve glanced around her bedroom, which was as lavish and pretty as a duchess's bedroom should be. She wished she could just stay here all evening, perhaps seeing if Gran and Byron wanted to visit for tea.

But she had to face everyone. She did. She wouldn't be able to do what she had to do if she wasn't willing to mingle with people of her class. How could she persuade anyone she was a good, thoughtful person if she was a stranger to them all? If she was just the reclusive woman in a position only men held?

She couldn't.

Thus armed—with a gown instead of weaponry, although she supposed a lovely gown was weaponry for some—she left the safety of her bedroom and walked down to where her houseguests and relatives waited for her.

Archie didn't mean to be waiting as she walked downstairs. It just . . . happened. Because he knew she and the Garrys were going out for the evening, and he would be busy reviewing the accounting that Wickes had sent for approval. So he was headed to the small room they'd designated as the office in her London town house. It was mere coincidence he had stopped to speak with Chandler, then waited as Chandler introduced him to one of the new footmen, then had to stop and take a bite of a biscuit the new cook had just sent up for tasting. Mere coincidence.

The crumbs of the biscuit caught in his throat as he spotted her at the top of the stairs. She seemed to hesitate, not yet looking down, her foot poised to the next step. And then she nodded to herself and did look down, leaving Archie breathless and wishing he was standing beside her. Could tell her how lovely and elegant and beautiful she looked. Not just because she was the duchess, the air of which she'd started to capture through her Duchess Practice, but because she was just herself. Beautiful, and strong, and intelligent, and caring, and—damn.

He started to cough as it hit him, and he put his hand up to his mouth to smother the noise as well as to keep himself from telling her.

Damn it. He had gone and fallen in love with her, hadn't he?

And damned if he knew what he was going to do about it.

"Good evening, everyone," she said in a low voice that very nearly trembled. "Goodness, Miss Evelyn, you look very pretty."

The younger woman ducked her head and smiled, a blush staining her cheeks. He was so proud of Genevieve for seeing that Miss Evelyn was just as shy and in need of attention and kind words as Genevieve had been—likely still was. And she knew just what to say and how to say it, to put people at ease.

That wasn't something she had learned since assuming her title. That was something that was intrinsic to her, whether learned or acquired.

"Mr. Salisbury." He braced himself to meet her gaze. Why did she have to be a duchess, of all things? Why couldn't she have been one of Lady Sophia's neighbors, or perhaps the local schoolteacher in the village? "I wish you were able to join us; you would make a fourth for the party." Genevieve's grandmother had refused to attend, saying she couldn't very well see if she needed to chaperone anyway, so it would be ludicrous for her to leave the comforts of home—and Byron—when Genevieve's relatives could lend her countenance.

"Inviting a steward to a party would be quite . . . egalitarian of the Estabrooks," Sir William said.

Archie wished Sir William were anyone else also. Preferably an anyone else who was also anywhere else.

"Sir William, I believe Mr. Salisbury to be otherwise engaged this evening. Or I would ask him to join us," the duchess said in a fierce, surprising tone.

Archie bowed, trying not to let his chest swell as he felt her championship. "Thank you, but as Sir William indicates, it would not be appropriate." Or it would be too appropriate, since it was very likely his family would be in attendance, and he had no wish to reunite with them. Or more likely be snubbed by them. "And I do have work," he added, seeing Genevieve's expression become set and determined, as though she were going to demand that he join them just because Sir William was a snob.

"The carriage, Your Grace," Chandler said, going to the door before there could be further class conflict. Genevieve looked at Archie one last time, a look that might have said she truly wished he were joining them, for her sake, or a look that said she knew just what he was thinking and she wished they could be kissing at this moment also.

Or none of those, just a look that indicated her gratitude for his work. Nothing more.

* * *

"The Duchess of Blakesley," the butler intoned. Genevieve took a deep breath, then stepped forward, feeling as well as hearing the hush of the crowd. As though time had frozen just because she had put one evening slipper onto the stairs.

Miss Evelyn and Sir William were behind her, as was correct. Appropriate. Even though she wished she could have Miss Evelyn beside her, at least. A companion to run the gauntlet of aristocratic eyeballs currently regarding her with as much interest as a pack of wolves eyeing a chicken. A duchess chicken, but still a chicken.

She started to laugh, then realized she should not at such a moment. She needed regality. *Duchessity*. Whatever it was that would make these people accept her as one of their own, despite the unusual circumstances of her inheriting.

"Your Grace, what a pleasure it is for you to join us. I am the Countess of Estabrook, your hostess for this evening." The woman accompanied her words with a deep curtsey. She was perhaps fifteen or so years older than Genevieve, with auburn hair just beginning to turn gray, and an honest, warm smile as she spoke. "This is my husband, the earl," she said, gesturing to a gentleman who had stepped up beside her.

"Your Grace," the earl said, bowing. He looked nearly as friendly as his wife, and Genevieve began to hope that things wouldn't be as terrifying as she'd imagined back in her bedroom.

"Thank you so much for the invitation," she

said. "These are my relatives, the Garrys. Miss Evelyn and Sir William."

The two murmured their thanks at being included and then the countess returned her gaze to Genevieve. "We will be having the Italian soprano Isabella Fortunato singing later on this evening. She is divine, I do hope you enjoy her."

What I'll enjoy is the chance to sit and be silent as I listen, Genevieve thought. "Thank you, that sounds lovely," she replied.

"Your Grace, could we offer you some refreshment?" The countess didn't wait for a reply but turned to her husband. "Dear, can you go fetch the duchess and Miss Evelyn some wine?" She looked at Sir William. "Perhaps you can accompany my husband, Sir William, so he can carry back all the glasses. Not that we don't have perfectly capable footmen, of course, but I would like a chance to speak with these ladies alone."

The earl's mouth curled up into a smirk, and he bowed to his wife. "I know when I am being dismissed, my dear. Come along, sir, the ladies have some very important items to discuss."

The two men walked away from the group, leaving the three ladies by themselves.

"Is this your first time out since assuming your title?" The countess's gaze was sharp.

"Yes, it is. Is it that obvious?" Genevieve asked, glancing around the room. Several of the guests were looking at her, and she felt like a bug under a microscope. Bugs, at least, were small and could scamper away out of sight. She had no such recourse.

"It is not," the countess said in a reassuring tone. "I had just not heard of you being seen yet, and the earl and I attend many events. It is truly a pleasure to meet you; your situation is so unusual. If you don't mind me saying so."

"The duchess is a wonderful person," Miss Evelyn said in a fervent tone. "She has been so good to me and my brother."

Genevieve felt herself start to blush, both at the countess's insight and at Miss Evelyn's staunch support. "Thank you, Miss Evelyn," she said, nodding. "It has been a pleasure finding relatives . . ." and then she paused, because she really wished she could say, *that don't want my money or my power.*

"Well, of course. Family is all that matters, isn't that right?" the countess replied, glancing between the two women.

Family. Of which she had very little. But the family she was making for herself—Clarkson, Miss Evelyn, Wickes—were excellent substitutes. And Gran was there, as was Mr. Salisbury. Archie.

If only she had merely familial feelings for the last-named gentleman. Unfortunately, she thought her interest in him was probably not what one would desire, so to speak, for a family member.

"Here are the refreshments," the earl said as he and Sir William returned to the group. "Are you done gossiping?"

"Just barely, dear," the countess replied, smiling at the ladies. "I was speaking with the duchess about her entry into Society. I cannot imagine how difficult it must be to meet everyone."

She firmly quashed the panic rising within her at the words. "Yes, well," she began.

"She does not find it difficult at all," Sir William interrupted. "The duchess is well-equipped to handle her position, she certainly doesn't need any practice." And at the last word he looked significantly at Genevieve, whose blush was now an all-out fire on her face. Which sounded just as painful and odd as it felt.

Was he referring to her time with Archie? Her Duchess Practice? She didn't think she'd spoken the phrase in his hearing, but she had already noticed Sir William had an uncanny way of knowing about things.

"Duchess, do let me show you to your seat. Our entertainment will begin in fifteen minutes or so." The countess nodded to the rest of the group. "I will save seats beside the duchess for the rest of you; just stay here for a moment so my husband can get the chance to know you. Thank you, dear," she added, speaking to her husband.

Genevieve allowed the countess to lead her away and into a large room adjoining the one where the majority of the guests were. Servants were setting up chairs, placing things on tables, and a few guests had already seated themselves, but it was a marked difference between the first crowded room and here.

"I thought you would be more comfortable here for a moment before everyone comes in to sit," the countess explained as she walked toward the front of the room. Genevieve followed, holding her head up as she'd practiced. As though nothing of import occurred below her nose.

"Are these seats acceptable?" the countess asked, gesturing toward chairs placed directly in the middle of the front row.

"Uh," Genevieve began. How could you tell your hostess you didn't want to be the object of all the scrutiny?

"Or perhaps over here," the countess continued, leading Genevieve smoothly to the far side of the room. "That way if you get tired and need to leave it will not be so noticeable."

"Yes, thank you," Genevieve said as she sank into the chair. The countess sat beside her.

"I really do appreciate your coming this evening," the countess said. "It will be quite a coup to have the new Duchess of Blakesley make her official debut at a party at my house."

"I am glad to have helped you with your coup," Genevieve replied, feeling as though she was truly the duchess, and not a complete fraud. "I am also available to foment revolutions, if you have that in mind."

"Excellent!" the countess exclaimed, laughing. "And I have no doubt there will be a revolution within certain communities of unmarried titled gentlemen when they discover you are not only a duchess, but also so charming and pretty."

Genevieve didn't know the countess well enough to tell her that the thought of that was enough to make her want to squeak louder than any Italian soprano could. So she settled on a distant smile and a nod.

"In fact," the countess continued, glancing behind them, "I see several young men right now, although your Sir William seems to be leading the fray."

Genevieve turned around as well, her breath catching as she saw there was, indeed, a phalanx of gentlemen, all relatively young, all wearing clothing they could do nothing but stand around in.

Not at all like Archie, whose physique seemed suited to hard work and rolled-up shirtsleeves. The thought of which did some interesting things to her insides.

"Thank you for saving the seats," Sir William said, stepping past Genevieve and the countess to sit closer to the middle. "My sister will be here in a moment; she has found an acquaintance she knew before."

"My lady, might I beg an introduction?" Another young man had burst from the pack to stand at the end of the row of chairs, a hopeful look on his face. He looked familiar, only Genevieve knew she had never met him before.

"Of course." The countess and Genevieve stood, which meant that Sir William did as well. "This is the Honorable Mr. Salisbury. He is the heir to the Viscount Salisbury."

Genevieve felt herself freeze as she looked at who could only be Archie's older brother. Or oldest? She didn't even know if he had other siblings. How many other Archie brothers were there out there? Or even a sister?

Meanwhile, the Honorable Mr. Salisbury was speaking to her. "It is a pleasure to meet you, Your Grace."

"Mr. Salisbury. That is interesting," Sir William said. "A Mr. Salisbury is assisting the duchess as her temporary steward. A remarkable coincidence, don't you think?"

Now it was the Honorable Mr.'s turn to freeze. His eyes widened, and he looked at Genevieve as though asking a question.

"Yes, that is correct," she replied, as smoothly as she could. Which didn't sound very smooth. If she were honest, she would have to say she was squeaking again. "Mr. Salisbury is engaged as the steward to Lady Sophia Waterstone, an old family friend. She was kind enough to allow Mr. Salisbury to help me temporarily."

Mr. Salisbury opened and closed his mouth a few times, Sir William scrutinizing the newcomer with some definite curiosity.

"Well," Mr. Salisbury said at last, "that is quite a coincidence." He swallowed.

"It is, isn't it?" Miss Evelyn said brightly, her brother giving her an exasperated look.

"Mr. Salisbury, would you like to sit down?" Genevieve gestured to the seat beside her, the one that Sir William had yet to claim. Thank goodness.

He sat elegantly, crossing one leg over the other. "Your Grace, I hope you—that is, I—"

"I understand it is a shock." *At least I understand that now.* She wished she had pressed Archie for more details about his family so she would better understand just what, besides his joining the army, had caused the rift. Because it seemed as though there was more than just that—or perhaps that was her own feeling about family. Because how could any family turn its back on a person who belonged to them?

But maybe people who had family didn't realize how precious it was.

"I've tried to find him since his return." Now that she knew why he looked familiar, it was easy to see the family resemblance. Like Archie, this Mr. Salisbury was tall, although not as tall. He was handsome, yes, but not as handsome. And he had an easier air to him, not as though he were always on the verge of fighting a battle or righting a wrong.

Probably the privilege of being the oldest son. Or the older son, she wasn't sure which.

"Do you have any other siblings?" she asked abruptly. Even though it felt oddly like spying to ask his brother about his family.

He nodded. "A brother. Older than Archie. He is a vicar in the north. Very studious and a bit pompous, to be honest." He grinned as he spoke, and for a moment, Genevieve felt like she was seeing double. Seeing Archie in his brother's skin; the sly look of mischief, the honest appraisal. These two were definitely related, even though it seemed as though they hadn't spoken in some time.

"How long has it been?" she asked.

He didn't pretend to misunderstand. "Four years. Maybe as many as five." He shook his head. "He didn't have to go, he had plenty to do right here."

"Perhaps he felt that wasn't enough." Would she have refused to become the duchess if given the choice? If someone had said, *You could remain who you are, while another of your relatives assumes the duchy. You wouldn't need to be responsible, but you also had to watch as another relative—one of your port-swilling money-wasting ones—debilitated the estates. Destroyed the livelihoods of all the people dependent on the Blakesley heritage.* Not that she thought that Archie's situation was as dramatic, but she did know he wanted to help, to make a difference, to defend his country and support and sustain the people who remained at home, those same people who currently worked Genevieve's lands.

"It should have been enough," Mr. Salisbury said in a low, fierce tone. It clearly still rankled. Perhaps exacerbated by discovering that his youngest brother was in London and hadn't sought him out. Had Archie stayed away because he wasn't sure how he'd be received? Because he didn't want to hear the recriminations?

Or because he wasn't interested in resuming the life of a gentleman?

He was a steward, after all. He was more comfortable dealing with the land, and working people, than being in society. It was ironic he had been helping her to become a better duchess when it appeared he had no desire to return to Society.

Which meant that no matter how much she liked him, no matter how much she liked to kiss him, he could never be a permanent part of her life. Not if she wished to succeed in what she was supposed to be doing.

Mr. Salisbury interrupted her thoughts. Her lowering thoughts. "Let us talk of other things than my family," he said, that charming very-like-Archie smile on his face. "Have you heard the woman who'll be singing before?"

Genevieve shook her head. "No, I"—how did one say that this was the first time she had ventured out into Society? "I have just returned to town. Arc—that is, one of my estates needed my attention."

"Where were you before you inherited?"

Out of the corner of her eye Genevieve saw a petite, dark-haired woman speaking with her host. That had to be the performer, since her gown was just a bit flashier than those of the rest of the ladies in attendance, and she was nodding toward the front of the room as though planning where to stand. Genevieve really would like to be done with this conversation, even though it meant sitting still while the woman sang. But he did sound genuinely interested, and she supposed it was good practice—so to speak—to converse with a gentleman. Who wasn't that Mr. Salisbury, but this one.

"I lived in the country." That wasn't enough of an answer, was it? Because it didn't specify where. It just made clear it wasn't here, which he already knew. Almost as though she had said, *Before I was a duchess I was not a duchess.* Not helpful. What would Archie encourage her to say? She took a deep breath and continued speaking.

"I lived in the country on one of the ducal estates in the west. In Shropshire. It was quite isolated." Which was one way of saying she had very little experience speaking with anyone besides servants.

Rather like Archie had chosen for himself, actually.

Oh, she wished he was here. It would be so different if she could look over at him as she spoke to people and was on display. She wouldn't feel as anxious, for one thing. For another thing she would get to look at him, to know that if she said or did anything he would rush in to protect her.

But she couldn't rely on him. Not just for the very simple reason he wasn't here at this moment but also because he was not a part of her future. He couldn't be, because of who she was and the path he had clearly chosen.

"Do you like London?" Mr. Salisbury continued, only thankfully the dark-haired woman went to the front of the room with the countess, a hush falling over the crowd as everyone took their seats.

"Welcome, friends," the countess said, her smile encompassing the whole room. "I am delighted to welcome Miss Isabella Fortunato all the way from Milan. Miss Fortunato will be appearing at the Royal Theater in a few days, but we have her singing just for us before anyone else can hear her." The countess's tone was smug, as it seemed it should be; yet another of the privileges that were an element of being part of this world, even though Genevieve herself didn't particularly care one way or another about this privilege. Or many of the ones that it seemed she should be grateful for.

She'd have to practice saying thank you for something she wasn't grateful for. Which just made her sound very ungrateful, another perquisite of her class.

It made her head sore and dizzy.

And then the music began.

~~Dear Mr. Salisbury,~~

~~I have discovered that not only do I not like going out to parties, I do not like women who sing as though they are being stuck with pins.~~
~~I have discovered that I find that I like you most of all. I wish that were not so.~~

~~Genevieve~~

(NOT SENT)

Chapter 23

And of course Archie wasn't able to take himself off to bed, even though it was late. She wasn't home, and for some reason, a reason he tried not to examine too closely, he didn't feel as though he could go to sleep if he didn't know she was safe.

So he sat in the small office he'd claimed as his own, listening closely for the sound of the door, glancing at the clock, then listening again.

Was she having a good time? It was so very late, and he knew, better than anyone but her, that she wasn't accustomed to being out.

Although that made her sound like a tired child, and she was anything but. She was a strong, intelligent, kind woman. A woman whose mouth was soft and whose skin felt like the smoothest silk under his fingers. Although—not silk, no, not that. Silk was too refined for what she was. Not that she wasn't refined, but she wasn't a rarefied, for-special-occasion thing; she was meant to be touched, to be held, to be more than just admired.

Was he the only one who could see that? He

knew Sir William, her other—that is, her only
suitor—seemed as though he felt he should treat
her delicately when Archie wanted to handle her.
Thoroughly.

The thoughts of what he'd like to do were
coursing through his brain, causing him to completely lose focus on what he was purportedly
doing when he heard the door open.

"Thank God," he muttered, getting quickly up
from the chair. He strode out into the hallway just
in time to see the three arrivals returning home,
the duchess's face—since that was all he could
look at—paler than usual.

"You are back," he said.

"Yes, we are," Miss Evelyn replied, allowing
Chandler to take her cloak. Sir William was busy
assisting the duchess with her cloak, and Archie
felt his eyes narrow as he watched the other man's
attentions. And not just his eyes narrow; he felt
his fists clench, and his throat tighten as his whole
body seemed to want to go stake his claim on her.

Even though he had no claim to her.

"Mr. Salisbury," she said, her voice sounding
higher than normal, "could you wait a moment? I
would speak with you."

"We met a relative of yours this evening," Sir
William said, sounding smug. Archie's spine stiffened as he absorbed the words as well as the tone.

"Yes, your brother," Genevieve interjected.
"This way?" she gestured toward the sitting
room, the one where she and Clarkson—and now
her pesky relatives—took tea in the afternoon.

"Yes, of course," Archie muttered. He bowed to

both Lady Evelyn and Sir William and followed Genevieve into the room, not so distracted by thoughts of his brother—it had to be George; his brother Charles was off being virtuous—that he couldn't admire how she looked in her evening gown.

She turned as he closed the door behind them. Her eyes went past him to the door, and she nodded, as though deciding something.

"I presume you want privacy for our conversation," he said, knowing he was justifying his actions to both of them.

"Yes."

She sounded shaky.

"Are you all right?" he asked, his concern for her outweighing whatever thoughts he had about her meeting George. That could wait. She couldn't.

She shook her head and looked down, worrying her lip with her teeth. "I am. I got through the evening perfectly well; I can't imagine anybody could find fault with me." She sounded surprised.

He wasn't.

"But there was a moment there where I wasn't certain that I wouldn't fall apart." She held her hands in front of her and he could see how she clenched them together, her knuckles white.

"You knew you could do this. I am sorry you doubted yourself. What happened?"

"Nothing." She looked up at him then, her eyes wide. "Nothing. It was fine, it was just—there was a moment there, when the woman was singing,"

"What wo—never mind, continue."

"She was a soprano who was the entertainment

this evening, and I thought it would be fine. It was fine, only then there was a moment when I felt—I felt as though all my breath was being squeezed out of me, and the only thing I wanted to do was run out of there shrieking." She paused, and let out a soft laugh. "I didn't, of course."

Now he found he'd moved closer to her, so close that if he just lowered his head and she raised hers they would be—

And then they were.

Kissing. Again.

It felt so right. The perfect end to an imperfect evening. Genevieve reached up to touch his jaw, rubbing the palm of her hand against his skin. Rough with stubble, so incredibly different from her own skin. He grabbed her hand and held it, squeezing her fingers, then brought both their hands down, resting them on his chest.

She slid her hand out from under his and splayed her palm against his chest. Oh, this felt marvelous. His chest, as she'd expected, was firm, and she pushed up against him as she moved her hand—or hands, since the other had joined the first—to the small of his back. Still kissing him, his hands on her elbows now, holding her in place. As though she'd want to go anywhere else when she could be kissing him here. And now.

His tongue was in her mouth, not at all tentative, but fierce, and she welcomed the onslaught, his lips moving on hers, his hands now at her waist, his thumbs kneading her hips. She felt herself get more and more lost in his kiss, but—paradoxically—find herself as well. Because this was who she was, the type of woman who would be kissed—and would kiss—someone like him. Who would, of all things, be sliding her hand down his back to his arse which was just as firm as the rest of him. Stroking it as she raised up on her tiptoes to get complete access to his mouth.

He broke the kiss, his breath shuddering. "I should not have," he began, only to stop when she shook her head in a vehement motion.

"Don't say that," she said. "Don't even think it." She rubbed her palm again over his chest, feeling how his hardness pressed into her belly, loving just what she was able to do to him. Not to mention what he was able to do to her. "It isn't just you," she continued, sliding her mouth over his jaw, planting small, openmouthed kisses on the stubbled line, "it's me. This is me," she whispered, and then moved to his neck, licking the skin above his cravat just below his jaw. Wishing she could undo all of him, unwrap him like the best gift ever, and kiss him everywhere.

Now that was an intoxicating thought.

She drew back, meeting his gaze. His eyes were heavy-lidded, a sensuous haze gleaming from their dark blue depths. Her breath caught at the frank desire she saw there, but knew her eyes had the same look in them. They had to, even though she didn't have as much—which was to say *any*—experience.

"I want to take this off," she said, gesturing to his cravat.

His answer was to raise his chin, giving an implicit yes.

Her fingers went to the fabric, undoing the knot, wrapping the folds around her fingers before drawing the entire thing away from his neck.

Oh, and then. And then. All that bared skin that positively begged her to bite it. To kiss it, to run her tongue over all those intriguing crevices.

Yes, he had been kissing her for—for what? Comfort? Sanctuary? But now she felt as though something had changed between them. Something darker, and more equal, and entirely provocative.

Something she wanted more of. Preferably now.

"And now what?" he asked, his voice strained. The cords of his neck stood out, as though he were experiencing tension. *You're not alone*, she wanted to assure him, even though she was fairly certain the tension between them could be alleviated. But was also a delicious tension, one she wanted to prolong.

"Now," she began, only to realize she didn't know what. She didn't know, because of who she was, and what she was. "Fine," she continued, biting her lip, "now what?" Might as well ask him what to do next since she had no idea.

It seemed that was the best response, since he smiled, but not in a thank-you-for-passing-the-sugar kind of way. Or even a good-morning-it's-been-nearly-ten-hours-since-last-we-saw-each-other kind of way.

This was—this was an I-am-so-glad-you-asked-since-I-have-many-ideas-and-I-plan-to-put-them-into-action kind of way. The kind of way that made her heart flip and her stomach tighten and other parts of her—well, other parts of her get all squirmy in a way she had never experienced before.

"Go onto the sofa," he commanded, and she felt a thrill run through her own self—yes, those other parts as well—as she stepped away from him to go do as he'd ordered.

Knowing that whatever he wanted would benefit her as well.

She sat as she'd practiced sitting as a proper duchess—knees together, back straight, her hands clasped loosely in her lap. Watching as he stalked toward her, her eyes wide.

Instead of sitting beside her, however, he dropped to his knees in front of her, sitting back on his heels and looking down at the floor. No, looking at her feet.

Why was he looking at her feet? Was this another one of the things she didn't know that she hoped she was about to find out?

And then his eyes went up, his dark blue gaze making her gasp. Aloud.

He smiled again, that same feral smile that made her knees—still pressed together—want to buckle so she fell onto the carpet with him.

"Did you dance this evening?" he asked, his words coming out so low and rumbly she didn't entirely comprehend the words at first.

"Dance?" she repeated, feeling stupid. She shook her head. "No, no dancing. Just listening." *To the Italian soprano, to your brother, to the countess, to Sir William.*

"So your feet aren't tired," he said, sounding disappointed. Why?

"I did stand quite a bit," she replied, wriggling her ankles.

He chuckled, then placed his strong, large hands on the tops of her feet. Beginning to undo the ties and buttons and laces and whatever else held her shoes onto her body.

Each yank and undoing of a button made her gasp, her throat tighten, even though she didn't know why. Perhaps—almost certainly, in fact— because he had his hands on her, his clever fingers removing her shoes, leaving her in her stockings, letting him place his hands—

"Ahhh," she moaned as he rubbed his thumb into her instep.

"Your feet were sore," he murmured, bending his head to the task.

"Yes," she said again, hearing her words come out in a squeak. Again. But not in an I'm-the-duchess? squeak, but something else. Something more . . . intriguing.

Something that caused him to look up, his eyes narrowing. But not as though he were angry. As though there was some other emotion roiling inside him.

Likely the same one currently flooding her senses.

His hands rubbed her feet, hard, a few more times, then they moved to her ankles, his fingers encircling her. The skin of his palm touching her through the thin silk stockings she wore.

Could she—how could she? And then she just

decided to say it, since she couldn't seem to push it out of her mind.

"Can I take my stockings off?" she asked in that same voice.

He froze, then shook his head slowly. And she tried not to show how disappointed she was.

"No, because I am going to take them off."

Oh. Well that was another thing entirely. If he took them off, that would mean that—"Oh!" she exclaimed as his palms slid up her legs, over her calves, to her knees, spreading them, then up farther, the skirts of her gown flowing over his arms so she couldn't even see where he was touching.

But she could certainly feel it.

And it felt wonderful. Everywhere he touched it felt as though he left a trail of sparks behind, sparks that lit her from the inside out.

His fingers reached the tops of her stockings and he hooked a finger, one on each side, between her skin and the stocking. The contact made her inhale sharply, and then she couldn't help but hold her breath as he began to roll each stocking down. Painstakingly slow, carefully, each inch an agonizingly exquisite moment.

She heard how he was breathing, too—labored, intense, each exhalation sounding as though it came from deep within his soul.

Fanciful, but true nonetheless.

And then he reached her ankle and slid the stockings over her feet, tossing them onto the ground beside him as he raised up on his knees again, those strong, warm hands on her calves. On her knees.

On her thighs.

He leaned forward, her knees widening to accommodate his size. He captured her mouth, his hands pushing her skirts up, his tongue demanding entrance, which she was only too happy to give.

Her hands were on his shoulders, shoving his jacket off, pushing them off his arms. He let go of her legs only long enough to let the jacket fall onto the floor, then his hands were back, stroking the soft skin of her thighs, a low growl coming from his throat as he kissed her.

And then her fingers were somehow at the buttons of his shirt, undoing each one until they were all undone and she could slide her palm onto his chest directly.

Oh goodness. He was warm and hard and soft all at the same time. His chest had a sprinkling of hair that was soft, so soft against the firm planes of his muscular chest. She moved her palm to where his heart beat, strong and solid.

Just like him.

He was still kneeling on the floor, leaning forward so he was pressed against her, her leaning forward to touch him as well.

His hands now at the apex of her legs, very close to where she burned.

He drew back from the kiss, his eyes gleaming with a low, banked desire that made her ache.

"Can I touch you, Genevieve?" he asked, his fingers moving on her thigh.

She didn't know much, certainly, but she knew to what he was referring.

"Yes, please," she replied, withdrawing her hand from his chest. "If I can touch you." One corner of his mouth edged up in a smile, and she took that as assent, moving her hand down his chest to the waistband of his trousers. Stopping there as his fingers began to move.

And then she couldn't do anything but let him touch her, his fingers caressing that place, moving lower to where she burned.

She gasped aloud when he rubbed a particular spot, and then moaned as he—*as he slid his finger inside her?* My goodness. Who knew that could cause such a strong sensation?

Well, he did, obviously.

"How does it feel?" he asked, a knowing grin on his face. Knowing because he could clearly tell how it felt, judging by how she was wriggling on the couch and making inarticulate noises.

She found boldness enough to move her hand down lower on his body, putting her palm directly on that part that stuck out at a gravity-defying angle.

And he hissed in response, closing his eyes as his finger—now joined by another—kept moving inside her.

"How does it feel?" she echoed, nearly unable to say the words because of the sensations flowing through her.

He opened his eyes and smiled. "Saucy wench," he replied, increasing the movement of his fingers. Making her unable to speak, squeak, or make any kind of noise at all beyond a general gasping that, if she were to think about it, was a sound quite unbefitting a duchess.

But entirely befitting a woman in the throes of passion.

"Come for me, Genevieve," he said, his tone urging her to somewhere, even if she didn't understand the specific words he was saying.

And then she felt as though she were falling and flying all at the same time, a force of something flowing through her whole body. She uttered a noise, louder this time, and he leaned forward and silenced her with a kiss, a ravaging, possessive kiss that she welcomed.

The feeling lasted for what seemed like hours, and yet seconds, obliterating everything else she was aware of or felt.

At last, she settled, and blinked to clear her gaze, only to see him smiling in supreme satisfaction.

"That felt good, didn't it?" he asked.

"You know it did," she replied. Her hand was still on him, and he was still huge and hard under her palm. "Is there—?" and then she stopped, not certain just how to ask.

"No, I will take care of that later," he said. He leaned forward and kissed her again, this time a soft kiss that still felt as though he owned her. As though they belonged together.

Which was the opposite of the truth.

~~Dear Genevieve,~~

~~I thought of you as I took my cock in my hand.~~

~~Archie~~

(NOT SENT)

Chapter 24

Archie wasn't sure quite how he managed to get back to his room without embarrassing himself. He did try to hide things by holding his jacket in front of himself, wrapping his cravat loosely around his neck. If he saw anyone, he'd just say—well, he didn't know what. His mind was too full of images of her to come up with a complete sentence. Likely something about stables and emergency and help.

But he didn't see anybody. He flung his bedroom door open and closed it just as firmly, leaning against the door in relief. Tossing his jacket to the floor, even though he certainly didn't have a valet to clean up after him. He was essentially a servant, after all.

She tasted so sweet. He wished he had been able to taste her, there, but it was enough to bring her to pleasure with his hands. He lifted his fingers to his mouth and licked them.

So sweet. And her face when she came— startled, and passionate, and satisfied all at once.

He would be replaying the memory of her face in his mind for a long time, he knew.

He staggered over to his bed, falling onto it gracelessly. Lying on his back and immediately reaching his right hand down to the fall of his trousers, undoing the placket to release his erection.

What would it feel like if she were to touch him?

Her hand would be smaller. It might not encircle his cock, as his own hand was doing now. His thumb and index finger met, and he began to stroke himself.

"Slowly," he said in a whisper, a reminder to himself as well as what he wished he could say to her. "Just like that," he said, closing his eyes as he thought about what she would look like if she were here.

She'd be concentrating on her task, biting her lip as she eased her palm up and down his shaft.

Would she be naked? He paused as he considered it. Partially naked, yes. Perhaps wearing only her stockings and some duchessy pearls or something.

In between there'd just be Genevieve. Her breasts, released from her shift. He hadn't seen them yet. He wished he could lick her nipple, drag his teeth gently across it as he cupped their fullness in his hands.

That would be for next time, getting to see her breasts. If there was a next time.

The unpleasant thought intruded before he could push it away. He had no place to be touching her. He was a servant. She was a duchess.

There was no way they could be together in any way, and yet here he was—well, he was by himself. He wasn't doing anything that would hurt her in any way, so he might as well continue with the fantasy, now that he'd started.

He took a deep breath and began to touch himself again. Rubbing a little faster now, thoughts of how her breasts would bounce as she moved making him even harder. How she would lick her lips as she looked at his cock, thinking about what it would feel like if he pushed inside her soft, wet warmth.

Fuck, he wanted to bury himself inside her, thrust until they were both panting. He was panting now for real, his hand moving even faster, his thumb rubbing across the slit on top, rubbing the moisture he found there down his shaft.

She'd watch as she moved her hand up and down, watching his face to see what he liked. Her gaze returning to his cock as she brought him close, so hard, so fast, so—"Uhhh," he groaned as he climaxed.

He lay there for a moment, his chest heaving, his hand still on his cock.

It was hopeless, he knew that, and yet he couldn't keep himself from imagining it.

Imagining what it would be like if he could be naked with her, as an equal, with her being his partner. For now, forever.

What would it take to make that happen?

He didn't know. But he would do his damnedest to find out.

* * *

"Mr. Salisbury?" Archie heard the tap on his door through the thick miasma of sleep. He'd dropped off fairly quickly the night before—a satisfying climax had a way of ensuring that—and he'd been dreaming of something unpleasant, he could tell, from how his chest was pounding.

It didn't mean he wanted to be woken up at—he glanced over at the clock—seven o'clock in the morning, but it didn't seem he had a choice.

"What is it?" he called. He thought the voice belonged to Chandler, the butler, but he wasn't certain.

"A Lady Sophia is waiting for you downstairs. I've already informed the duchess that she is here."

Archie froze, then scrambled out of bed, his gaze darting around the room for his clothing. "Here?" he said, nonsensically, since why would Chandler say she was here if she wasn't?

"Yes," Chandler replied, his tone not revealing what an idiotic question Archie had asked. Thank goodness for good servants, Archie thought.

"I'll be down in ten minutes," Archie replied, donning fresh linen and then finding a pair of trousers that hadn't been lying on the floor all night and putting those on.

What was his employer doing here? The thought struck him that perhaps there was some sort of emergency—after all, Lady Sophia did not generally like London and tried to avoid it as much as possible—and he would have to leave soon, if not today.

And he wouldn't see her again. Not until after she was married, since it wouldn't be long before some gentleman persuaded her to marry him.

If he hadn't thought of how *he* could marry her. She'd have to get married eventually, wouldn't she?

He felt his chest tighten at the thought.

It was with a feeling of foreboding that he descended the stairs to the sitting room only eight minutes later.

"My dear, you look in such good health," Aunt Sophia exclaimed.

Genevieve returned her compliment with a smile that was only slightly yawn-tinged.

She hadn't slept much the night before—how could she, when thoughts of what he'd done and where he'd touched her were running through her mind? She hadn't known it was possible for a body—specifically, hers—to feel that much pleasure. And she very much wished she could feel it again, even though she knew she should not.

It would be her fault if they continued to interact in such a way. She knew he wouldn't have approached her if she hadn't indicated she was approachable.

"Thank you," she replied. The door opened and her grandmother came in, looking remarkably awake.

"Good morning, Sophia," she said as Genevieve sprang up to guide her to her chair. "It is very early, is it not? Byron woke me to chatter at the birds," she said, smiling.

"It is early, but I just had to come," Sophia replied. She was looking at Genevieve as she spoke, and Genevieve felt herself awash in guilt. Did her godmother know what Genevieve had done? And what had been done to her by Mr. Salisbury's clever fingers?

And now she was starting to blush, so if her godmother didn't know anything before, she certainly would suspect something now.

"The estate is doing well, of course, with Mr. McCready in charge," her godmother said. Or Sophia wouldn't notice anything at all because she was too engrossed in telling her own story. "But now that Mr. Salisbury is off the estate helping you it is so lonely at Waterstone Manor. Nobody comes to visit, not the way they did before." She smiled in satisfaction at Genevieve. "So I thought I should just come for a visit so I could see people. And I am expecting that Mr. Salisbury will be able to return with me, since it appears that he has helped you enormously. The butler was all that he should be, and the house looks lovely. And you," she exclaimed, peering at Genevieve. "You do not look at all like someone who has just come into Society. You are so fashionable, if I didn't know you I would think you were too high in the instep to speak with me."

Genevieve returned her godmother's smile, inwardly wanting to smirk at the old-fashioned slang she used.

Thankfully, she'd been unable to sleep anyway,

so Clarkson had already gotten her dressed, which meant that she only had to keep her godmother waiting a minute or so.

The door opened again, and this time it was Chandler opening the door for Archie—Mr. Salisbury—who came in with a faint blush staining his cheekbones. What did he think about what had happened? Was he appalled at her behavior? Was he wishing it didn't happen?

Was he wondering if it would ever happen again?

"Mr. Salisbury!" Lady Sophia waved at him as though she were worried about being seen, dislodging Truffles, who tumbled to the ground in a disgruntled heap. The dog got up and shook himself off, glaring at Archie as he did so.

"My lady," Archie replied, bowing. "Your Grace," he said, turning to look at Genevieve, whose breath caught as she saw him.

It wasn't fair that he was so handsome all of the time. She knew that Chandler had just woken him up, and yet he looked . . . perfect. Perfectly dressed, perfectly appropriate. Not as though he had kissed her senseless, then did whatever he'd done to her to make her feel those things.

"Good morning, Mr. Salisbury," her grandmother said in a cheerful chirp. As though she were channeling her cat.

"Good morning," Genevieve murmured, feeling her cheeks start to warm. Why wasn't there some sort of protocol for what a duchess should do when the man who'd brought her such passion greeted her the next morning?

Perhaps she should write an etiquette guide for similar duchesses in the situation. Of whom she was the only one.

So never mind.

"Mr. Salisbury, I was just telling the duchess that the manor has been very lonely without you." Lady Sophia scooped Truffles up again and placed him on her lap. "Not so many people visiting, and I thought I would pop up and save you the trip home. You can return with me in a week or so."

Genevieve's throat tightened at her godmother's casual announcement. And then her cheeks really started to flush as she couldn't help but look at him—only to find him staring at her. If looks could kill, could they kiss?

Because if they could, she was getting thoroughly kissed right now, judging by the look in his eyes.

She lowered her gaze before even her grandmother could see what was going on between them.

"A week." Archie's tone sounded strained, and her heart fluttered in a fierce joy. He didn't want to leave. But she couldn't keep him, not without betraying her godmother's trust and causing potential scandal.

She would have to let him go.

"A week, maybe two," Lady Sophia replied. "I know I am not fond of London but I thought perhaps that would change if you were to show me around the city," she said, nodding toward Genevieve. "And it appears you have done a wonderful

job, even better than I'd imagined, Mr. Salisbury,"
Lady Sophia continued. "I know you won't be-
grudge his return, Genevieve, since he's done so
well for you."

"Of course," Genevieve said in a soft voice. She
wished she weren't so relieved at the prospect
of having him around for longer than she'd first
thought. That would only make the inevitable
parting even more painful.

"And I do apologize for arriving so early. It is
just that I had the thought in the middle of the
night, and I discussed it with Truffles, and we decided we just wouldn't wait." Lady Sophia smiled
as though her impetuous behavior wasn't in the
least bit odd. Probably because she didn't think
it was. Nor did Truffles, it seemed, who had also
been consulted.

And now she was thinking the dog had actually had a part of the conversation. She really was
not thinking properly today.

Genevieve felt sorry for the servants, who
would have had to scamper around preparing
her godmother for the journey. They were likely
wishing Mr. Salisbury to the devil since he was
the cause of everyone's early rising.

"So what are we doing today?" Lady Sophia
continued, smiling brightly at everyone in turn.

Uh—*I was going to review just what your steward
did to me the night before*, Genevieve thought. *And
then wonder if it would ever happen again, and if so,
when was the earliest that could be?*

"I—I didn't have any plans," Genevieve replied
when no one else spoke. Because she couldn't

really share her true thoughts. Not without explaining all sorts of things she could barely explain herself.

"Excellent! I have been wanting to go look at St. James's Palace. Do you think the Queen will be there?"

"Perhaps," Genevieve began, "but it is not likely that she will be outside sweeping the steps or anything."

"But you're a duchess, you could call on her, couldn't you? I'd love to meet the Queen," Lady Sophia said in a dreamy voice.

"Oh, me too," Gran chimed in. Making Genevieve glare in her direction, only of course Gran couldn't see her. Thank goodness.

"We can't go meet the Queen," Genevieve said in a squeakier voice than she'd had a few minutes earlier.

"The duchess is right," Archie said in a smooth voice. Genevieve glanced gratefully at him, then kept looking at him because she wasn't an idiot. "They announced in the papers that the Queen has gone to one of her summer houses. No, I don't know which one, either," he said, forestalling the ladies' inevitable questions.

"Oh, well, but I still would like to see the palace. Mr. Salisbury, you can stay here and review the accounts Mr. McCready sent up for your review."

Genevieve opened her mouth to object, only to realize that she couldn't. Not only was Mr. Salisbury a servant, he was not even her servant. She couldn't in any way ask that he accompany them, she couldn't say that it wasn't appropriate for him to be doing anything but serving her, and she couldn't—well, she just couldn't. None of it. Any of it.

She swallowed hard against the lump in her throat and nodded. "Perhaps you would want to rest a bit from your journey, Aunt? I need to have something to eat"—*although nothing will fill up the ache in my heart*—"and I want to ensure that Chandler knows of our plans over the next few days. Our new cook will be very excited that I have company; I am certain thus far she has been sadly disappointed in how much I am able to consume."

"Wonderful. Meanwhile, your grandmother and I will just sit and have a gossip. Perhaps talk about some young men you might have met?" Lady Sophia said in a leading voice.

Some young man—oh goodness! She'd entirely forgotten! "Uh, as it happens, there is a young man staying here. One of my relatives, a Sir William Garry, is here, as is his sister, Miss Evelyn Garry."

"And he is young? And unmarried?" Lady Sophia asked. "Perhaps he should join us on our trip?" She settled back and gave Truffles a firm pat on the head. Truffles did not seem pleased. "That means it makes even more sense to wait a bit until the household is entirely up. I am looking forward to meeting your young man."

"Now that she is established as the duchess, Vievy will have no shortage of young men," her grandmother added. Unhelpfully, in Genevieve's eyes.

She couldn't help it, she glanced at him. He

wasn't looking at her any longer, instead keeping his focus at the other end of the room, for
some reason. She craned her neck to see what he
might be looking at; nothing there, unless he was
passionately interested in that shepherdess her
relative had manhandled only a few weeks ago.
Someone had removed it from its prominent position on the bedside table to another table out of
the way. Had the shepherdess complained? Had
he heard about it?

What was she even thinking?

She shook her head and returned her attention
to the conversation between Lady Sophia and her
grandmother, which was nearly as ridiculous as
her own conversation regarding the harassed
shepherdess.

"One of the members of the royal family would
be a fine husband for our Vievy," she heard Lady
Sophia say, not only adopting her grandmother's
nickname for her, but also suggesting she marry a
man she'd never met who wasn't Archie.

It was a safe bet that the unknown gentleman
couldn't get her nearly as worked up as Archie
could. Could any man?

She had to say she highly doubted it.

"But we want Vievy to be happy," her grandmother replied. Finally, Genevieve thought.
Someone who was concerned about her needs,
not what the title could garner. "So I would think
she would want to inquire about one of those foreign kings, someone who would show her new
exotic lands."

So much for that thought.

"Excuse me," she said through gritted teeth, "I need to eat something." And try to swallow her words so she wouldn't say everything on her mind—*I want you, and only you, I do not want to be married to someone just because of his title, and I do not want you matchmaking for me when I have no desire to marry anyone. Because I cannot marry him.*

Dear Duchess,

As the time for my departure comes closer, I would like to ~~stop time~~ remind you of a few things that your next steward should keep in mind (this oversight can be turned over to your husband, when you marry ~~Please don't marry~~).

Chandler is an excellent butler, but he has no experience managing a large ~~respectable~~ party. It will be up to you to remind him that your needs for a party are very different from those of your father. Also, I would remind you to retrieve the jewels that are part of the ducal holdings ~~are there pearls? Dear God, let there be pearls~~ so you can begin to wear them in the evenings.

~~I wish I could see you in them. I wish I could see you forever.~~

Mr. Salisbury

Chapter 25

"You didn't tell me that your family lived in London," Lady Sophia said with an offended sniff.

That is because I wished to forget it myself, Archie thought.

His employer had requested he join her for tea, of all things, so they could go over the plans for their return.

When he would no longer see her.

"My family and I are not in touch," Archie replied, trying to keep his tone light. "I didn't mention it because it is . . . awkward." A pause as he tried to figure out what to say. How to say it so she wouldn't scamper after it like a dog chasing a rabbit. "I am a working man now, and my family would not want it to be known that someone with their name is working for a salary." It was terrible enough for them when he'd joined the army; now that he was back in the same country, actually doing labor was more than they could possibly stand.

He knew his brothers didn't feel as strongly

about that as their parents did, but as long as his parents lived—and as far as he knew, they did—he wouldn't ever return. His brother hadn't come to call after discovering he was here; that was proof enough of the discord between them.

And now he'd unearthed another place he could never return. Here, with Genevieve. *Vievy.*

Was his life going to be just a series of places he had once belonged and now he didn't? London at his family's home, abroad fighting various battles, London again with her.

The only place that did welcome him was Waterstone Manor, and that only because of the skills he brought to the position. If he were to quit, Lady Sophia would mourn his loss for a time, mostly because she would have fewer visitors, but anybody could perform the same work.

It was a lowering thought.

"Well, I think you should be reconciled with your family." Lady Sophia addressed Truffles, who was in his mistress's arms. "Don't you think family is everything?"

Truffles did not reply.

The door opened to admit Genevieve, who paused as she took in the scene; the corners of her mouth lifted when she saw the tea things in front of them. Archie stood to look at her, an answering grin on his face. Lady Sophia couldn't see his expression, so he allowed some of what he was feeling to show.

Her eyes widened, and she shook herself as though from her imagination.

He wondered what she was thinking about,

and if they were thinking about the same thing. The same thing being them alone, with both of them wearing less clothing.

And no tea.

"I am just in time," she said, crossing to sit in the chair beside Archie. He sat himself down again and gestured to the table. "I do love tea," she said, with a sly look toward Archie.

"I was just asking Mr. Salisbury if family was not the most important thing."

Actually, she was talking to her dog, but maybe she viewed both of them interchangeably.

Genevieve paused in the middle of preparing her tea, her smile frozen.

"I don't know that I am the right person to ask that question, Aunt." And then she did actually smile, a smile that settled right in Archie's heart. "My family are people not actually related to me, besides Gran. There's you, and the people at home in the country where I was raised. Sir William and Miss Evelyn are relatives, but they aren't yet family."

And he hoped to God they never would be.

He wanted to be her family. He wanted her, forever. If she was his, he would want her to do whatever she wished. Not always, but preferably unclothed.

She was more than capable of handling her new duties, even if she herself wasn't entirely convinced of that. But he knew she was strong and capable and smart, and she would do what had to be done to right the wrongs her father had inflicted.

"And Mr. Salisbury has been invaluable as well," she added. She looked at him, her eyes saying so much more than her words.

"Thank you, Your Grace." He took a sip of tea, swallowing the unspoken words along with the beverage.

She couldn't stop herself from going to his room later that night. After they'd all eaten together, Aunt Sophia and her grandmother shooting meaningful looks toward Archie and herself, but not in conjunction with each other, thank goodness.

The last thing she wanted was for either of those two ladies to take it into their heads that something was going on. Because she knew full well that neither one of them would approve.

But Aunt Sophia was almost painfully transparent on continuing on the theme of a family's importance, while her grandmother was talking about all the gentlemen Genevieve would meet, including Sir William in that conversation.

It was agonizing. Made even worse or possibly better because he sat opposite her, and she was able to catch his eye every so often and share a look of commiseration.

But it was mostly agonizing.

She knocked again, louder this time, her hand freezing in midair as the door swung open.

He didn't look surprised to see her.

"You shouldn't be here," he said in a low growl, but accompanied his words by taking her arm and drawing her inside.

So did she want to believe his words or his actions?

And then he kissed her.

Definitely his actions.

It was a fierce, angry kiss, one that spoke of the frustrations of the evening and likely the anticipation of their separation. She felt precisely the same thing, and she returned his kiss, dragging her fingers through his hair, over his shoulders, down his arms and to his waist.

He dragged her backward, his arm around her waist, lifting her feet off the ground. And then she felt herself falling as he tumbled them onto the bed—my goodness, his *bed*—and then he had flipped her over and had thrown one leg over her, his mouth still locked on hers.

Her hands still continuing their exploration of his body.

She really liked exploring his body. Perhaps more than she liked—no, definitely more than she liked—being a duchess.

Exploration meant touching all that firm muscle, and the interesting curves and strength his body held.

And it seemed he liked the same thing, because his fingers were at the neckline of her gown and he was tugging it down, now breaking the kiss to mutter a few unintelligible words as he exposed more of her skin.

And then—and then his mouth was on her breast, and he was kissing her nipple as thoroughly and as delightfully as he'd kissed her mouth.

She had her hands in his hair, raking her fingernails on his scalp, muttering her own unintelligible noises. Noises that appeared to indicate to him that he should continue just what he was doing, only also reach down and begin to draw the bottom of her gown upward, his palm eventually touching her leg, running his hand up closer to where she ached.

Just as she was trying to twist herself closer to him, he stopped. Stopped everything; his lips on her breast, his hand on her leg, everything.

And she felt bereft.

What would it be like when he left?

"We shouldn't be doing this," he said, his voice ragged.

"No, probably not," she agreed. Wishing that they didn't have so much in common—both knowing, for example, that they didn't have a future together because of who he was, and more importantly—in so many ways—who *she* was.

He withdrew and moved away from her on the bed, but grabbed her hand as he did so. Just touching her fingers with his, making that small point of contact between them the only way to show their connection.

And it was so huge, that connection. From how she knew to glance his way when someone said something ludicrous or pointed or both, to how she felt so comfortable with him as he pretended to be Lady Arch or whoever during Duchess Practice.

To now, when all she wanted to do, even though she was supposedly a respectable female, a duchess no less, was to remove all his clothing so she could examine and explore every inch of his skin while he did the same to her.

"What are we going to do?" she asked, after a few moments of silence.

He took a deep breath instead of answering. Until at last the words seemed as though they were dragged out from him. "There is nothing to do."

Her throat got tight. "But—" she began, only to stop as he squeezed her fingers.

"But nothing. You are you. I am only me, and that is the third son of a viscount who has disowned the same said son."

Oh. Put that way it did seem rather hopeless.

"There must be something," she said again. How could all this be worth it if her life was so empty? Although she doubted the hundreds of people who depended on the duchy would care about that very much.

He sat up, releasing her fingers. He ran his hand through his hair, making that one piece fall onto his forehead. She didn't think she would ever stop wanting to push it back.

"You should go," he said in a rough voice.

She should. She would. She sat up also, pulling her gown back up so she was almost respectable. Smoothing her hair where it had gotten mussed by lying on his pillow.

Calming her breathing.

She swung her legs over the side of the bed and stood, her knees nearly buckling underneath her.

And glanced back at him, still sitting, gazing

at her with an implacable gaze. It was terrible and also wonderful that he was so honorable. Too honorable to continue when there was no hope of a future.

"I'll see you tomorrow." She spoke in that damn squeak again. "And then you and Aunt Sophia will be leaving," she continued on a sob. *Do not cry, Genevieve. Do not.*

She swallowed the lump in her throat and spoke in a stronger voice. "I will miss you, Archie." She waved her hand. "Not just this, but our friendship. I don't know if I will ever find another person with whom I have so much in common in so many ways." A pause. "The only thing we disagree on so far is the importance of tea," she said, trying to lighten the tone.

"I'll see you tomorrow, Genevieve."

And she walked to the door, acutely aware of his watching her, just as acutely aware that they had no future. That after she left this room, that would be it.

Archie flung himself back down on the bed as soon as the door shut behind her. And then vaulted off the bed, too agitated to sit still.

What was he going to do?

There was nothing to do. She was not for him. Even if he reconciled with his family, a duchess would not marry the third son when the first was available.

No doubt his parents, if not his brother, were planning how to snare the unmarried and elusive duchess for George. As every other single society gentleman was no doubt doing. They should just set up a queue and have them all state their case to Genevieve, who could choose the most suitable gentleman and be done with it.

What if she chose him?

He sat up at the thought. It wasn't as though he hadn't considered it before. But that had been wishful thinking. But what would it look like if they were to do the unimaginable and marry?

They could live in the country, where both of them would be more comfortable. They could work together on her holdings, and argue about what farming supplies were needed where. If she—*when* she was pregnant with their child, he could oversee things until she was ready to return to it.

He would encourage her to continue Duchess Practice, but not so she could learn how to navigate social waters, instead working on more important things, like taking care of her people and her lands. Taking ownership of her holdings and showing all the Mr. BetterThanYous who was in charge. Giving a voice to people who wouldn't otherwise be heard.

He found himself back on the bed, stretched out, his hands behind his head, thinking about it. About how it would look.

It would be worth whatever stigma they might face. Although the stigma would be worse for her, of course. She'd have to decide if she was willing to face it.

He'd have to convince her.

He allowed his mind to return to the difficult times in battle, when he'd persuade his men to march to the front line, some of them knowing they'd never return.

Not that marriage to him would be the same as facing certain death—at least he hoped not—but he would have to put as much effort into convincing her as he did to convince his men to follow him into battle.

Because their being together was as right as a just cause. He wanted to put order to things, to put the things that belonged together *together*.

Because he loved her. He wanted to be with her for the rest of his life.

And now he would just have to convince her of that, too.

Dear Archie,

I think I know what we should do, even though it is terrifying and not at all conventional. I will come to your bedroom after I return home from attending the theater with the Countess of Estabrook to speak with you.

Genevieve

Chapter 26

"Have you been to the theater before?" the countess asked, her words kind and not dismissive.

Had she found another friend? Genevieve wondered.

It rather felt as though she had.

They were sitting in the earl and countess's private box, able to see and be seen. Genevieve wore one of her new gowns, of course, the gown made from a sky blue material that seemed so light and lovely that it would float up to rejoin the sky.

She felt beautiful, but she hadn't gotten confirmation from Archie—he hadn't joined them for dinner, since Aunt Sophia had asked him to accompany her to visit an old friend. And of course, since she was his employer, he'd said yes.

It had been just Sir William and Miss Evelyn, and Genevieve had found herself glancing at the clock, willing it to move faster. She couldn't wait to speak with Archie, to see if he'd agree to what she'd proposed.

Proposed. Now that was an ironic word.

Meanwhile, she was at the theater, a place she had never been before. Of course. Since she had been to so few places.

"I have not, my lady," Genevieve replied with a smile. She glanced down at the pit, noting the wide variety of people, from the grand members of Society to people who appeared to have worked all day, and were crowding into the standing area for a moment of entertainment.

She didn't feel anxious, as she had those times before, being out in public. Maybe she was growing accustomed to being a duchess? That would be wonderful. And also sad, because it would most definitely mean that she no longer needed Duchess Practice. And her teacher was leaving soon anyway.

She didn't need him anymore, not for this. Though she did need him.

"It is a treat, even for someone who's been in town for years," the countess said. "The only trick is to get lost in the story rather than paying attention to the company. Not that it isn't lovely, of course," the countess added, a faint blush on her cheeks.

Genevieve laughed in reply, and she patted her friend's—*her friend's!*—hand. "I would like to get lost in the story," she said. *Especially if it is a love story with a happy ending.*

She leaned over and looked at the crowd below again, this time distinguishing more clearly between the groups—working-class types in dark, worn clothing, merchant families with many children in their finest garments, and—"Who is that?" she asked, pointing toward a woman in a particularly bright dress, a color Genevieve couldn't even name, except that it was somewhere between lemon yellow and orange, only brighter than either one of those.

The countess followed her gaze, and her lips tightened. "That is Mrs. Foster. She is the Viscount Salisbury's . . . special friend."

Genevieve's interest quickened at hearing Archie's last name, and then the meaning of what the duchess had said hit her. His . . . special friend? So his mistress?

She wished she could see the woman better. She could see a few plumes and large necklace taking up all the available space on her décolletage—which was vast, owing to the low-cut neckline—and she saw how the woman's face looked brighter than those of the women near her.

She must be wearing cosmetics. Genevieve didn't think she had ever seen a woman wearing cosmetics so obviously before. Now she really wished she could see better.

"Do you think the viscount's wife"—Archie's mother—"knows about Mrs. Foster?"

The countess nodded as she exhaled. "Yes, I am sure she does. It is not usually a secret about these things. And Mrs. Foster has been kept by the viscount for nearly five years."

So perhaps Archie knew about her as well.

She wished she could excuse herself and go home right now to speak to him, only it would be terribly rude, and besides, she wasn't yet sure what she was going to say. Except to tell him how she felt about him, and see if he felt even close to that.

And if he did, then they could discuss the future.

He was hoping she would stop by again this evening, even before he received her letter. And then it arrived, and he welcomed the chance to explain everything, to resolve it in a way that hadn't been resolved before.

So when the knock came just at midnight, he was waiting, and sprang up to open the door before she could knock again.

She stood outside the door in her nightclothes, a candlestick in one hand. The light cast flickering shadows on her face so she looked like something he'd conjured from his imagination for a minute.

"Can I come in?" she asked in that high voice she got when she was nervous.

Well, he was nervous, too. He'd spent most of the evening thinking about what to say, and he still wasn't sure. The only thing he was certain of was that he would say it.

"Of course," he said, stepping to one side as he glanced around the corridor to make sure nobody was lingering outside. Or would hear them.

Although if she said yes, then it wouldn't matter much. Yes, there'd be scandal that the duchess had been seen with her betrothed late at night, but then there'd be the betrothal to rebut the talk, plus she was a duchess, and could wield her power . . . powerfully.

Archie wanted to roll his eyes at himself for being so bad with words. If he was this stuck when he had thoughts inside his head, what would happen when he had to ask her?

"How was your evening?" he asked, gesturing for her to sit down. She shook her head, but then went and sat down on the bed.

He felt his mouth curl up into a grin at how he had anticipated her doing that—saying she didn't want to sit, then sitting anyway.

He knew her.

He loved her.

He hoped she'd say yes.

"My evening was interesting," she said, narrowing her eyes in thought. Her focus was beyond his shoulder, as was usual for her. It made him start when she flicked her eyes back to his. "I saw someone—that is, someone you might know." Her voice was still squeaky.

He closed his eyes and took a deep breath. "My brother George again?" With any luck, he would leave London without seeing his brother at all.

"No, not your brother. It was a Mrs. Foster."

The words hung in the air between them, suspended as though they were lighter than air.

Even though they most definitely were not.

"I know who she is," Archie replied in a grim voice. He hadn't thought about her for years. It seemed she was still in his father's protection, if Genevieve knew enough about her to tell Archie she'd seen her.

"Yes, well, the countess didn't want to say too much."

Thank goodness for the countess, Archie thought.

"But she did tell me that she and your father . . . that they . . ."

"Yes. They did. They apparently still do." Archie stood, unable to sit still, and began to pace the short distance between the chair he'd been sitting in and his bed—where she was sitting. He turned and faced her. "Why are you here, Genevieve?" He didn't think it was to discuss his father's mistress. He knew it wasn't because she thought he would be proposing.

Instead of answering, she gazed off past his shoulder at that red painting again. He really needed to remove it; it seemed to be far more fascinating to her than it should be.

"I—" she began, then shook her head, now looking down at the carpet. At any place but where he was, apparently.

"What?"

His chest tightened. What could be so difficult to say to him?

Was she getting married?

Oh hell. Was he too late?

"Tell me." His voice was raw.

She looked up at him then, her eyes widening in confusion. "You seem upset yourself. There is nothing—that is, I am hopeful that we can come to an agreement. This is not usually what a female would ask, but . . ." and then she inhaled, and he felt himself mirror her breath, his chest easing as he considered her words.

"If you're going to ask what I think you are, what I should be asking, then the answer is yes," he said in a low voice.

He saw the incredulity of her expression. Was it really so difficult to imagine he'd want to marry her? To be with her for the rest of their lives?

"You will?" she squeaked. "Won't it be awkward?"

He shook his head, kneeling onto the carpet in front of her as he did. He took her hands in his and placed both of their hands on her thighs.

He couldn't get distracted by the thought of what was under that night rail now. Although now he could actually, couldn't he? She'd agreed.

She would marry him. She would allow him to join her life and be with her.

He opened his mouth to tell her he loved her— to finally say it aloud, so she knew. So it was spoken. But she spoke first.

"We can find accommodations for you not far from here." She shrugged, and her cheeks started to turn pink. "I am not certain how it is usually done, and you can understand how it would be difficult to ask anyone."

He blinked at her, his hands still holding hers, his mouth hanging open. What on earth was she talking about?

"And you'll be able to continue helping me with the estate, if anyone were to ask." Now her cheeks were bright red, her eyes darting frantically around the room.

Not looking at him any longer.

"If anyone were to ask?" he repeated. He still had no idea what she was talking about.

"If someone suggests—that is, if someone wants to know why we spend so much time together. Why we seem to be so close." The last few words were spoken in the highest squeak he'd heard her emit yet, and he still couldn't understand what she was meaning, until—

He did.

"Are you saying," he asked, dropping her hands as he rose to stand, his legs touching the bed so she had to lean her head far back to look at him, "are you saying that you want me to be your mistress?" He shook his head as though to clear it. "That is, the male version of a mistress? Whatever that word is?"

Because if there was a word for it, he certainly had never heard it.

"The countess referred to Mrs. Foster as your father's 'special friend.'" He kept his gaze on her, so sharp and intense it seemed she had to look away. Back at that damn painting.

"I thought you wanted to marry me," he said in a low rasp. Because if he spoke in a normal tone he'd shout, and he knew he did not want the entire household to come running.

Even though it would result in what he wanted—marriage to her—since to be found together in this position would compromise her irreparably.

The irony was not lost on him. Nor was the possibility of losing his honor if he were to give in to his temper. But he couldn't do that, not now when she'd made herself so clear.

"Marry you?" Now she looked startled. Why?

Was it such a far-fetched idea? He felt his pride—that pride that had caused him to walk out on his family—start to churn inside his gut, and he felt sick. Aghast that she would have thought of such a thing, that she would have thought he would be willing to do it, that he'd misunderstood her feelings for him so thoroughly that he actually thought she might want to marry him.

"But you don't want to marry me," she said in a small voice.

He stepped back, knowing he was probably intimidating to her now, what with his towering over her as she sat on his bed. His *bed*, for God's sake.

"How would you know that, Genevieve?" He raked his hands through his hair in frustration. "You didn't ask me. You told me." He took another breath. "You didn't even think of it."

She opened her mouth as though to protest, and he held his hand up. "You might say you thought of it. Maybe you did. But you must have rejected it for you to come up with this ludicrous idea of me being your—your special friend," he finished with a snarl. "Did you even think how that would make me feel?"

He began to pace again, not wanting to look at her. To look at the possibility of her, which she had just discarded without asking him.

Like a true aristocrat.

"Congratulations, Duchess," he said, sneering. "You have completed your training, you are fit to take your place among the ranks of Society. Treating people as though they were lesser than you because of who you are and who they are not."

Her hand was at her mouth, her eyes bright with tears. He wished his chest didn't hurt at seeing her in pain. He wished he didn't care.

Didn't love her.

"I should go," she said in a low, trembling voice. She stood and swayed, and he went to catch her—he couldn't help himself, he didn't want her to fall, no matter what he was feeling at the moment about her—and held her just for a moment in his arms.

As he'd hoped to hold her for the rest of his life.

And now that dream was shattered. And all he had left was a bruised heart, wounded pride, and the knowledge that he would never again feel the connection he had with her.

She shut the door and he dropped onto the bed. Alone. As she'd managed it.

Genevieve felt her knees wobbling the entire walk back to her bedroom. She just had to make it back to her room where she could close the door, close the world, away from her.

What had just happened? One moment they had seemed in perfect agreement and the next he was furious with her.

What had she done?

She reached her bedroom door and turned the handle, stepping inside. Alone. As she would be forever, no matter who might enter her life.

She leaned against the door, closing her eyes as she tilted her head back. "What have I done?" she murmured, pressing the heels of her hands against the wood. The physical pressure against her skin a mirror of the emotional pressure weighing her down. Although the better question was "What have I not done?" she said again. "I am so stupid," she continued, shaking her head as she stepped to the bed. Her own bed, now hers completely alone, never a possibility of his coming to join her there. To hold her, to kiss her, to be with her in all the ways a person could be.

She crawled onto the bed, dropping on top of the coverlet without sliding inside. It felt like too much effort even to pull back the covers. How had she bungled it so thoroughly?

Because duchess or not, she didn't feel as though he'd want her forever. Because she was hesitant to even ask him to consider such a thing because she didn't trust he cared for her enough. Even though every one of his actions indicated he did.

Because she didn't trust herself.

Even after all this time, her growing confidence in herself as a duchess, and most importantly, a woman, she didn't trust she would be enough.

So she'd made sure of that by not being enough for him.

The tears took longer to come than she might have anticipated, a distant observant part of her brain remarked. But when they did, they were a torrent, a storm that felt as though it originated from the bottom of her feet and swept up through her entire body, wrecking everything in its path.

She didn't know when she fell asleep, just that it was nearly dawn, and the remainder of her life was looming before her, lonely and distant and filled with duty and responsibility, but not love.

Never love.

Dear Duchess,

I wanted to let you know Lady Sophia and I will be departing very early tomorrow morning. I have instructed Chandler on what needs to be taken care of immediately, and I will be in correspondence with him to ensure progress on your ~~affairs~~ business matters go smoothly.

Sincerely,
Mr. Archibald Salisbury, Capt. (Ret.)

Chapter 27

"Are you enjoying yourself, Your Grace?" The countess sounded concerned. Probably because Genevieve was most definitely not enjoying herself, and wasn't yet a good enough aristocrat to be able to pretend well enough to fool people she was.

Was it ironic that she needed more Duchess Practice? Or was it just sad?

She'd have to go with sad.

She'd been sad since he left. Or more precisely, since about two days before he left, meaning she'd been sad for nearly three weeks.

"I am, thank you, my lady." Genevieve's smile to her friend was honest, at least. Anne had become a good friend during that same time, although Genevieve hadn't felt as though she could confide her heartache. But she knew Anne could tell something was bothering her, but she didn't press; she just made it clear she was there when or if Genevieve wanted to talk.

"Oh, there is Mr. Salisbury," the countess observed, and Genevieve's heart leaped, only of course it wasn't the right Mr. Salisbury.

Archie's brother was a pleasant enough gentleman, and if Genevieve had met him before meeting his brother, she might have even considered him as a partner for life. But his easy charm and mild good looks were nothing compared to the intensity his brother had—he wasn't easily charming, but he was compelling. And he was ruthlessly handsome, not just nice to look at.

He wasn't easy. He wasn't charming.

He wasn't hers.

"Good evening, Your Grace, my lady," Mr. Salisbury greeted them. "This is a fine party, wouldn't you say?"

"I was just commenting on that to the duchess," the countess said, shooting Genevieve a conspiratorial look. As though somehow Anne understood, even though Genevieve hadn't said anything.

Like how she'd been able to communicate with him.

"The Musgroves are renowned for their entertainment." Mr. Salisbury moved in close and lowered his voice. "It seems they have managed to secure the talents of Mr. Velasquez, the famous Spanish tenor." He nodded and smiled at both of them, as though he were the one responsible for the rare treat.

Oh, wonderful. Not only was her heart broken, she would have to endure more caterwauling by people from warmer climates.

The countess clapped her hands. "Excellent! I

have been dying to hear him, the earl and I have tickets for his performance in a week. And yet the Musgroves managed to lure him for tonight? I must go find Mrs. Musgrove and ask her how she did it. Excuse me," she said, darting away without waiting for a reply.

Leaving her alone with Mr. Salisbury. The wrong Mr. Salisbury, who was enthusiastic about some man who'd likely sing about love and loss, and frankly, Genevieve didn't want to hear anything about it.

"Have you—have you heard from my brother?" Mr. Salisbury asked in a hesitant tone.

Her throat got thick, clogged with so much emotion she was surprised she didn't explode. "No. That is, he is in contact with my butler, but I have not heard from him myself." She missed his letters. Along with the rest of him.

Asking herself why, for possibly the thousandth time, she had to be so stupid, to misread what he wanted so thoroughly she ruined her life. She couldn't make the same judgment about his life, but she imagined it was less pleasant than before. She wasn't so foolish as to think he didn't care about her, at least.

But she couldn't imagine he cared about her as much as she cared about him.

"I was hoping—that is, could you send this to him from me?" He held a letter out to her and she froze, just staring down at the envelope in his hand. "He won't open it if he sees the return address, so I thought if you could just include it with one of your letters." He stopped, looking at her with eyes so close to his, and yet not his, it made her heart hurt.

She took the letter from him, wincing as she thought what he might say when he received it. About both of them.

"I'll send it, but I can't guarantee anything." She couldn't guarantee, for example, that he wouldn't shred her letter with his brother's letter inside.

At least it would be a mode of efficient disposal he would no doubt applaud.

"Thank you, Your Grace," he said, bowing low over her hand.

It is the least I can do, she wanted to say, *given how badly I treated your brother.* But of course she couldn't say it. Not to this Mr. Salisbury and most definitely not to that Mr. Salisbury.

She could barely even say it to herself.

"No, Mrs. Coster, I wouldn't advise treating your sheep with the same hair refiner you use." Archie barely managed not to roll his eyes. "That is, your hair looks lovely, of course"—at which the older woman preened and touched said hair—"but wool is very different from human hair."

"Oh, do leave Mr. Salisbury alone, Hetty," Lady Sophia said, plucking a biscuit from a tray and feeding it to Truffles. "He has so much work, what with preparing for the festival and continuing to help the Duchess of Blakesley. She's my god-daughter, you know," she added in an aside.

Mrs. Coster couldn't resist the temptation to roll her eyes. "You've only said a few thousand times.

I wish she had never inherited the title, then she would be a normal woman."

Nobody wishes that more than I do, Archie thought. He'd immersed himself in work, but he couldn't keep his employer from mentioning, only about a hundred times a day, that her goddaughter was a duchess, and speculating on what she might be doing at any particular moment.

He wished, for selfish reasons, that she was less inclined to be doing things so he wouldn't have to hear about her quite so often.

"What will you be exhibiting at the festival?" Lady Sophia asked.

Mrs. Coster took a sip of tea and began to list all the embroidery, cakes, and livestock she was claiming ownership of, but hadn't done anything to produce.

And since when had he gotten so cynical?

Oh, of course. Since about a month ago.

Still, he did have his work, and right now he was in the thick of helping Lady Sophia do her planning for her own festival showings, which meant he didn't have time to think. Much.

"Mr. Salisbury, you're not even listening!" Lady Sophia's voice cut—thankfully—through his thoughts.

"Pardon, my lady. I was—I was thinking about Mrs. Coster's sheep," he said. "Perhaps you could wash them in whatever your laundress washes your clothing in, to make them sparkle." Sparkling sheep. Had he ever thought he'd be sunk so low?

"Sparkle! That sounds perfect." Apparently Mrs. Coster thought his idea was brilliant. Although judging by how she kept appraising him, if he'd told her to dye her sheep green she'd probably be as enthusiastic.

The thought made him want to chuckle, which meant, perhaps, that he was on the road to recovery. Excellent. He'd only have to suggest a few dozen or so more ridiculous things to do to livestock to get him feeling like himself again.

It was a plan.

"Are you feeling well, Mr. Salisbury?" Mrs. Coster asked, looking worried. "You are breathing oddly."

"Oh, fine, ladies. I feel fine," he replied, straightening up in his chair and concentrating on not laughing.

It was better than how he'd felt in a while. Since—well, he knew since when.

"I'm going to throw a ball," Genevieve announced.

Given that she was alone at the time, the announcement was not particularly noteworthy. But it was to her; if she was going to do this, was going to continue trying to do what she'd set out to do, she'd have to succeed on her own, without any man in her life.

It hurt, but it was what she'd practiced for. If she could just show them, show all of her new world, that she was perfectly able to handle being who she was on her own, then perhaps she could decide her own future, without worrying about gossip or being challenged.

Her mind shied away from what she would do after she'd proven herself. "One step at a time," she reminded herself, walking to the wall where the bellpulls were. She yanked the two for Chandler and Clarkson and waited.

"It's the right thing, you know," Clarkson said. She stepped back to appraise Genevieve's appearance, nodding after a few tension-filled moments.

Mrs. Hardwick had delivered the remainder of the gowns Genevieve had ordered, and she was wearing the most beautiful evening gown of them all: pale pink, it fit her curves perfectly, and had an overlay of sheer material studded with sparkles. Clarkson had dressed her hair in a more elaborate style than usual, and Genevieve had taken ownership of the ducal jewels, so she wore a diamond necklace and matching earrings. Her gloves were an even paler pink, as were her evening slippers.

She looked like a princess from a fairy tale, which was only slightly more unbelievable than what she was, a female duchess in her own right.

She just wished he was here to see her. But the whole point of this was that he was not here, she didn't need anybody to succeed in this whole duchess venture.

He'd given her the guidelines she needed, but now it was up to her. Alone.

"There are so many people coming," Genevieve murmured.

Clarkson patted a curl, since there was only one ribbon on the gown. "Everyone who is anyone, plus a few people who think they're someones," she said with a sniff.

The countess was coming, thank goodness, so at least there would be one friend in attendance. The Garrys were coming as well, and Genevieve had promised herself to try to find a nice young man for Evelyn. Sir William hadn't yet made clear his intentions, and she was hoping he held himself back from it for just a bit longer. It would make things awkward between her and his sister after her refusal.

Because if she couldn't have Archie, she didn't think she wanted anybody. She was a privileged person, the most privileged person in England with the exception of the Queen, and if she didn't want to marry someone, she shouldn't have to. That was the point of tonight's event; to show everyone who she was, and who she was not—she was not a mealy-mouthed, husband-accepting-for-the-good-of-the-title person. She was Genevieve, Duchess of Blakesley, and she was throwing her own party.

She just wished she felt happier about it all. This kind of thing had been unthinkable a few years ago, when she'd been tucked in the country with no friends and fewer hopes and dreams.

She was content to be proceeding, however, and that would have to be enough. Unless she could somehow undo the mess she'd made, it would have to be enough. Forever.

* * *

"How are you, dear?" the countess asked. Her friend had arrived nearly as soon as the party had begun, for which Genevieve was grateful. The countess wore a gown of dark blue satin, setting off her dark hair and blue eyes perfectly.

She couldn't think about dark hair and blue eyes, however, or she would cry. And that would not be appropriate for her own party. Or anyone else's, for that matter.

"I am perfectly well," Genevieve replied, widening her mouth in what she hoped was a credible smile. It wasn't that she was miserable—well, fine, she was miserable—but she could find pleasure in a few moments, and spending time with her friend should be one of them.

So why did she keep wishing he was here to share it with her?

Oh, of course, because she loved him and he had helped her with all of this and he should be here to share in the triumph.

Because it was a triumph. Chandler had ensured that the newly hired staff was properly trained in how to plan and execute an event on this grand a scale. The food was delicious, the wine was flowing, and there were no histrionic singers in earshot. Instead, Genevieve had hired a trio of musicians to play continuously during the party, providing a pleasant backdrop of sound rather than being the focal point of the evening.

"You have done well," the countess said, speaking in a low tone so as not to be overheard.

"Everyone is saying what a success tonight is, and how perfectly you suit your new position, despite not having been trained since birth for it, as so many of the males in your situation were."

"Thank you," Genevieve replied. "That is good to hear. And thank you for being a good friend, I have so few of them." One less, now that he had left. And left furious with her for suggesting something she should have known would never suit him.

For perhaps the millionth time, she found her mind wandering back to when she'd said it. Wishing she hadn't assumed he'd want something like that as well, that he wouldn't want to be affiliated with her permanently. That it didn't mean as much to him as it would to her.

She was an idiot. Truly.

Albeit a titled, wealthy idiot. Meaning she fit in even better in her new world than she could have anticipated.

It was comfort. Cold comfort, to be sure, but comfort nonetheless.

She plucked a glass of champagne from the tray of a passing footman and toasted her new life before taking a sip.

"It was a wonderful party," Miss Evelyn enthused the next afternoon. Genevieve had been up until three o'clock in the morning, dancing and talking and ensuring everyone was having fun.

Everyone except her, that is.

When had she become so—so morose?

Ah. Of course. When she had completely ruined her own life with her thoughtlessness.

"Thank you, I am so pleased you were able to come." And Genevieve had introduced her to several young gentlemen, including Mr. Salisbury. The lesser Mr. Salisbury, she had come to think of him. Because he wasn't anything close to his brother, although he was perfectly pleasant.

"You have served our family well, Your Grace," Sir William added.

She opened her mouth to retort that merely not being an addlepated drunkard would serve their family well, but she did not wish to point that out, not if he harbored the misconception that their family was tolerable.

Perhaps he had relatives she hadn't met yet, perfectly respectable relatives who didn't discard their children when it was inconvenient to have them around, or who hadn't squandered great wealth at the gaming table.

Hope springs eternal, she thought ruefully.

Genevieve was dressing for more afternoon calls when the post arrived, including a letter from her aunt Sophia. She sat at her dressing table as Clarkson worked on her hair, opening the letter and trying not to wish too hard for news about him.

She shook the pages out and tried to make sense of Aunt Sophia's letter. Which was nearly as confusing as Aunt Sophia herself. She scanned the letter, chortling to herself as she read the convoluted thoughts.

"Is that from your godmother?" Clarkson asked. She'd finished Genevieve's hair, and was picking things up around the room.

"Yes, it is. She goes into great detail about what is happening," though she doesn't mention him. "Apparently there is a very grand event she refers to as the festival. She says that 'the annual festival showcases the best in a variety of items,' but she doesn't say what items, or what the point is. Or showcases to whom." She waved the paper in the air and looked over at Clarkson, who was fussing with yet another ribbon. This time on a gown that was not currently worn by Genevieve, but still fussing.

She'd been fussing nearly continuously in the time since Mr. Salisbury had departed, as though she knew something was amiss, and wished she could fix it, but couldn't. Hence the fussing.

"I would assume the festival is similar to what occurred in my own village," Clarkson replied, her hands stilling. Thank goodness. "It's primarily an excuse for everyone to come together and socialize." She shrugged. "The local farmers would bring the best produce and livestock, there would be food for sale, and entertainment. The highlight for me was always in the evening, when the best musicians would begin to play and we'd all dance under the stars. If it wasn't raining, of course," her ever-practical lady's maid said.

"It sounds delightful," Genevieve said. "I believe there were such things in the village in which I grew up, but of course I was never allowed to attend them." Because she was a duke's daughter, even though she had been entirely forgotten.

"Perhaps you should go. Get out of London for a while." Clarkson smoothed a ribbon. "You have not been quite yourself for the past few weeks."

Three days and three weeks, Genevieve corrected in her head.

But if she went, she'd see him.

But if she went, she'd see *him*.

"I think I will," Genevieve said, her tone just a bit shakier than before. Clarkson shot her a suspicious glance, but then resumed fussing even faster.

She'd go to see him. If he'd listen to her—which she wasn't sure he would—she'd explain. Or try to explain.

Or something.

"If you can just bring the tables over here," Lady Sophia said, gesturing to the spot they'd just been in, before she'd asked Mr. McCready and him to move them.

Archie exchanged a glance with Bob as they hoisted the first of the three tables up again.

"Remind me why this is better than the army," Bob muttered as they began to shuffle back to where Lady Sophia pointed.

"Because you won't run the risk of dying?"

Bob snorted. "No, there's only the chance I'll kill someone," and he glared at their employer.

Archie couldn't help but laugh.

"That's the spirit," Bob said. "I haven't heard

you laugh in weeks. I'll need to remember this moment, maybe make other inappropriate jokes about work just to bring some sparkle to your life." Bob emphasized the word "sparkle," which made Archie want to kill someone now, too. Preferably Bob.

Mrs. Coster had run with the idea of "Sparkle Sheep," and now all the local ladies were using a variety of hair products on their poor livestock.

"Is it time to rinse?" Lady Sophia called.

Including their employer.

"Not yet, my lady," Archie replied, steadfastly avoiding Bob's snicker. "Another half an hour."

"They'll be dry by the time we bring them to town, though?" She sounded worried now. As though a damp sheep was going to ruin the festival.

"Yes, my lady."

Plus she had asked the same question only fifteen minutes ago. Perhaps he should just make up a sign that displayed the answers to all of Lady Sophia's questions: "Yes, we will leave in enough time to make it to the festival by nine o'clock." "No, I don't think so." "Only if Mr. McCready counts to ten." And so on.

Her constant questions kept him from thinking too much of what he had turned down. The possibility of being with her, even in the capacity she'd suggested—well, he couldn't deny he was tempted. Had even gone so far as to put on his trousers in the middle of the night, preparing to rush to London to see her.

But he couldn't and wouldn't do that. She'd have to get married eventually, he knew as well as she did that she wouldn't allow the title to fall to one of her ne'er-do-well relatives. She'd have to get married and have legitimate heirs.

And he'd seen his mother's face often enough when his father had left the house for several hours "on business." He wouldn't do that to another man, even though that sounded so odd, and even though another man would have the legal honor of sharing her bed.

"What do you want done now, my lady?" he called to his employer, who was currently consulting with Truffles.

He'd immerse himself in work for the foreseeable future, until he was too old or too tired to care about the state of his heart.

Archie

   ~~I am on my way.~~

Genevieve

                    (NOT SENT)

Chapter 28

"*Y*our Grace!" Genevieve heard Sir William's voice from behind her and winced. She had been trying to depart without running into the gentleman, since she knew he was set on proposing, and she did not want to put either of them into that awkward situation, since there was no possibility she would say yes.

Even if *he* said no.

"Yes, Sir William?" she replied, turning back around. She was relieved to see Chandler walking up from the coatroom carrying her cloak. He slowed his steps, clearly not wishing to intrude, but she shook her head and held her hand out to him to indicate she wanted her cloak.

"I—I was hoping we could speak on a private matter," Sir William replied, nearly glaring at poor Chandler.

"No time, Sir William, I am afraid," she said in a breezy voice, allowing Chandler to assist her into her cloak. "I am on my way on very important business." *More important than anything you might have to say*, she added in her own head. Even though she knew it was important to Sir William—from what his sister had said, he was in debt up to his eyeballs, and marrying Genevieve would obviously solve that problem.

He was also trying to marry his sister off to the highest bidder, which made Genevieve want to invite Miss Evelyn to live with her permanently, so she wouldn't be in danger of ending up with some gentleman who wouldn't appreciate Evelyn's quiet manner.

Sir William was not to be so easily dissuaded, however, stepping closer to speak quietly into Genevieve's ear. "I understand you are quite busy, Your Grace. I wish to ease your burden, if I might. That is, I would like to share your burden"—*and my money*, Genevieve thought—"and I believe if you could just spare a few moments of your time, it would be to our mutual happiness." And then he looked at her with a significant expression on his face, so there was no doubt about what he was talking.

She was going to have to have this conversation after all, wasn't she?

"I can spare a few moments. Just tell Coachman I will be out shortly," she said to Chandler. "In here, Sir William," she said, gesturing to the library.

She preceded him and wasn't surprised when he shut the door behind them.

"I know you cannot help but have noticed my marked attentions," he began, clasping his hands behind his back.

"Yes, I have." How was she to answer that anyway?

He looked startled, so apparently she'd answered that incorrectly. She wished she had a book on *How to Receive and Politely Decline Marriage Proposals from People You Don't Wish to Be Married To*. Then again, perhaps she would have done better with a book that was about *How to Trust That the Person You Love Loves You Back and Wants to Marry You After All, You Idiot*.

"Well, then," he said, and began to lower himself down onto the carpet. She started at him as he positioned himself just so. He looked up at her and smoothed his hair with one hand, placing the other over his heart. "Since you understand my intentions"—and wasn't it ironic that she understood this man's intentions when she hadn't understood the other man's—"I would like to ask if you would do me the honor of accepting my hand in marriage."

He smiled, a satisfied smile that seemed to anticipate her assent to his question. He was going to be so not satisfied in a moment.

"Thank you, Sir William," Genevieve replied in a firm voice. "I very much appreciate your honor, but I must decline."

Now he looked confused. "Decline?" he repeated, still on his knees, his hand coming away from his heart.

"Yes. Decline," she said, even more emphatically. "I must say no." And this time she used the voice she'd acquired during Duchess Practice, the tone that should indicate, if she was doing it properly, that she knew best and she was altogether far better than you.

He struggled to his feet, his face taking on a purple hue. "You cannot mean this," he said, sounding furious.

"I do." She raised her head and looked down her nose at him. Archie would be proud.

"You know that people are talking about your—your unusual situation," he said, as though she weren't aware of it. "And while I wouldn't have mentioned it, it has been made clear that there are certain members of our family who are considering challenging your right to be duchess. As your husband, I could assuage those concerns."

Genevieve felt her eyes narrowing as she glared at him. He swallowed, and his expression got more belligerent.

"You will marry me," he said. "Or else—"

"Or else what?" She stepped forward, placing her hands on her hips. "Or else you will allow the family to tear the duchy apart as you attempt to toss aside a written legal document? Or else you and whoever you have found to speak against me will come face-to-face with my *noblesse oblige*, and you can be sure I will oblige you with how much *noblesse* I can muster." She spoke in a low, furious tone that made him blanch. Good.

"You will not force me to marry you simply because I am a woman in a position you wish me not to be in. I dare you to try to challenge my position. Or I could just offer your sister a dowry so she can be free of your machinations." The thought emerged from her mouth before she even knew she'd had the thought. But once she had, it made perfect sense. She did like Evelyn, after all, and this way he would have to accept her refusal without then trying to unseat her as duchess.

"If you will excuse me," she continued, nodding as she strode to the door. "You can think about what you want to do while I am away"— *trying to persuade someone to marry me, of all farcical situations.*

Even though she didn't much feel like laughing.

"Everything is running smoothly, then?" Lady Sophia asked. Only for the hundredth time.

Archie bowed. "Yes, my lady." He gazed over the crowd, which was substantial. They'd all begun pouring into the village in the morning, and now it was nearly two o'clock, and it seemed that every single villager—plus people from all the surrounding towns—were there in various states of happiness.

It was difficult for Archie to stay glum also, despite how he'd been feeling for the past few weeks. There was too much sunshine, too much laughter, and, yes, too many sparkling sheep to stay miserable.

Besides which, Bob had promised he would tell Lady Sophia—who would tell every other lady—that Archie had mentioned his love for pickled fish, but that he had been unable to get some he truly liked while he'd been here. Unless he laughed or at least smiled every so often.

The thought of being drowned in pickled fish

was enough to make him grin, even though there were moments when his smiles were definitely forced.

"I do so love the festival," Lady Sophia said, accompanying her words with a contented sigh.

Archie glanced down at her and felt himself start to smile—an honest smile, not just a pickled-fish-avoiding smile. He did like it here, even though of course he missed her.

But he didn't miss London, nor did he miss the opportunity of running into one of his family. It was enough that he'd heard she had seen his brother.

"It is a lovely event, my lady."

"I wish to take a hayride," Lady Sophia declared, pointing to a cart piled with hay and several young children.

Archie raised his brow. His employer did manage to surprise him every so often. She had a zest for life that could be obfuscated by her dithering, but she was joyful in a way he envied.

Like Genevieve was joyful.

Damn, he missed her.

"Let us take a hayride then," Archie said, taking Lady Sophia's arm and guiding her to where the farmer was unloading some of the children. He concentrated on guiding his charge through the crowd, leading her to the cart before she could decide she wished to engage in some target practice or toss rings into a fountain.

Though he could probably guess she would wish to do those things after.

The farmer looked doubtful when Archie told

him what they wanted, but relented in the face of Lady Sophia's constant questions, laying down a coarse wool blanket on top of the hay so that "the lady's dress won't get all wispy."

He was assisting Lady Sophia up when her expression brightened and she yelled directly into his ear, making him jump.

"Vievy!" she called, waving her arm and hopping up and down in her seat.

Archie forced himself to take a deep breath before turning around to see.

She stood there, not twenty feet away, clutching a bundle of papers in her hand and biting her lip.

He didn't change expression. He couldn't. He was frozen in place, his heart pounding, his chest feeling as though someone was squeezing it until his lungs popped.

"Help me down so I can go see her," Lady Sophia said from behind him.

"Of course," he replied, turning back around, feeling his hands start to shake.

She was here. Why was she here?

Then again, why wouldn't she be? It wasn't as though she thought anything had occurred between them, at least nothing much of import. She had asked, he had said no, and that was that.

Even though he knew that was most definitely not that. Not for either of them.

"Vievy, what are you doing here?" Lady Sophia had looped her arm through Archie's and both of them were making their way toward Genevieve, Archie feeling as though each step was more and more difficult to make.

"I—I came with some letters," she said, thrusting the packet toward Archie.

Letters. Of course letters. Had she written to him? But if she had, what was she doing here when everything could be said on paper:

> *Dear Man I Wish to Persuade into an Illicit Relationship,*
> *Even Though You've Said No:*
>
> *I would like to be illicit with you. Please do reply at*
> *your earliest convenience.*
>
> *Illicitly Yours,*
> *The Duchess of Blakesley*

Or something like that.

But Archie didn't say anything beyond a murmured "Thank you, Your Grace" as he took the packet. Thick, so maybe she had gone into great detail about what she wanted to do to him, and vice versa?

In which case he should probably be alone to read the letters.

"You have not seen each other for weeks," Lady Sophia said. Stating the painfully obvious, for Archie, at least. "Go ahead and take my spot on the ride, Vievy; you will love it."

"Will I?" she said, glancing past Archie to where the farmer was presumably waiting for them.

Right. She wouldn't know if she did love a hayride, since she'd never experienced any typical childhood entertainment when she was young.

"You are certain to, Your Grace," Archie said,

donning his most charming smile, even though smiling was the last thing he wanted to do. He caught Bob's eye out in the crowd and gestured for him to join them.

"Mr. McCready will escort you to the carriage, my lady, and I will take you on a hayride later. May I?" he said, turning to address Genevieve, holding his arm out for her.

He held the packet of letters in one hand, and she slid her arm into his on his other side. They began walking, slowly, him glancing around at the crowd, smiling at a few of the people he knew. Not to mention some of the sheep.

"You're surprised to see me."

It wasn't a question.

"Yes."

The hand on his arm tightened. "I tried to write. I did write. And I couldn't figure out how to say what I wanted to." He felt her shrug. "So I decided to come myself."

"Should I thank you?" Now that she was here, the feeling he'd had when he'd realized she'd misunderstood him hit all over again, making that furious ache well up again, his chest tightening, a fierce course of anger flowing through his veins.

"No."

The word, spoken in a soft voice, did more to deflect his anger than a lengthy speech could. Not that he wasn't still angry; he was. But he was slightly less angry, hearing the hopelessness in her voice.

That seemed less than honorable, to take pleasure that she sounded sad.

But he couldn't lie to himself; that's what he felt.

They reached the cart without speaking again, him helping her up onto the blanket, the farmer frowning as he saw Genevieve's general splendor.

And she did look splendid. She wore another new gown, at least one he hadn't seen before, a bright yellow day dress that almost outshone the sun. Her hat was festooned with feathers in varying shades of yellow, and she completed her outfit with pale yellow shoes that did not look as though they could withstand walking around the village, more suited to paying visits in elegant drawing rooms.

But that was just her appearance. He knew, probably more than anyone, how foreign she felt in her new world. How she struggled to belong, how she had to resort to practicing—with him— in her new role.

Was she practicing with somebody new now?

The thought brought a return of those feelings of aggression he'd had when he'd thought Sir William was a viable suitor. Perhaps he still was. Perhaps she was here to tell him she'd accepted her relative's offer, since she did have to get married eventually.

Didn't she?

In which case, though, why hadn't she just written? It would have been easier.

The cart lurched forward, making her shoulder bump into his. He caught a whiff of her scent, something delicate and floral and expensive. Not that it necessarily smelled expensive, but he assumed it was.

"How are you?" she said in that same low voice.

"What am I to answer to that, Genevieve?" He kept his voice as low, but heard the anger threading through it. "The last time we saw one another, you . . ." He paused, shaking his head.

"I know. I . . ." and then her voice caught on a sob, and he wished he could comfort her, as the friend he considered himself. Only he'd be comforting her because she had insulted him, so that seemed backward.

"Is there somewhere we can speak privately?"

He glanced around at the cart's other inhabitants, noting how the children were all staring, no doubt because of the novelty of having adults in the cart, never mind that Genevieve was more appropriately dressed to meet the Queen for tea than jostle about in a cart.

Though—"Hold on to me," Archie said, wrapping his arm around her and leaping off the cart. They tumbled onto the grass, Archie cushioning her fall by making sure she landed on him.

"Don't stop!" he yelled as he heard the sound of raised voices emanating from the cart. "We'll make our own way back."

He looked up at her, him still holding her, her lying on his body.

Her. Lying on him.

Oh.

She looked back at him, her lips parted, her eyes dark, and he knew—he knew—she wanted to kiss him.

And he wanted to kiss her; that hadn't changed. But so much else had.

He sat up, still holding her so her gown would have less contact with the grass. She wound up on his lap, and he gathered himself—in strength and in willpower—to get her upright without entirely ruining Mrs. Hardwick's work.

"Not yet." Her voice shook slightly, and she raised her eyes to his. "Not yet." She licked her lips and he found himself watching her tongue as it darted out, leaving her mouth moist.

He glanced around; the cart was retreating, but they were still on a road, one that presumably offered less privacy than either of them wanted.

"Let's go over there," he said, nodding to a row of trees behind which was a meadow he'd used as a shortcut a few times. The trees would provide cover in case anyone happened down the road. He didn't want her to be the focus of more gossip, of talk that she'd been inappropriate when she had just barely started to try to make herself as appropriate as possible.

With his help.

She stood, looking as beautiful as he'd ever seen her, and he had to swallow against the thickness in his throat.

"Come," he said as he stood as well, starting to walk toward the trees. He heard the rustle of her gown as she followed, and he resisted the urge to drop his hand back for her to hold—it wouldn't be appropriate.

Even though it was what he wanted. Which was the whole problem, wasn't it?

They ducked under the trees and arrived in the meadow, the whole area covered with tiny blue flowers, making it look as though the ground was a blue carpet.

She pushed him down to a seated position, then lowered herself as well, back onto his lap. To keep her dress from getting dirty? Or was there another reason?

"I have something to say," she continued, after a few moments of silence. "And oddly enough," she said, humor in her voice, "I find it easier to say it sitting like this."

"Do I have any say in this?" he asked, his tone sharp. "What if I don't feel comfortable like this, Duchess?" He stressed her title, and he felt her stiffen in his arms.

"I don't blame you for being angry."

"So you're here to tell me you don't blame me for having a reasonable response to your unreasonable request? That's very kind of you." He sounded like an ass. He was an ass. But he was also fiercely, ferociously angry, and that her soft sweetness was currently on his lap wasn't helping matters.

"Just listen," she said in a stronger voice. One that sounded almost duchesslike.

Had she been practicing?

"Fine. I'll listen," he replied ungraciously.

She didn't speak right away, and he caught himself holding his breath, waiting for her words.

Dear Archie,

    I love you. Forgive me.

Genevieve

Chapter 29

*F*or a moment, she wondered if she could just sit here, on his lap, until they both withered up and died.

But not only was that entirely impractical, it also sounded unpleasant.

So never mind that.

"I wrote you a letter," she began.

"So you said."

He was not going to make this easy.

"And in the letter," she continued, taking a deep breath, "I said I—"

Now she wasn't going to make it easy for herself, given that she felt the tightening of her throat as her tears threatened to come.

"You said what?" A slightly less harsh tone now.

"I said I regret saying what I did. I regret assuming what I did. It was a misunderstanding. A big misunderstanding." She turned to face him, meeting his gaze, even though it hurt to see the guarded look in his eyes. "And not just a big misunderstanding, but a tremendous, enormous, and—and tremendous misunderstanding," she said, her voice strained. "I just—I just never thought that you would want me that way."

His eyebrow drew up sardonically. "What way? The wanting-to-be-with-you-forever way?"

"Uh," she stammered, feeling as though she should vault off his lap, that it was all too much. But he clamped his hands on her arms and held her in place, his eyes fixed on hers.

"Tell me what you did think, Genevieve."

The way he spoke her name—as though he didn't hate her. Not that she was thinking the opposite—that he loved her—but she didn't feel, at this moment, as though he loathed the very sight of her.

It gave her the strength to tell him. To finally and absolutely tell him the truth.

"I thought I loved you." She felt him stiffen, then realized what she'd said, squeezing her eyes shut in response. "No, I mean, I didn't think I loved you. I do love you." She opened her eyes again to find him still looking at her, that intense gaze sending a reaction, she didn't know what kind, through her entire body.

"I love you, Archie. And yet."

"And yet you asked me to be with you in a less than loving way. You asked me to do something that you should have known was something I would never do."

She bit her lip and looked over his shoulder, unable to look at him. To acknowledge the enormity of hurt she'd put him through.

"I did."

"Why?"

"I didn't think you felt the same way." She spoke in a small voice, and he lowered his head to hear her.

"Why wouldn't you think that, Genevieve?"

His voice was low as well. So low it seemed to rumble through her.

"I didn't think anybody could love me."

Silence.

The truth of it, of how alone and lost she felt, hit her as palpably as when she'd first realized how little her father cared for her.

"Why would you think that?" His arms were around her now, holding her tight against him. She buried her nose in his chest and inhaled his warm, strong scent.

"Because nobody did."

His arms tightened, and she felt him rest his chin on her head. Still silence, but it wasn't an uncomfortable silence.

"You're an idiot," he said at last.

She started to laugh, only she was still on the verge of tears, so her laughter came out accompanied by a few choked sobs. No doubt making her sound entirely insane—maybe even idiotic. Which only made her laugh and cry harder.

"Shh," he said, lowering his mouth to her ear. "Stop whatever you're doing."

That made her laugh more than cry, at least, and he kept holding her, murmuring incoherent things into her ear, which made it tickle.

"Your grandmother loves you. Some of the staff

at the house where you grew up love you, is that right?"

She nodded.

"Lady Sophia loves you."

"Mm."

"And I love you."

She froze. Had he just said that? She tilted her head back to look at him. He returned her look, one corner of his mouth curled up in a knowing smile.

"Yes. I do. I love you, Genevieve." Then he pressed his lips together into a thin line. "Which is why I couldn't believe you were so willing to throw all of that aside. Why I couldn't believe that you wanted to tarnish our feelings for one another in such a sordid relationship." He reached forward and drew his fingers along her jaw, sliding them down until he cupped her chin in his hands. "You are a rarity, Genevieve. A lady duchess, one not beholden to a man for your position. But true love? That is even more of a rarity." He shook his head, his fingers smoothing the skin on her face. "I want to believe in you, Genevieve, but I don't know that I can trust you."

His words hurt.

"I thought my family trusted in me, and I in them," he continued, still gazing deep into her eyes. She saw the hurt there as though it were a palpable thing. "And then when I wanted their trust, their love, they turned their backs on me." A moment of silence. "How will I know you won't do the same?"

"I won't. I can't," Genevieve replied in a fierce, low tone. She rolled off his lap onto the grass, heedless of the stains that would no doubt make Clarkson fuss and her look as though—well, look as though she'd done things out here under the summer sky.

She hoped she would be able to validate by actually doing something that would warrant the gossip.

"What are you doing?" he said, trying to return her back to the safety of his lap.

As though his lap, or anywhere near him, was safe. It was most definitely not.

At least, she hoped it wasn't. If he would only believe her. Believe in her, and trust her. How could she make him see?

"You're going to ruin your gown, and people will—oh," he said, nodding his head in understanding.

"People will what?" she asked. He might understand, but she most definitely did not. She swung her legs around so she could sit on them, probably looking like a little yellow mushroom on the grass.

His expression was puzzled. "You don't know?" He stood in one graceful motion. She wished she could glower at him for being so athletic, but she didn't dare. Because she had broken his trust.

"I don't."

He shook his head, a rueful grin on his face. "Then I won't tell you."

"Fine. Don't." Whatever it was he thought "people will" do, it wasn't as important as what he would do. Which was dependent on what she was about to do.

She got onto her knees and shuffled closer to him, feeling her gown dragging in the dirt and the grass and no doubt a few ant colonies.

She didn't care.

He stared down at her, openmouthed. "What are you doing now?" he asked, putting his hands on his hips.

She had to say, she liked the view from down here. Him standing straight and tall in front of her, his strong, masculine hands on his even more masculine hips. The long length of his legs directly in front of her, his shirt sticking to his chest in a few spots because of how warm it was.

That made her warm, too.

She didn't reply to his question, instead reaching one hand up and taking his fingers in hers. "Archibald Salisbury," she began, trying to keep her voice from wobbling, "would you do me the very great honor of accepting my hand in marriage?"

More silence. How did men ever do this, when the object of their affections just stood there gaping at them? It was a good thing men were men, and so confident, or else there would be many fewer marriages.

At last he spoke. "No."

Had she—"No?" she repeated, not sure she'd heard him correctly.

He lowered himself back onto the ground, a warm, genuine smile on his face. Perhaps she hadn't heard him.

"No." He placed his palm on her ankle, nudging the fabric of her gown aside. Now his expression was less friendly and more feral. He slid his hand up her leg onto her calf. She felt her breath hitch. "I won't have you thinking you can just say a few words and I'll forgive you." His hand was on her knee now. "You'll have to prove it to me."

"And—and how will I do that?" She sounded breathless, and his hand was only on her knee.

Another few inches, and his warm palm was on her thigh, at the tops of her stockings. He hooked his fingers between the fabric and her skin and rubbed his fingers together.

"You'll just have to trust me." Left unspoken was that she hadn't trusted him to love her. That he wasn't certain he trusted her.

Hopefully this would go a long way to convincing him.

"So you're—ah," she said as his hand slid up to cup her there, underneath her skirts. His eyes dropped to her mouth, and she watched as he licked his lips.

And felt it as though he had licked her there.

Did people do that? Specifically, did he do that?

Oh my goodness. She had never thought of the possibility before, but she really hoped he had, and did, and was about to. Because it seemed as though it would be heaven to have his mouth there, kissing her there, making her fall apart as he had with his fingers.

Something of her thoughts must have shown on her expression. One corner of his mouth lifted in a sly grin, and he slid one finger inside, moving his body closer to hers as he did.

"What are you thinking about?" he asked, his voice rough with desire. At least, she presumed it was desire. Unless he'd caught a cold in the last five minutes.

She swallowed. Now was not the time for prevarication. She had to tell him what she wanted so he would trust her. So this would be more than just this.

Even though this was fairly spectacular. But it wouldn't last her a lifetime.

"I was wondering," she began, and her voice sounded . . . odd. Squeaky, but in an entirely different way.

"What?"

"I was wondering if you, if people, if it was possible—?" and then she stopped, because how could she possibly ask what she was thinking? What if he was appalled, what if people never did do these things?

Only she thought that they probably did. She might not have a lot of experience in things, but she definitely had imagination. An imagination that had been sparked when he put his fingers there, and made her feel that.

"What?" he asked again, sliding another finger in.

"How am I expected to speak in coherent sentences when you are doing that?" she blurted out, then caught his startled expression and began to laugh.

"My fault, Duchess." He smiled slyly. "Perhaps you can ask me your question again, that one about accepting your hand at another moment?"

"Oh," she said, not in a squeak so much as a sigh.

"Oh," he repeated, lowering his mouth to cover hers.

Dear Archie,

    Don't stop. Please don't stop.

Genevieve

Chapter 30

*H*e didn't just kiss her; he devoured her, his lips moving on hers, his fingers—three of them now, she thought—stroking her down there, his other hand caressing her breast. She was now lying on the grass, a tiny part of her mind knowing that her yellow gown was about to be grass-stained, but not caring in the least.

Because he was here, and he was kissing her, and she wanted to practice this, as often as he would let her. Why had she spent so much time pretending to meet people and be proper and show disdain?

This was the practice she wanted. Him and her and them.

He broke the kiss, withdrawing his fingers as he leaned back on his heels to look at her, his chest heaving. She had done that to him. They had done that together.

"You should be naked."

The blunt words shocked her, but not as much

as they likely should. After a few seconds' hesitation, she got back onto her knees, pulling the material of her gown up and over her head.

Unfortunately—or really fortunately, given the circumstances—Clarkson wasn't there to undo the buttons, so Genevieve's head got stuck, and she was in darkness. Knowing her lower half was exposed to his gaze, and yet not able to remove her gown.

"I don't want to be a lady anymore, if this is what I have to go through," she muttered as she wriggled.

"Just a moment, I didn't expect you—well, never mind, I should have," he said, and she felt him move around to her back, undoing the buttons as swiftly as Clarkson would have.

And then a moment later she was free, and unclothed out in the open.

Well. So that had happened.

He held her gown and met her gaze, an appreciative smile on his face. And yes, she was naked, but she didn't feel naked. Or at least badly naked. If such a thing existed?

"And now it's your turn," she said, casting an appraising look up and down his body. She hadn't seen any more than his face, his throat, and his forearms yet, for goodness' sake. And she the privileged aristocrat who was supposed to have everyone do what she wanted.

He wasn't naked yet, and she wanted it.

"As you command, Duchess," he said, smirking. He kept his eyes locked on hers as he removed his jacket, tossing it onto the grass. His shirt was next, and he pulled it up and over his head, revealing his chest.

"Hold on," she commanded, putting her hand out. "I want to look first before you're all done." She twirled her finger. "Turn around so I can see all of you."

He grinned and began to turn, slowly, so she could see each and every part of his upper body. The firm curve of his biceps, the definition of the muscles on his chest, the intriguing indents lower down leading into his trousers.

"What do you think?" he asked.

"You're gorgeous," she replied. There was no need to be coy about it; he wanted honesty and trustworthiness, didn't he? "And now the rest, please."

"Didn't I remind you not to say please?" he teased, his fingers going to the placket of his trousers.

"You did. Trousers!" she commanded, trying to keep herself stern and unsmiling, and failing utterly.

"Much better," he said as his trousers dropped down to the ground.

He stood in his smallclothes, his male thing sticking out in a gravity-defying way. That was impressive in and of itself.

And then the smallclothes were gone, too, and she was staring at him, at all of him, all that smooth, hard skin curved and bunched in intriguing ways.

Much different than how she looked, for certain.

And then he had lowered himself onto the

ground again, onto her, so her back was pressed into the grass and the earth and probably those darn ants again, and she couldn't care, even though she knew she would likely get sunburned—it wasn't often, which is to say never, that she was exposed so thoroughly to the sun.

And then what would Clarkson say?

"Are you uncomfortable?" he asked, his tone low and rumbling.

"Yes," she admitted, because she wanted to be honest. "But I don't care." She placed her fingers on his side and smoothed her palm down his warm, bare skin, running her hand over the curves of his arse and then, daringly, slipped her fingers between their bodies to find that part of him that was so . . . insistent.

"Ahh," he said, nearly gasping as she encircled, or tried to encircle, him with her hand.

"Are you uncomfortable?" she asked.

He opened his eyes, which it seemed he'd shut when she touched him, and smiled. "Yes. But only in the most comfortable way."

He shifted off her then, reaching behind himself to grab his jacket. "Lie on this," he commanded, spreading it out on the ground.

"There's no need," she began.

"Oh, there is, Duchess," he interrupted. "Because I don't want your lovely back to get scratched by the grass and the twigs that are on the ground when I thrust into you as far as I can go." He accompanied his words with a demonstration of what he meant, thrusting himself into her hand, his male part all hot and hard and demanding.

"Oh," she said, not even squeaking now. Just . . . breathless.

"Do you want me to do that, Duchess? You can command me, if you wish. If you paid attention to our lessons you should know how to quite well by now." He lowered his mouth to her ear and licked her lobe, making her shiver all over. "Just tell me to make love to you, Duchess." He spoke in a whisper, but the specificity of his words made her feel as though he'd shouted them from the rooftops.

From the rooftops while entirely naked.

Now was not the moment to laugh, and yet she was.

He laughed along with her, but his laugh was one of pure joy, not a laugh she thought she'd ever heard from him before.

"Make love to me," she said in her most authoritative voice. Which would be impressive if she weren't naked outside lying on a steward's coat while said steward was preparing to ravish her. At her invitation.

"Your command is my wish," Archie replied, clamping his hand on her side. He ran it back down to there, right where she longed for him to be, nudging her thighs aside so his fingers could gain entrance again.

"Oh." She sighed, wriggling into his hand.

"Tell me what you want," he murmured, his fingers caressing her, causing her to feel that uncomfortable comfortable feeling, too.

"Actually," she said, trying to sound conversational rather than breathless—a fruitless task—"I was wondering if people ever kissed . . ." and she stopped speaking, instead closing her eyes tight in embarrassment.

Because apparently she wasn't embarrassed to be stark naked outside with a gentleman who was not her husband, but she was embarrassed to say things.

"Kiss . . . there?" he asked, a smile evident in his voice. "Duchess, you shock me," he continued, even as he began to move so he could put his mouth where she most wanted it.

Amazed she had even thought of it.

And then, when he did kiss her there, she wondered why she hadn't thought of it before. Preferably at their first meeting, when she was all awkward and resentful and he was dismissive and controlling.

Well, perhaps not exactly at their first meeting. But shortly thereafter.

He licked and kissed her there, making her breath go faster and faster as she writhed on the ground—no, his jacket. But still.

And then, just then, she exploded, feeling as though she was a part of a million stars falling from the sky.

He looked up at her then, his mouth moist from her, his lips curled into a self-satisfied smile.

"Now I'll ask you, Duchess. Would you do the honor of accepting my hand in marriage?"

"No," she replied, a sly grin on her face.

Archie had had sex before, of course. But it had never felt like this—so intense, so passionate, so—

fun. She was fun. It was a delight to feel how she came apart in his mouth, how she lured him to her with her unselfconscious charm, how happy she was to be with him.

How she'd apologized.

He wasn't angry anymore, now that he knew why. That is, he supposed he might be again at some point, but it was difficult to stay mad at someone who was wonderfully and thoroughly naked and who was very interested in having you ravish her into next week.

"Well?" she said, after he didn't reply. "How are you going to convince me?"

He raised himself up on his arms and moved up her body so they were face-to-face. She arched an eyebrow and he felt the urge to make her so well-pleasured she couldn't speak, let alone refuse his offer.

Which was precisely what he was going to tell her.

"I cannot convince you with my words, Your Grace. I can only convince you with my tongue"— and then he leaned down and claimed her mouth, withdrawing to speak again—"and my body"— and he moved one hand, which she'd placed on his back, to his penis—"and my cock." And he kissed her again, putting his hand on top of hers and showing her how he wished to be stroked.

She learned quickly, and if he weren't interested in thoroughly and completely compromising her, he would have let her continue.

But he knew what he had to do. It was the only—ironically enough—honorable thing to do, since she loved him, and he loved her, and that meant they should be married.

He'd have to ruin her, figuratively and literally, for anyone else.

He stilled her hand and broke the kiss. "Are you ready for me?" he asked.

She nodded vigorously, her eyes wide. Not in shock, but in interest. He was already anticipating just what their married life would be like, and he had to admit he was very much looking forward to it.

"Please," she said, rubbing his cock on her mound. She closed her eyes and emitted a little moan that went straight to his—well, all over his body, but there in particular.

"Don't say please," he admonished, a part of his brain wondering how he could possibly be making jokes at this time. But that was what she brought out in him—that joy of life, no matter how difficult things seemed.

"Then just enter," she commanded, tilting her chin up.

"Yes," he replied, entering her with one deep thrust.

She gasped, and he froze, but she shook her head at his questioning look. "No, it's fine. Continue," she ordered, the curve of her mouth showing she was sharing the joke.

He did, pulling back out and in again, her wet heat surrounding him, her hands clutched on his arse, biting her lip as he thrust in and out.

It would be too much to expect that she would climax her first time, but he could tell that she was finding pleasure in it, her body moving to meet his, her fingers digging into his skin.

He set himself a steady rhythm, trying to think of haying equipment and ledgers so he could prolong the moment.

And then he couldn't wait, his motions getting faster and faster, hearing his breath ragged, exploding from his lungs in short bursts.

He shouted an inarticulate groan as he came, a bone-deep feeling of satisfaction accompanying the waves of pleasure suffusing him.

And then he collapsed on top of her, heedless of his weight, knowing she could handle him no matter what. That she would handle him no matter what, now and forever.

"Yes," she murmured. "Now I'll say yes."

Dear Genevieve,

Have I told you today how much I love you? Perhaps I should show you instead. I'll come by your room after dinner.

Archie

Chapter 31

"Yes, please do come in," Genevieve said as the earl and countess arrived. Chandler helped them off with their coats, and Genevieve gestured to the dining room. "This way. We are just waiting for two more."

One of whom was to be her husband.

Husband.

Her entire life, she'd longed for a family, an enormous family with loads of people and animals and conviviality and love.

She'd ended up with Gran and Byron, Aunt Sophia, Miss Evelyn, and Archie.

It was more than enough.

The door opened again, and her head swiveled to see. Was he here? At last? Aunt Sophia walked in, followed by Archie, resplendent in formal evening wear. She'd never seen him dressed as a true gentleman, as he must have looked before joining the army and then working for a living. His coat and trousers were pitch-black, his shirt a snowy white, his evening neckwear ornamented with a small gray pearl.

That lock of hair still fell forward, though, and she suppressed a smirk at when she'd last pushed it back—after their mid-meadow romp, when they'd been lying together entirely naked, talking of their plans for the future.

Getting a sunburn she couldn't seem to adequately explain to Clarkson.

"Good evening, Vievy," Aunt Sophia said, rushing forward with both her arms out. "Thank you for inviting us to dinner; you know I love food."

Genevieve blinked at her godmother's statement, glancing back at Archie, whose eyebrow was raised. He shook his head in fond tolerance, and her heart swelled all over again at seeing him be so kind.

"Mr. Salisbury said you'd invited him as well, and I hope that wasn't a mistake, because here he is," Aunt Sophia said, gesturing to him behind her.

"No mistake, I promise," Genevieve replied, to him as well as to her godmother. "No mistake," she repeated, more softly.

"Allow me to escort you into the dining room," Archie said, holding his arm out to both ladies. Genevieve stepped over to his right side, while her godmother took his left. She squeezed his forearm as they walked, breathing in his scent.

He was here. He was here, and he was hers forever.

They walked into the dining room, the formal

table studded with candles, the silver glinting in the soft light. Sir William looked up at their entrance, his expression tightening as he saw Archie.

"What the dickens is he doing here?" he said. Sir William hadn't renewed his offer, thank goodness, and he had agreed to accept a dowry for Evelyn. But they hadn't, for obvious reasons, had any conversation beyond ironing out those details.

"That is an excellent question," Genevieve replied. She waited as Archie seated her godmother. "That is one of the many reasons I wished to invite you for dinner."

Archie came to stand beside her, and she took his hand in hers. All of the guests' eyes were riveted to their clasped hands.

"Mr. Salisbury has done me the very great honor of agreeing to become my husband," she said, glancing at each guest in turn. Noticing how everyone—save Sir William—looked exceptionally pleased. "I wanted to let you know first. We'll be calling on Mr. Salisbury's family tomorrow to let them know." That would be much less comfortable than tonight, but it was necessary. She knew the value of family, and she wanted him to have the benefit of it, even if it just ended up that he was reconciled with his brother, and not his parents.

His brother's letter had already done a lot of good toward mending the rift between the brothers—Genevieve hadn't read it herself yet, but she'd watched Archie's face as he did. By the end there were tears in his eyes, and she had every hope that he and the lesser Mr. Salisbury—in her eyes, at least—would be true family again.

His parents sounded as horrible as her father had been, albeit in an entirely opposite way—cherishing duty and propriety above anything else. Still, there would be times they would see each other, and she was determined that it not be the subject of gossip.

Their marriage would already cause gossip, but she was willing to endure that if it meant she got to have him.

"And the duchess has done me the great honor of agreeing to become my wife," Archie added, looking down at her and smiling.

"Oh, wonderful!" Gran said, clapping her hands as a disgruntled Byron leaped off her lap and went scurrying for the corner. "I can see you will have a perfect life together," she said, stressing the "see" part of her sentence and chuckling.

"We will," Archie said in a low tone, a fierce promise meant for Genevieve's ears alone. "We will."

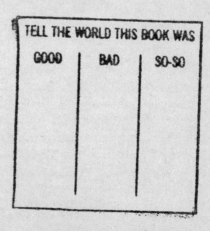

TELL THE WORLD THIS BOOK WAS

| GOOD | BAD | SO-SO |

The Truth About Love and Dukes
by Laura Lee Guhrke

Henry, Duke of Torquil, wouldn't be caught *reading* the "Dear Lady Truelove" column, but when its advice causes his mother to embark on a scandalous elopement, Henry decides the author must be stopped before she can ruin any more lives. Though Lady Truelove's identity is a closely guarded secret, Henry has reason to suspect the publisher of the notorious column, beautiful and provoking Irene Deverill, is also its author . . .

You May Kiss the Bride by Lisa Berne

Gabriel Penhallow knows he must follow "The Penhallow way"—find a biddable bride, produce an heir and a spare, and then live separate lives. It's worked for generations, and one kiss with the delectable Livia Stuart isn't going to change things. Society dictates he marry her, and one chit is as good as another. But Livia's transformation makes Gabriel realize he desperately wants the woman who provoked him into that kiss.

Dangerous Games by Tess Diamond

Maggie Kincaid left the FBI two years ago and didn't look back. But when a senator's daughter is abducted, the nightmare isn't just familiar to Maggie, it's personal. She'll need all the help she can get to bring Kayla Thebes home alive—even if it comes from a hot-as-hell ex-soldier, Jake O'Connor, who plays by his own rules . . .

REL 0317

*G*ive in to your Impulses!

**These unforgettable stories only take a second
to buy and give you hours of reading pleasure!**

Go to *www.AvonImpulse.com* and see what we
have to offer.

Available wherever e-books are sold.

AVONIMPULSE

IMP 0811